D0257859

The
Song
House

The
Song
House

Trezza
Azzopardi

First published 2010 by Picador
an imprint of Pan Macmillan, a division of Macmillan Publishers Limited
Pan Macmillan, 20 New Wharf Road, London N1 9RR
Basingstoke and Oxford
Associated companies throughout the world
www.panmacmillan.com

ISBN 978-0-330-46103-0 HB
ISBN 978-0-330-51393-7 TPB

A CIP catalogue record for this book is available from
the British Library.

Typeset by Ellipsis Books Limited, Glasgow
Printed by CPI Mackays, Chatham ME5 8TD

Visit **www.picador.com** to read more about all our books
and to buy them. You will also find features, author interviews and
news of any author events, and you can sign up for e-newsletters
so that you're always first to hear about our new releases.

Like the
Touch of Rain

Like the touch of rain she was
On a man's flesh and hair and eyes
When the joy of walking thus
Has taken him by surprise:

With the love of the storm he burns,
He sings, he laughs, well I know how,
But forgets when he returns
As I shall not forget her 'Go now'.

Those two words shut a door
Between me and the blessed rain
That was never shut before
And will not open again.

Edward Thomas

She's hearing things: the noise her skirt makes as she walks, the low grumble of a distant tractor, a crow laughing in the tree-tops. There's a half-remembered melody playing in her head. She removes her jacket and slings it over her shoulder, humming the tune out loud, aware of how slight her voice sounds in the open air. It's high summer, hot and arid, but the overgrown hedges on either side of the path cast a welcome shade; walking between them is like being in a tunnel. A right bend leads her to a clearing. From here, set back behind a dense thicket of rhododendron bushes, she sees the upper half of Earl House, its tall windows mirroring the sky. She is surrounded by fields of crops; she recognizes the burnt gold of barley, and the silver feathering of ripe wheat. There is no wire to keep her out. She takes a detour off the dirt path and steps between the rows of wheat, feeling hidden and exalted: the only one here. The heels of her sandals sink slightly into the earth. Removing them, she picks her way barefoot over the rutted ground, deep into the centre of the field. Her watch says two-fifteen. All she can see is the wide sky, all she can hear is the tractor drone, very faint now, and the wheat shushing as she moves through it. She doesn't know why she must do this; she has no reason except that it seems a natural thing, a childhood act revived. Despite the awkwardness of the ground, she picks

I

up speed, turning one way, then another. She doesn't know what she's searching for until she finds it. And now it's here, as she knew it had to be all along: the bowl barrow. She lies down on the mound, splays her arms and legs like a skydiver in free fall, and then she is still, quietly panting into the blue space above her.

On the top floor of the house, standing at the window, Kenneth is watching.

part one

bless the weather

one

Her hair is darker than he thought. When he first caught sight of her, it looked like copper wire, but now he sees that it has an earthy hue, streaks of auburn and chestnut brown. He's pleased with this subtle difference; he thinks it more sophisticated. The woman stands quite still before his desk, her hands loosely clasped in front of her, the suit jacket back on and buttoned – one button done up – so if he hadn't seen her just half an hour earlier, her body spread out in the field below, he would never have known.

Maggie Nix? he says, to which she nods and smiles without showing her teeth, Please, do sit down.
Kenneth Earl does not sit down; he walks to the window again and looks at the wheatfield, then back into the room at her. He has interviewed three others this afternoon, has seen them all walk up the path, has waited while the rhododendrons lining the drive eclipsed and then revealed them again, counted the beat of their footsteps on the staircase. All three were unable to enter the room, to stand or to sit, without first saying something. What a hot day it was, such a nice walk up to the house, what a magnificent room. And it *is* beautiful, Kenneth's office. Situated on the west side of the building, the two original windows give a sweeping view of the Berkshire downs; the interior has plaster crisp as snow, a few discerning antiques, a

thick cream carpet underfoot. Maggie has said nothing about the room; she does not gaze up in wonder at the intricate ceiling rose, or admire the painting hanging on the wall behind Kenneth's desk. She sits and waits, and watches his movements with a clear, open expression. In the sunlight, she looks flawless, a study in oils. Her eyes are completely and unnervingly fixed on him.

Can I get you a drink? A tea, coffee? he asks. She will have to say something to that. She begins to shake her head, and then an intake of breath,

A glass of water, please.

From the closet in the corner of the room, he draws some water, walking back towards her where he sees a bent stalk of straw caught in the curls of her hair.

I'm afraid it's only tap, he says, expecting her to speak again. Kenneth watches her drink it, in quick gulps, like a child would drink, and then place the glass on the low table next to her chair.

Thank you, she says.

He'd advertised in the national papers, not wanting anyone local, anyone who might know of him. He thought he required an assistant, but it was an applicant in the last round, an ambitious young man who had ideas, who heard him out and finally told Kenneth that what he needed was an amanuensis. Or slave, the young man added, going on his way. An amanuensis. Immediately, Kenneth liked the sound of it; it was musical, perfectly right. He wanted to talk and have someone listen, someone to note his words, exactly as he spoke them; someone who did not interject or question or make noise. But he did not specify these skills in the advertisement. An assortment of women had come down on the train from London, with their telephone voices and lacquered fingernails, strident perfume announcing their arrival. Each thought they were progressing their careers by becoming a personal secretary, or a PA, as one of them insisted on calling the job. Maggie, now, he doesn't know where she has travelled from; he doesn't know what she thinks.

As she sits and listens, he outlines the work. She nods and, once or twice, opens her face with a quick smile. It worries him, this eagerness; perhaps she hasn't taken in the scope of the task he's proposing.

You mention here in your letter that you have shorthand, he says, It's a rare skill, these days.

I have a kind of shorthand of my own, she says, It's quite fast, like texting.

Texting, he says, See you later.
Maggie narrows her eyes at him, and Kenneth's finger draws a squiggle of hieroglyphics in the air.

C, U – you know, I do know what texting is.

Good, says Maggie, Well, it's just like that.
He glances again at her letter, turning the single sheet over in his hand.

What was your last post? he says, I can't seem to find your references.
The blush growing on Maggie's face tells him she hasn't got any.

I was a carer, for a relative, she says, But then – she looks down into her lap – I wasn't needed any more.

I don't suppose they're in a position to write you a reference? Kenneth asks, not unkindly. Maggie answers with a shake of the head.

Actually, she says, raising her eyes to his, Before that I used to manage my stepfather's shop in Dorset. Charmouth. Do you know it?

Can't say I do. Nice part of the world, I believe.

It has lots of fossils, she says stupidly.
Kenneth bares his teeth in a pained grin.

Well, there's your qualification for the job, he says. He gives her a quick look to see how the joke is taken, is gratified to see her smiling again.

Maybe I should show you the library. It'll give you a better idea of what's in store.

Kenneth's plan is simple enough; he wants to catalogue all the music in his collection. Not details of artists or labels or conductors; most of these he already knows, and the ones he's forgotten he can read from the cover. His idea is to insert inside each sleeve a page of notes; memories, associations, what the piece means to him, when he'd obtained it, and why. He wants to be able to draw out a record and say: this is why I love this, or: this is what listening to it does to me. He wants to remind himself of his life – episodes of joy, romance, desire – and so relive it. Kenneth is nearly sixty-eight. Apart from Freya, who comes in once a week to clean the rooms still in use, he sees few people. And lately, he's felt his days merge seamlessly into each other, felt how quickly time can pass; how quickly, and how slowly.

Taking her elbow – a light touch, barely that – he leads Maggie down the stairs. Close up, she's not as tall as he thought, and older; not a girl at all. She must be in her thirties. Under the curls of her fringe he glimpses a scar, pale against the suntanned skin, a thin strike from hairline to eyebrow. He is delighted with this flaw, the most perfect imperfection; and is as quickly mortified by his urge to stroke it. He ushers her in front of him so that she can't read his face, and sees the back of her head again, the piece of straw clinging to her hair. In the light from the landing window, he thinks he also sees a small red mark on the collar of her blouse. From a crushed insect, perhaps, a spider mite or beetle.

The library, down a long painted corridor on the ground floor, is shuttered from the light. Kenneth opens one of its two doors, standing aside to let Maggie pass through. Adjusting his eyes to the dimness, it takes a moment for him to realize that she hasn't moved.

What? he asks.

Like a library in a book, she says, her face flushed with delight.

She puts out a hand in front of her, but still doesn't venture into the room. The darkness inside is so brown and stained that she can't possibly see how not like an ordinary library this is. He feels disappointment nip at him, and doesn't hear the playfulness of her remark. He strides ahead of her, crosses to the window shutters and folds one back: *now* she will see.

Any particular novel? he asks. Maggie steps into a bar of sunlight on the floor.

The Great Gatsby, she says, gesturing to the far wall, The scene where Owl Eyes talks about the books being real.

And then she laughs, as if the idea of having actual books in a library is a peculiar thing. Kenneth laughs too.

Can you hold a silence? he asks.

Do you mean, can I keep quiet?

That's right, says Kenneth. He edges nearer, trying to place her accent.

Because some of the things you'll hear, he says, making his large hands into fists and holding them in the air between them, Some of these things will be quite . . . intimate.

I can keep quiet, she says, And I can keep a secret. But words on a page, they're going to be read, aren't they?

Kenneth nods in agreement.

They'll be read by me. And when I'm dead, they'll be burnt. Not the recordings, just the notes. I've left instructions.

Maggie looks at him keenly now; he sees in her eyes something like recognition.

How many records?

Three thousand five hundred and counting, he says, But we won't be cataloguing all of them, of course.

Green, her eyes are green.

What kind of music?

Blues, jazz, classical, rock, he says, swaying slightly on his heels. To cover his embarrassment, he leads off along the windows, folding back the shutters one by one until the room is sparkling with light.

And rather a lot of Frank Sinatra, Ella, Satchmo. Look, here, I'll show you what there is.

There are no books. Lining the walls, from floor to ceiling, are rows of records, each row divided into columns by a thin strip of wood. In the dimness, it had looked like a design on wallpaper. He hears her catch her breath.

It's amazing, she says, So much to choose from.

So you do *like* music, Maggie? Because, as you say, there's a lot to choose from – a lot to hear.

She turns from the wall, an incredulous look on her face.

Do I like music? she asks, What a bizarre question. Do I like music?

Kenneth is now properly embarrassed. He feels as though he's managed to insult her, but can't think how.

It's just that I've interviewed quite a few applicants. None of them seemed very interested in the actual music. Salary, conditions of employment – he flicks his fingers out in a count – Holiday leave, sick leave, maternity leave—

Maggie splays her own fingers in the air between them.

Music is power, she says, her face serious.

Is it? he whispers, Who says so?

Richard Ashcroft. You'd put him in the rock section, she says, and seeing Kenneth's bewildered expression, she adds, Under 'Gods'.

Kenneth grins with relief. He finds her intensity refreshing after meeting the other candidates, with their laptops and their assured manner, their dead eyes. And he likes it more that she seems so interested in the task.

You won't tease me about the rock section, he says, Will you?

Ah. Let me guess.

She closes her eyes. He fixes on the pale bluish tint to her lids, can't concentrate on the list she's reciting.

. . . The Rolling Stones, Pink Floyd, and – The Who.

Bill Haley. Elvis Presley. Eddie Cochran, he counters, Bruce Springsteen.

Really? I didn't know he recorded on 78s.

So she is teasing. He can easily go along with that.

Actually, I'm quite clued-up on the latest technology, the pods and downloads and that. I like to keep abreast of these things.

You have an iPod, she says, not even attempting to keep the disbelief from her voice.

A birthday present. But those little headphones—

Buds.

They make my ears ache.

Maggie nods in agreement,

And they don't do much for the sound. But they're useful, you know, for blocking out other people, their noise.

You'll be listening to my noise. I hope you won't mind that. But at least it will be on vinyl. This here is the system, he says, with a little introductory cough.

He opens the door of a sideboard to reveal a stack of silver equipment, which they both stare at.

It's all made by Linn. The best, apparently. Don't tell him, but I much prefer listening on this.

Kenneth pats the smoked-perspex lid of an ordinary-looking record player.

Who should I not tell? Maggie asks.

My son, Will, he says, You'll meet him. He sometimes pops in.

He gives her a wry smile,

Not too often, he adds, And usually only to raid my wine cellar, or try to sell me some dubious piece of art.

Maggie blinks at this, gesturing to the wall of records.

How many a day, do you think? she asks, Only, you said it was a three-month contract.

It will depend, says Kenneth, On the day, on what I hear first, on what I *feel* like hearing first and what I feel like hearing next. A three-month contract, yes, possibly extended, all depending on how we get on.

I'd like us to get on, she says, moving to a long glass-topped display cabinet. She bends over it, using her hand to try to block out the reflections on the surface.

We won't be bothering with the sheet music, says Kenneth, dismissive, Those in there, they're relics. They used to have singing lessons here.

They?

The children, he says. He wants to draw her away from the cabinet, eager to make her understand. He's decided she's right for him.

This is what we'll do, Maggie, in here, in the mornings, in silence – silence from you, that is. We'll resurrect history, make the past into a story. I mean, not invented but . . . personal. I'll sit there – he points to a wing-backed chair in a corner of the room – And I'll speak and you'll transcribe and—

He stops himself, hearing how pompous he sounds, and ridiculous, his breath coming quick and excited. But his belief that she could help him, his sudden sense of needing her, pushes him on again,

– And you don't interrupt, you listen to the music and you listen to me talk and you take it all down. Understood? And in the afternoons, you type up the notes.

On a computer?

On a typewriter. There's one in the prefect's office, under the main stairs.

The prefect's office, she echoes, her eyes fixed on his face.

This place used to be a school.

Ah, the singing lessons, she says, Yes.

Not quite, he says, returning to the windows and closing the shutters one by one, After we bought it – after the school closed – the choir still came to practise here.

Must've been exquisite, she says, lifting her head as if to hear the sound of their voices.

It wasn't always *that* tuneful, he says, furrowing his eyebrows,
But it was only on Sundays, so we coped.
He watches her turn from him, and turn back again.

On Sundays, she says, Of course, the choir sang on a Sunday.
He's not sure he's understood her correctly, wonders if she's
religious.

Do you have any more questions, Maggie?

The advert said 'live in', she says, So, where do I stay?

two

She doesn't know where she is. The light has woken her, pale green, tracing an unfamiliar pattern on the wall. Her body is covered by a smooth tight sheet with the weight of the quilt on top. She doesn't know *who* she is. It's a familiar feeling for Maggie, this fleeting moment when she's caught between the waking and the dead. She'd been dreaming of her mother again. Pushing one leg out across the bed, Maggie feels the coolness of the cotton under her foot: she must have lain in this position all night. The bed is high, like a princess's bed: like the princess and the pea, she thought, but didn't say, when Kenneth first showed her the room. A high bed with a thick floral-patterned quilt and a mahogany headboard, and a dark wooden wardrobe and bedside cupboard and, in the corner, a marble-topped washstand. On top of it is a television set with a dust-sticky remote control perched on the edge. Maggie thinks it is a fine room. It smells amberous and heady, the scent of baked summer. It is nothing like anywhere she knows, and that is good. There's the coo of a wood pigeon, a chatter of other birdsong she can't identify, a power saw off in the distance. From the window, her view is of a cobbled courtyard, in the middle of which stands a tree with massive, hand-shaped leaves and a thick trunk. She looks at it for a time: there are definitely eyes in the trunk. She doesn't know the name of the tree. She will ask Kenneth about it.

She arrived last night, just before dinner, as Kenneth had instructed. They ate in the dining room. It had wall cabinets full of fine china, plates with gold-leaf patterns on them, but the crockery they ate from was just ordinary; plain and heavy. He's laid the table especially, she thought, looking at the candles and place mats and napkin holders. She imagined him on his own in this big house, eating a ready-meal at the end of the long table, and the thought of it brought a tightness to her chest. He served her pasta, vegetarian, because, he said, he didn't know if she was or wasn't, and no one objects to vegetables. He looked proud when he told her that he'd cooked the meal himself, and made the sauce. It was a mixture of tinned tomato, hard courgette chunks, chopped onion that squeaked between her teeth. Kenneth was very different in this role; slightly bashful and eager to please, and when he gave her some wine, Maggie understood the effort involved: as he poured, he placed his free hand on the base of the glass to steady it.

Call me Kenneth, he said, No need for formalities, which made her feel stiff and oddly angry, as if he were granting a privilege to a servant. And you can call me Maggie, she replied, which made them laugh, and easy again, because he had been doing just that all along. Afterwards, he wanted to show her around downstairs.

So if you get lost, you'll know where you are, he said. He pointed to a half-closed door,

Kitchen. Where I've just spent three hours concocting. And where you will often find me concocting. I am, if I may say so, an adventurous cook.

Maggie glimpsed a large rectangular space with a stove set into a brick hearth.

And the dining room you've seen. I sometimes eat in there, but quite often you'll find me down here. C'mon.

He led her further along the corridor until they arrived at an atrium, stuffed full of tall hothouse plants and wicker furniture. Despite the hour, the heat was intense, trapped by the blinds on the sloping glass roof. It reminded Maggie of a picture in a catalogue, with its pamment flooring and French windows leading onto the courtyard. There was a coffee table in the centre with a wedge of magazines on it, shaped into a careful fan. She couldn't quite see Kenneth deliberating over which type of conservatory blind would best complement the chintz, but someone had definitely styled this space. They passed a closed door with an engraved plate on it.

Music room, she said, reading it.

True, true, but it's where I keep most of my books. The library is oak-panelled, you see, with a coffered ceiling.

Maggie struggled to keep up with him.

A coffined—? she asked.

Coffered. Good for listening to music. So I switched them about. The music room's now my library, and the original library is my music room.

And this is where the schoolchildren came to practise? asked Maggie, perplexed.

What? No, no. It's full of books! The main hall. They used that.

The corridor grew narrow; Maggie had to walk behind him to avoid bumping her elbow into his.

Don't you find yourself rattling about in this place? she asked, just as he came to an abrupt halt. They'd reached the end of the tour, and were facing a painted white door.

I do, he said, Which is why I spend a lot of my time in here: the den!

He opened the door onto a room saturated with colour; the walls were maroon, the curtains midnight blue and covered with golden stars and planets. Two brown leather armchairs were placed either side of a marble fireplace, itself a repellent, mottled purple.

It's very . . . full, said Maggie, eyeing the books and papers stacked up all over the floor. Kenneth smiled at her.

A full life is a wonderful life, don't you agree, Maggie? She wasn't about to contradict him. Instead, she pretended to study the gallery of paintings stretched along one wall: a stag in oils, a stern-faced portrait of a man in a dog collar, a ruin in a garden.

Lots of stuff, she said, moving on to the collection of clocks on the mantelpiece. Each one told a slightly different time: ten past, twelve minutes past, a quarter past. Closer, she could hear their panicky ticking. Her eyes fell to rest on a large glass orb housed in a tubular frame. It looked modern, out of place. As Maggie approached, she was able to separate it from the background. It was an aquarium, swirling with brightly coloured fish.

That, said Kenneth, pointing, Is not my idea. It's a work of art, apparently. But it has a *function*. The fish are intended to keep me active.

Active how? It's not as if you can take them for a walk. As she ducked forward to watch them more closely, the neons flashed away to the far side of the globe.

I'm supposed to remember to feed them, you see, otherwise the little beggars die.

Well, it seems to be working, said Maggie, straightening up again, They look healthy enough.

He drew closer, suddenly serious.

You don't think it's cruel? he asked.

Maggie shrugged,

No more cruel than eating them, she said, Perhaps that's the way to go. Fried in batter, like whitebait.

Kenneth bent his head and put his hands on either side of the globe. He looked like a fortune-teller about to reveal her future.

When they die, they float to the top, he said, I find it quite sad. Like they say, the water gives up her dead.

The sea, corrected Maggie, I think it's from the Bible.

I found a man once, he said, still staring into the bowl, Drowned. Well, I didn't find him myself, but I saw him. What remained. He'd been washed up after a storm. Baggs, his name was. Huge man, lived in one of the estate cottages. It's an awful thing, the smell. You never forget it.

Maggie turned away from him. She didn't want this conversation any more, didn't like the way it had cast a shadow on the room.

These are just little fish, Kenneth, she said, And if you really don't want them, why don't you advertise them for sale? Or donate them to the local school? Or you could sell them to the pet shop at the retail park. That's probably where they came from in the first place.

Can't. Will bought them. One of his less brilliant gifts. You see, Maggie, that's what happens, as you get on. You acquire stuff you don't want. People give you all sorts of rubbish, football-shaped radios, painted china kingfishers, a stacking rooster teapot— he was in full flow now, sweeping his arm across the array of objects on the shelves – A tartanware bloody decanter! His face had gone very pink. Maggie tried not to laugh at him.

Show me the worst thing, she said, offering her palm.

Kenneth rummaged on the shelves, brought down a black mug with the Playboy logo etched in gold, and passed it to her. She weighed it in her hand, held it out at arm's length.

You really hate it, she said, her eyes glittering.

Yes I do.

She took it over to the hearth and let it drop.

Whoops, she said, glancing down at the broken pieces, I'm so clumsy. Any more?

Kenneth thought for a second, then fetched an ornate round dish with a transfer image of Frankie Dettori on the front.

Present from a lady friend, he said.

She gave you a *plate* with a *jockey* on it? said Maggie, astonished, And now she's in a home, yes?

Kenneth's laugh turned into a coughing fit. He wiped his tears on his sleeve as Maggie waited.

Ali's – well – she's in a stable, so to speak. Lambourn. It's a village not far from here. Full of horsey types. Breeders, trainers . . .

Plate-givers, finished Maggie.

Kenneth held it over the hearth and dropped it. It bounced, twirled on its rim, and settled with a scuttering flourish.

I don't seem to have your knack, he sighed, bending to retrieve it.

Maggie crossed to the shelves, scanned them.

Seriously, though, if you don't want to live with all this, why keep it?

Ah, well, I'm on to that, he said, fanning the plate in his hand, I'm sorting it out. See, here, I'm cataloguing everything. He moved to a low table near the window and fetched an exercise book from the top of a pile. She saw for the briefest moment an emblem on the cover, before he opened it to show her what was written inside: three long columns of words, some of them scored out and rewritten, and on the facing page, lists and bullet points and a great many exclamation marks. It was a wild, meaningless scrawl. And she saw plainly what he'd neglected to mention at the interview: he was unable to put anything down in a coherent manner. His thoughts were everywhere on the page. Maggie perceived his tone, his plea for acknowledgement.

So you're far too busy to do this *and* make your music notes, she said.

That's right, he agreed, and suddenly lit with a new idea, Would you like some more wine? It's such a nice evening, we could sit on the terrace, watch the sun go down on the river. What do you think?

Maggie has her own kitchen up here, off her bedroom: a narrow space with a high window. This first morning she eats, standing up, a piece of toast and marmalade, waiting for the kettle to boil.

It was only three days ago they'd agreed the terms of the job, but nothing in the kitchen looks newly purchased, except for the milk and bread. The cereal packet has dust on the top, the marmalade has a faded price sticker on the lid, and the coffee granules in the jar are solid: she has to dig repeatedly with a spoon to excavate them. It takes her back, as everything does, to her mother, for whom the simplest things became an act of deep concentration. Place the spoon in the jar, scoop the granules up and hold the spoon steady while you carry it to the cup. It was agonizingly slow to watch. Maggie would have to grip her hands behind her back to stop herself from snatching the spoon or the kettle or the plate — whatever implement it might be — and doing the job herself. After the feat was achieved, she'd sneak back into the kitchen, wipe away the stains and spillages as if they had never happened.

She tries not to think of her mother, because it feels wrong, at this, the start of her new life, to let her old life in: she would like to keep them apart for a while longer yet. But there's a prickling at the back of her neck, a sense that if she were to turn round, quickly, she would find her mother standing there in the doorway with one hand on her hip, shaking her head in disbelief.

And what do you hope to achieve by this?

It was her mother's idea that if Maggie would be staying in Berkshire for a while, she should get herself a job: nothing too demanding, just so that she wasn't stuck indoors all day, she'd said, fussing over nothing, *fretting*. They ordered the local and national papers, and in the evenings they'd look together, Maggie half-heartedly, her mother with more determination, reading out the most ridiculous posts.

Fork-lift truck driver, that's local. Arborist. You could do that. You know about trees and everything.

But the illness progressed so quickly that the prospect of even a few hours away from her mother frightened Maggie; the idea of hours, suddenly, being all they had left together. So she never did apply for work, but they continued to look, all the same; for amusement, for distraction, to pretend that everything was normal. Towards the end, Maggie would sit on the edge of the bed and read the advertisements out loud, one eye on her mother, watching as she slipped quietly into sleep, like a child being told a bedtime story. Then Maggie saw the advertisement for the post at Earl House; a large blocked-out rectangle in the *Times*: unmissable, beckoning. She didn't read that one to her mother.

Unable to finish her toast, Maggie throws it in the bin and rinses her cup, forcing herself to concentrate on the moment, and on Kenneth: she considers how long he might have waited for the right person, feels a thin pulse of satisfaction that he's found her at last. And she's conscious of how long she has waited, too. Thinking again about what he told her at the interview, she is struck by a way of laying her ghost to rest. Make the past into a story, Kenneth said. Resurrect history. Her plan, if she had thought it through, was not dissimilar: to resurrect history, yes – if she only knew what that history was. She has heard stories, has lived inside moments, has memories scattered like light. She thinks these things aren't facts. But Kenneth can tell her, if she can only lead him to it. If he supplies the facts, she'll do the rest. Time to go to work.

She comes down to find the library empty. No sign of Kenneth, no sound from the kitchen. On a low table next to one of the chairs, she finds his instructions. 'Make yourself at home. Here's the office equipment! Be with you soon, K.' Beneath his note is a single slim exercise book, an exact copy of the one he showed her yesterday, the same herald on the front displaying a badge, the words *Veritate et Virtute* scrolled beneath it. The paper inside is ruled with pale blue lines. Placed next to it is a cheap gel pen. In the dimness of the shuttered room, Maggie sits on the edge of the chair, opens the book and turns to the back. She presses the page down flat with her hand, and begins to write.

three

My mother names me Maggie, after the song by Rod Stewart. She decides this as she lifts me in her arms and angles me to the window, where both of us can watch the rain fall on the glass. You'd think I'm an unexploded bomb, the way she holds me.

Look, Baby, she says, That's called rain, that stuff. You'll see lots of that.

Outside the window there's an overgrown garden with a shed at the far end. Abandoned deckchairs are grouped around a burnt-out bonfire, with cups and glasses strewn across the grass. A washing line stretches from the back door to the shed, the whole length beaded with shimmering pearls. Everything is sodden. The rain comes down fine and steady, softening the view.

Ed is sitting at the kitchen table, rolling a joint. All the paraphernalia — the silver tin, lighter, Rizlas, the torn-off strip of an Embassy packet, the greasy wrap of red Leb — are set out before him on top of a copy of yesterday's newspaper. He ducks his head slightly to lick the edge of the roll-up. His thick beard hides his lips.

You can't call her Baby forever, he says, nodding at the newspaper, My family will want to put a notice in the *Telegraph*. 'We are delighted to announce the birth of Cassandra Crane.

Mummy and daughter are both doing splendidly.' Ed laughs at his joke, looking up to see my mother, still at the window, facing away from him.

What would you like to call her? she asks, not rising to the bait about his family. Of course they will want a christening, as they wanted – will still want – her and Ed to get married.

Whatever you like, he says, It's all cool.

So she decides, if it's all cool, that she'll call me Maggie, but she won't mention it just yet, because if she sees him pull that shrugging, artless gesture again, she'll throw something at him. The sink is full of unwashed pots – any one of them would do.

My mother takes me upstairs and lays me down in the centre of the bed, then she undoes the buttons of her smock and steps out of it. She'd like to take a bath, but she knows there's no hot water unless she lights the fire downstairs. She considers the idea; Ed will grumble about burning wood in June, and she'll have to lug it in herself from the shed when he's having a sleep because otherwise he'll insist on doing it but then he'll forget. And then it'll be night, and she'll have to go down there in the black and scrabble around among the mice and insects. She takes a flannel out of the drawer and calls downstairs for Ed to put the kettle on. She'll wash me and then she'll wash herself, squatting in front of the unlit fire as if the memory of it will keep us warm. I'm a week old, she's a month off twenty, and this is the dampest, coldest summer she can ever remember.

My mother's called Eleanor but everyone calls her Nell, and Ed, my father, is called Edward Harper Crane. His father is a circuit judge and his mother is a charity worker, which, he tells Nell, means that she does bugger all except hold a coffee morning once a week. Ed doesn't appear to do anything either, although when he first meets my mother he tells her he's an artist. There's not much evidence of his work around the cottage – a few drawings, the odd painting – and no hint of his interest, except for the glossy catalogues he sometimes brings back from his trips to London, full of pictures of glass bowls and distressed wood.

Nell sits with her hands in her lap and surveys the room. The furniture is old, remnant stock from when the cottage was tied to the Lambourn estate. It was let to the Weaver family for generations, and it's still called that, despite the fact that the Weavers vacated years ago, years before the Cranes got hold of it, before Ed persuaded his father to let him use it. Nell likes the simpleness of the place; the artisan patterns etched into the dressing table and the wardrobe, the blunt iron crucifix set into the wall cavity. She likes the walnut headboard of the bed, and the way the mattress slumps in the centre, so no matter how much you cling to the edge, no matter how angry you were with him when you turned off the light, your bodies would find themselves rolling together like ships in a storm. My mother and Ed do a lot of fighting, and a lot of making up. Now she has me. At night, holding me to her, she imagines all the babies that have been born in the bed, the moans and sighs and happy tears. Rather that than the piss, sweat and blood-stains that darken the old mattress like a map of moil.

The walls are plain off-white, dusty to the touch, the distemper cracking and falling onto the floorboards in wafer-thin flakes. My mother doesn't mind this, nor the way the floor slopes down towards the back of the building, so everything is on the tilt. What she minds is the river. It runs at the bottom of the garden, behind the willow trees. Businessmen come at the weekends to fish for brown trout. It's part of the deal with Ed's parents, that Ed and Nell can live in the place rent-free as long as they don't interfere with the clients, who pay handsomely to fish the private waters. The men bring hampers and metal boxes full of kit, trudging up and down the path at the side of the cottage, their laughter ringing off the stone walls. Their Range Rovers, parked on the verge outside the living room window, block the daylight.

Since meeting Ed, Nell doesn't see many people. Through

accident or design, he keeps her close: he says she is his forever, she was meant for him and he was meant for her. He wraps a lock of her hair around his fingers as he says it, winding the auburn curl tighter, and tighter, singing it, crooning it, tugging her near. He couldn't bear anything to come between them, he says, his mouth so close to her ear she can feel the wetness of his breath. Nell's happy enough to hear it. She thinks they are what a real couple should be like; not like her mum and dad, who couldn't stay in the same room without it ending in a slap, or his mum and dad, who live separate lives under one cold roof.

She enjoys the solitude, and she can put up with the aimlessness of their days, the lack of adventure it brings. Nell's not one for adventure. Most of her friends are out in the world; they send postcards from stops on the Silk Route, or from Amsterdam, Paris, South America, with tales of their travels: drunken nights on the beach, stoned nights in a blues den, sober nights in a dank cell waiting for word from the embassy. Others, the more serious girls she knows from school, have become involved in liberation and consciousness-raising and protest. The USA is the enemy, the state is the enemy, men are the enemy. Nell understands this, but she isn't convinced. And anyway, it simply doesn't apply to her. She is in a real relationship; she thinks she is quietly growing up. She and Ed stay in most days, and only go into the town to buy food or tobacco, supplementing his allowance with their own vegetables, fizzy home brew and elderberry wine. Their friend Cindy visits from time to time, and Ed's cousin Leon calls in when he isn't touring with his band. Occasionally, Nell sees Bryce, the water bailiff, with a young lad in tow, patrolling the river. The bailiff has a spaniel called Sonny; sometimes it swims across the river to greet her. Nell tells herself she isn't lonely, but can count the faces she recognizes on one hand – apart from the men who come down to fish.

She tries to ignore them until, one day, quite early on in

this new, shuttered life, one of the men comes close to the window and peers in, thinking the place uninhabited. He takes fright when he sees her, staring back out at him like a pale reflection. She hears him call to his friends; hears the words 'squatter', 'peasant', their broad laughter trailing behind them. She would go and have it out with the men, tell them what she thinks of their remarks, but Ed is away, in London. She knows it's not her place to make a scene. And she would have to follow them down to the river.

It isn't visible from the house, but still Nell can feel its presence everywhere; brought in on the stagnant, oily air of a summer's night, in the wheedling sound of the mosquitoes as they trace her skin in the darkness, that sweeping metallic chill before dawn. In winter, the river seeps into her clothes, her hair, her bones, makes everything clammy to the touch. She's had to put her books on a high shelf above the fireplace, hoping the rising heat will keep them dry, but she's wrapped her most precious ones in old blankets, swaddled them like babies: the Shakespeare her mother gave her when she passed her eleven-plus; an illustrated collection of myth and fable; her irre-placeable copy of the Brothers Grimm. Its drawings of goblins and witches terrified and enthralled her as a child, and would do the same to me, later. These are her treasures. She won't let the river deform them with its slick caress.

If Nell imagines the river as an infiltrator, sidling its way up the path to spy on her, then she sees the house as her protector. It is her shield, repelling the invasion with its thick stone walls. The world outside can do what it wants; safe inside the house, Nell is queen.

When she first saw Weaver's Cottage, she thought it idyllic. Set low behind a thicket of trees, you could miss it entirely. The only visible part was the roof, half-covered in ivy. Up close, there were tall white hollyhocks in front of the windows and a short cobbled path to the door. The place looked so perfect, so unspoiled: a house a child might draw; a house in a fairy

27

tale. The occupant was Ed, and this was where she first met him, just two years before.

She heard him before she saw him: a steady rhythm of thumping, which sounded to her like giant steps. As she opened the gate, Nell felt the ground tremble underfoot, and paused, almost trembling herself.

What's going on? she asked, looking to her friend.

Go on, urged Cindy, waving her towards the door, You'll see.

Inside, the air was choked with dust, like an explosion of flour. Ed emerged from a cloud, separating himself from the background in two strides. He had a mallet crooked in his arm, and was completely white from head to foot, except where the sweat ran down his bare chest in shiny brown tramlines. He released the mallet with a clunk onto the threshold.

You must be Nell, he said, dipping his head to accept Cindy's kiss. He held open a grimy palm,

Won't shake hands.

He led them down the side of the cottage, through the long grass to the trees at the far end. Cindy, smiling, was wiping the dust from her cheek, picking her way through the rash of nettles at the edge of the riverbank. She turned to look at Nell, but Nell was craning her head, her eyes fixed on Ed's retreating form. Without stopping, he strode up to the bank and leapt into the water. He was under for such a long time, Nell began to worry. When he resurfaced, he had his shorts in his hand and was scrubbing them over his head. He pulled out the elastic from his ponytail and dived back into the depths.

What do you think? asked Cindy, wanting approval.

I'll let you know when I can actually see him, Nell said, relieved, waiting for Ed to reappear.

My mother loved this story; she'd tell it to me over and again. The odd detail might be added, a memory modified. Sometimes, Ed looked like a ghost coming out of a haunted house, sometimes like Windy Miller. Once, he was a bronzed prince; only once. But always, after he'd washed himself off in the water and pulled himself naked and dripping onto the bank, she'd end the story with her happy-ever-after: And that was it, my Bird, love at first sight, seeing as that was when I first actually clapped eyes on him, properly, I mean, without all the plaster dust and filth. Cindy wasn't best pleased, of course. But I'd made my mind up: I was there to stay.

★

Maggie hears footsteps, quick, almost military in their rhythm, coming along the corridor. She turns the notebook over and closes it, just as Kenneth enters the library.

Ah, Maggie, there you are, all ready with your pen poised, he says brightly, I trust you slept well?

Yes, thank you, she says, and to cover her guilt, holds the book up for him to see, I was just wondering about this badge.

Veritate et Virtute, says Kenneth, The old school motto. Truth and courage. Quite apt, I think, for the journey we're about to embark upon. Didn't you study Latin at school?

I didn't really go to school, she says, and seeing the surprise on his face, adds quickly, My mother taught me at home. But I went to the comp for my O levels. No Latin, though. It was quite . . . progressive. I don't think we had a school motto, unless it was 'Wake up, you at the back!'

Kenneth rewards her with a quick laugh. He moves to the window, fumbling at the shutters until he manages to open them; light spills over her and across the floor.

You know, you've given me an idea, he says, Because I was wondering where to start. Well, of course, we should begin at the beginning.

Lesson one, says Maggie, but Kenneth's not listening.

He scrutinizes the wall of vinyl, drumming his lips with his fingers.

Schooldays, he says, to himself, Music lessons.

His fingers track the row, stop, go back, until he finds the record he's seeking, slipping it out of the sleeve and holding it by the edges. He places it carefully on the turntable of the record player. It's a slow benediction, him bending over, mouth slightly open, dropping the needle onto the edge. In the stillness of the room, Maggie waits.

four

Lesson one begins with a click and a hiss. Kenneth, standing in shadow at the far end of the room, bends slightly at the knees, holding his arms out at either side of his body. He looks as if he's about to jump into the abyss. Nothing happens, neither of them moves; but Maggie listens hard for a sound. As he lifts his arms up high, it begins. To Maggie, the music sounds as if it starts in the middle, building too quickly to a crescendo.

'Jerusalem'! cries Kenneth, breaking into song: *And did those feet in ancient time, walk upon England's mountains green!*
Maggie writes it down, the shout that comes over like a war cry, and the breathless reminiscences that follow. The next – 'I Vow To Thee My Country' – is accompanied by more of Kenneth's full-throated singing, until he finally gives up, over-whelmed, and beats a teary retreat to a darkened corner of the library. Maggie makes notes, trying not to be distracted by the way he paces the room; he's not so much listening to the music as parading it in front of her. There's a sudden break in this activity. She pauses, waiting for the next stream of talk, a white noise whine in her ears. Kenneth stands with his broad back to her. He's muttering something about apple scrumping which she struggles to decipher.

Can you repeat that? she asks, but he waves away her request. Never mind that now; listen to this.

He places the record on the turntable, turns up the volume. Maggie hears a few simple opening bars, the asthmatic wheeze of an organ. Church music, she thinks. Kenneth slips behind her chair just as the choir starts to sing. The voices rise high, fall low: it is the singing of children. He's near enough for her to hear him, and speaking quite clearly, but Maggie can't put pen to paper. Her hand is stunned on the page.

Something wrong, Maggie? he says, seeing her rigid posture.

This song, she says, tilting her head like a bird, What is it? Kenneth moves back over to the record player and plucks the stylus off the record. He looks aggrieved at her interruption. The silence that follows is thick as wool.

'All Things Bright and Beautiful', he says, I was put in mind of it – if you'll forgive me for saying so – when I first saw you. He sees her again, down in the field, spread on the barrow. Despite the knowledge that she can't read his thoughts, his face reddens at the memory.

And I was saying, he continues, That this was a hymn we used to sing at school. Harvest festival time, I think. It's got such an innocent theme, so full of optimism. Don't you agree? Maggie holds her right hand with her left to steady it. She feels last night's supper repeat in her throat: bitter courgette, acid onion. Perhaps his cooking has given her food poisoning.

Did they sing it here, she asks, The children?

What? he says, frowning now, Oh. You mean when they came to practise. Quite possibly; I wouldn't know. It's a popular hymn; this version's by the Winchester Cathedral choir.

Would you like me to write that down? she asks, tasting bile.

Kenneth closes his eyes and sighs, as if dealing with a recalcitrant child.

Only, I can't actually hear you over the music, Maggie adds, quick with the lie.

Kenneth hadn't thought of this; she can see it in his eyes. His response is tense, commanding:

I will speak now. Please write down exactly what I say.

It was quite an amazing experience, made all
the more amazing by the fact - extraordinary
- that everyone brought something; fruit in
baskets and what else was there - um - there
was fruit, and vegetables. The day boys only
brought tinned stuff, tinned stuff, of
course. Mr Vaughan at the piano. He erm,
anyway, the singing was the thing. All things
so very bright and so very beautiful in those
days, the colours and the church—

Kenneth stops reading. They are in his office on the top floor,
a late sun slanting through the room. Outside, the fields are
nearly in shadow; the barley burning copper, wheat the colour
of pewter. Maggie has presented him with her afternoon's
work: two closely typed pages of his words. He stands at the
window, holding the papers in his hand, while she sits on the
sofa behind his desk. Kenneth can barely bring himself to look
at her, with her face lifted, and that expression she has; so
solemn, so eager to please. She has done well, he should praise
her efforts: she has given him precisely what he's asked for.
Except he can't get beyond the first page.

Something wrong? Maggie asks, fighting the urge to get up
and go and stand at his shoulder, Only, you tend to speak quite
quickly.

Everything's wrong, he says, It's terrible.
He sees her head twitch, her hair fall over her face.

Not you, he cries, Me! It's so ... God. I sound so
awful. 'The day boys only brought tinned stuff.' Did I really
say that?

I couldn't make it up, says Maggie.

And I go on and on, two pages of ... utter tripe.
Kenneth removes his glasses and runs a hand over his eyes.

Maggie sees the age in his face, the lines and creases magnified by the low sunlight.

Well, this won't do. We'll have to have a rethink, he says, Change of plan.

It's just for you to read, she says, feeling a rush of pity at his crestfallen look, That's what you said, didn't you? It's only for your eyes?

Kenneth's voice is very faint,

I suppose, he says.

Then what does it matter how it sounds? Maybe you just need a few words, you know, to get the feeling again.

Maggie looks keenly at him, her green eyes cool as glass. Kenneth flips the papers, moving towards her so quickly, for a second she thinks he's going to hit her with them. He scrunches the pages into a ball.

Maggie, I don't know what the prompt is. They came back to life, you know, those moments? But it wasn't just hearing the hymn again, it was—

It was telling me, she says, finishing the sentence he can't bring himself to utter, Telling me about your past brought it right back.

And why should that be? he asks, You don't know me, or my past. Why should I care about that?

He throws the ball of papers at the waste-paper bin, misses, picks it up again and dashes it into the basket. Maggie is silent for a second, waiting for his anger to subside before she continues. She weighs her words; she wants to make them count.

Because what's the point of memories, if there's no one else to share them with? You might just as well use a Dictaphone if that's what you believe.

Kenneth drops himself heavily into his chair, smoothes his hands across the blotter on his desk. He finds the truth of her words baffling.

But you don't believe that, do you? she adds, You want to share them.

Kenneth's laugh is cynical.

Oh yes, Maggie, I want to share them all right. I want to share them with *me*.

The pause that follows is a kind of reckoning. Kenneth's gaze wanders over the blotter, the leather-topped desk, his knuckles and his blunt fingernails. He won't look at Maggie. In the waiting, a shiver of fright courses through her, as if she has been found out, as if he's known right from the start who she is and why she's here. Her mind races back over the past two days; she's given nothing away. She could be anybody, nobody. He can't know, and he mustn't know, and she must keep courage. Truth from courage, she thinks, misremembering the motto. She jumps when he speaks again.

Why I hit on this scheme . . . I was standing down there in the library, a few months back, and I was watching the black-birds bouncing over the lawn, and there was the morning, the sharp air, and the light, everything rinsed and – it was brand new, you know, the way only an early spring morning can be – and I was listening to a flute sonata. It's by Poulenc. Some of his stuff is quite austere, but this is—

Kenneth throws his hands up,

The piece, for me, is how spring feels.

Maggie is nodding, calm enough to find her voice, Sounds good, she says, I'd like to hear it.

But I wanted to record the moment *exactly*, so that I could remember it again properly, without any . . . interference. So other thoughts won't sneak up on me, catch me off guard. Because that was when I realized. There are fewer spring days left now, for me. Who knows, maybe I won't ever see another spring day like that. So in the gloomy winter, I'd like to relive it. Properly.

Maggie searches for some conciliatory words. Finding nothing to stem his self-pity, she simply looks at him.

I'll let you into a secret, he says, My mind these days, it's a runaway train. One minute I'm doing something ordinary –

opening a tin of tomatoes or writing a memo – or, or listening to music – and the next, I'm thirty, forty years away from what I'm doing. As if I've been invaded. And I have to find some way to control it. Contain it. I want to bottle the memory, I want to pull the cork out and be back in that same time. That shining time. It might be hard for you to understand now, but one day, you will.

She doesn't know if she understands, but she knows there's no way to bottle a moment and keep it as it was; there's too much stale air trapped between the memory and the cork. Best to let it breathe, she thinks, but doesn't say.

So I have to get it right. And that— he gestures to the waste-paper bin – That is not how I wish to relive my life. I want the good stuff. I've read plenty of memoirs, Maggie, politicians and film stars and suchlike. And they're interesting – not like that drivel.

That's because they're ghostwritten, she says, You don't think celebrities spend their days dictating their life stories, do you? They tell them to other people, and then the writer goes away and does the research. Why don't we try it? You tell me your memories and then I'll write them up. I'll write a story for your story. I'll be your ghostwriter.

As she speaks, Kenneth moves from behind the desk and wanders back to the window. Maggie doesn't know if he's heard her.

Will they still be my memories, he says, finally, If you're writing them?

I'm a very good listener, she says.

And you'll be my interpreter, he says, catching air in his fist, That's what you said?

That's right, agrees Maggie, not correcting him, You see, we're both good listeners.

five

Maggie opens the notebook at the front, weighting it with her cup of tea. She switches on the electric typewriter, which makes a series of buzzing protests, and feeds a piece of paper into the slot at the back. The machine seizes it from her grip and winds it round the platen. Click, whirr, silence.

ALL THINGS BRIGHT AND BEAUTIFUL, she types. She pauses, looks around her. The prefect's office under the main stairs is no more than an angular cupboard: just enough space for a shelf, a chair, and a desk. This last is a long piece of oak running the length of the wall. Typewriter, paper, correction fluid. Maggie picks up the bottle and shakes it. Hearing nothing, she twists the top off: the fluid has long ago become solid, and now she sees only dried flakes of white on her fingers. She sniffs them for the faint scent of solvent.

All creatures, she says, staring at the page, All creatures great and small.

Above her is a casement window, glowing with leaded lights: blue diamonds in each corner and a circular motif in the centre depicting a woman in profile. She knows it's not the Virgin Mary; the robe is rose pink, and there's no halo. Maggie reaches up and releases the latch, pushing the window wide. Outside is the entrance, a gravel drive cut into a sloping lawn. Beyond lie the rhododendron bushes, their leaves dark and glossy, the space underneath them a deep spill of shadow. Nothing will grow under there. She feels, but cannot see, the river running in a black ribbon at the edge of the estate. Maggie breathes in the soft evening air and the sweeter tang of the honeysuckle growing up the wall. Wood pigeons throb out their song. Resurrect his time, she tells herself, and then your own. But she falters, her hands poised over the typewriter keys. It makes such a racket, the machine. Every key she strikes results in a flurry of noise. She takes up the pen, lifts her cup from the notebook, and turns to the pages at the back.

★

They spend most of the summer down by the river. My mother sits a little way off from the bank, so she can barely see the water. Ed loves it, though; he jumps in and out, in and out, shaking the droplets off his body like a happy dog.

If she had said nothing, the businessmen would still be fishing here, and she wouldn't have to spend so much time near the water. But Nell hasn't learned about consequences yet; there is talk in the papers about the butterfly effect, but she doesn't understand what butterflies have to do with CND or flood or famine: she simply wanted the fishing to stop. After the man had put his hand on the glass and looked in, she told Ed about it, how it frightened her. She told him about the names they called her.

The day before the men's next visit, Ed went to the iron-monger's shop in the market place. He bought two indus-trial-sized canisters of liquid soap and a long length of rubber hose, which he attached to the outlet from the bath. Early the next morning, he set to work, snaking the hose through the high grass, up to the corner of the field and down through the nettles at the far bank where he settled it at the river's edge. He filled the bath with soap and water, then emptied it, filled and emptied it, leaning out of the little window to see how the river was looking. He said it was like watching a cloudy sky go by. Nell was worried about the fish, whether it would kill them, but Ed just laughed at her.

There are no fish in that river, you dimwit, except when the river man stocks it. For when the *chaps* come down from town, he said, in a languid, mimicking drawl. In his ordinary voice he added,

Reckon that should buy us some peace for a while.

Nell is not sophisticated, but she's not stupid, despite what Ed thinks. She has simple ways – an innocent, Cindy calls her; a child of nature, says Leon – and she does have a childlike quality that certain types of men find attractive, and certain women think is an act to trap such men. But she's not thick. She knows what she likes.

She likes it when the cow parsley grows tall and the only thing she can see at the bottom of the garden is a mass of nodding white. Then mullein, willowherb, clumps of elephant-ine dock, all crowding together as if to shield her from the river beyond. She knows the names of the plants and herbs that grow in the hedgerows around the house; to her library of fairy tales she adds books of natural remedies, traditional cures, none of which she ever considers using. She reads avidly. She is *not* thick.

Ed keeps busy, devising a plan to make paintings from the colours of the earth. He's bored with the art scene and its labels; tired of the conceptual, of the minimal, the performance; fed up to the back teeth of fluxus and navigus and all the other us-es; he won't be pigeonholed. He tells anyone who will listen: his art transcends all that; it is transcendental. It's a transcen-dental-active-nature vibe. He calls the movement Trans-Act and declares himself the sole practitioner of the group.

Can you have a group of one? asks Nell, innocently snip-ping the heads off a bunch of dandelions.

We used to call them piss-the-beds, he says, nodding at the weeds, But you'd *know* that.

Ed's art is indeed very active. He digs holes in the garden, squatting over them naked, pouring in water and swirling it to mud with a stick. Finding a new use for his mallet, he pounds up nettles and berries and throws them into the mix. Soon, the garden is pocked with muddy hollows, so to venture out at night is to risk a broken ankle. Inside the cottage a collection of jam jars clutters the draining board and kitchen table, in shades of green and brown, algaeous and putrefying. After a while, the jars give off the same stench as the river. Ed won't allow Nell to throw them away; he paints pictures of rainbows in these hues, on the walls and occasionally on canvas, every one of which dries to a dull khaki brown.

My mother is productive too; she makes dreamcatchers, which sell well in the craft shop in town. She finds the feathers in the neighbouring fields, striped golden-brown and shiny blue-black ones, tiny white chick down clinging to the brambles on the verge outside the cottage. She uses the feathers sparingly, even though they're not hard to find; sticky clusters of them lie on the main road at the end of the lane, buzzing with flies. She leaves these alone.

Ed's cousin Leon comes to live with them. His band is finished, he says, the guys have had musical differences. He brings his tabla and a rucksack and a case of whisky, and overnight, Ed's Trans-Act movement comes to an end; he and Leon decide to form a duo. They sing to the tall grass, to the birds, to Nell and Cindy; and they swim in the river, drink whisky, roll six-skin joints that leave them parched and motionless under the shade of the trees. The evenings are long. Leon patters accompaniment on his drums, while Ed composes songs, inventing chords on his guitar. He calls to Nell to write his lyrics down, quick! before he forgets them. Nell is never still at this time. She treks in and out of the cottage, bringing fish-finger sandwiches, charred toast disguised with baked beans, anything left over in the pantry that she might pass off as edible.

The men like to sleep out in the open, like cowboys; it's not warm, and most nights they need to light a fire. When they've used up the stock of logs in the shed, they saw branches from the trees that border the property. Nell realizes she can be seen from the road when, one day, the water bailiff and the boy pass by and shout hello.

It gets too cold, or the wood they've cut is too green to burn; whatever the reason, they move back indoors. Now Nell can't listen to her records at night, because they want to sing – to rehearse – and cannot be disturbed by her noise. Gong and America replace Joni Mitchell and Carole King. The smell of Ed snoring next to her is the sweet and sour of hash and whisky.

Leon takes to sleeping on the couch in the living room under an Indian blanket. When Nell gets up to make breakfast in the kitchen, she can see him, wrapped up like a mummy, through the gaping hole in the wall. The improvements Ed has started don't progress: in the daytime, the hole becomes a serving hatch; in the evenings, they light the candles stuck onto the exposed brick ledge, and it becomes a kind of altar. When Ed peers through it, he looks to her like Christ bestowing a blessing. Nell's not unhappy: she has Ed and Leon, and sometimes Cindy, for company, and soon she'll have me, although she doesn't know it yet. Summer lags into autumn.

★

Maggie reads through what she's written: her handwriting, neat and right-leaning, looks like soldiers on the march. She takes pleasure in imagining her mother's past, and thus far, it's been easy: tales told and retold by Nell, at bedtime, to help them both sleep. It was a funny and sometimes strange amusement

41

for Maggie – at only five years old an attentive listener – but welcome relief from the silence and the dark. Through the history Nell created, they could both visualize a life only one of them knew. It avoided talk about the one they shared.

She turns to the typewriter and the heading – ALL THINGS BRIGHT AND BEAUTIFUL – at the top of the page. Beneath it, her fingers on the keys crash out just two lines:

```
He gave us eyes to see them
And lips that we might tell.
```

six

They spend the evening together again. Maggie hadn't intended
it. After writing up the music notes, she wanted to be away from
Earl House for a while. She caught the bus into town and bought
food at the supermarket: pasta and tomatoes and tinned tuna;
easy, thoughtless stuff. She treated herself to a bottle of Fleurie,
planning a night in front of the snowy television screen. Just
her and the remote control and the wine. But on her return,
she found a note had been slipped under the door: Kenneth's
writing, looping letters in a stylized, old-fashioned hand,
requesting the pleasure of her company. It ended with a large
flourish for the K. Underneath his signature he'd added, almost
as a plea, 'Come and try my latest concoction!'

Maggie finds Kenneth at the stove, peering into a rise of
steam wafting from a large metal saucepan. As she falters at the
kitchen door, he stretches across the worktop and switches off
the radio.

No music, he says, Not after the choir this morning.
He looks directly at her, a stern expression on his face, which
softens when he sees the paleness of her skin, the shadows
under her eyes. It's enough confirmation for him to pursue
this line of enquiry.

You found it troubling? he asks, Something in that hymn
affected you?

43

She makes to shake her head, to deny the plain truth of it, but then her words betray her.

Yes. It was a bad feeling, that's all. I'm sorry. I won't let it affect our work.

Kenneth lifts the wooden spoon to his mouth and blows on it.

Here, tell me what you think, he says, holding it out for her to taste. He watches as she puts her open mouth to the sauce.

Because I hadn't planned on that, Maggie. I mean, I thought the music was simply for me to have feelings about. Silly, isn't it? Of course, you would have a response too, even if you didn't know the piece.

Maggie flicks her tongue over her lips.

It needs salt.

She observes him as he searches about amongst the jars and pots scattered over the worktop. He's dressed casually, mustard-coloured slacks, a white linen shirt undone at the neck and with the sleeves rolled up. In contrast, Maggie has forced herself to make an effort. She feels like a gauche teenager, standing in a strange kitchen with a strange man, in her yellow flower-print dress. Her hair is squashed under a wide tortoiseshell clip; every time she turns her head, she feels it dig into her scalp, as if to remind her that her natural self has been disguised. She takes a moment before she delivers her speech, blinking at the sight of his forearms, the hairs on his tanned skin glistening under the kitchen spotlights. He looks so capable, so full of life and confidence; no sign of the trembling hands she'd witnessed last time. Her own hands are sticky with heat.

Kenneth, I must apologize for this morning. This is your history we're writing, not mine, she says, I'll try to be more professional from now on.

Finding the bowl with the salt in it, he takes a pinch between his fingers and dashes it into the stew. He wants to say, Please don't be more professional, just be who you are. Instead he says,

And what about your history, Maggie? You didn't give much away in your letter.

What would you like to know? she asks. She crosses to the sink as she says this, turning the cold tap on full. He follows her, puzzled at the way she puts one wrist under the flow, then the other. He ducks his head slightly, looks into her face.

Cools the blood, she says.

There's the scar again, a silvery strike on her brow.

Well, if we're talking about music, he asks, What kind do *you* like? What moves you?

I like all kinds. But what moves me? Maggie gazes into the running water, considering her response. Kenneth takes a step back from her to bring her into focus again.

Singing, choral music, and— she breaks off, unnerved by the intense way he's listening – I suppose voices affect me most. Music my mother used to play to me when I was little.

And your mother, he says, reading the answer in her face, Keeping well, is she?

She died a little while ago, says Maggie, and before he can offer condolences, she rushes on, She liked all kinds of stuff, blues, and soul, lots of folk. John Martyn, mainly, Nick Drake, Joni Mitchell, Bob Dylan—

I adore Dylan! says Kenneth, And Joni, too, of course. Not sure I'm familiar with the others. You must play me some.

And hymns move me, as you know, she says, shaking the water off her hands, Some of them. But maybe not in the way they're meant to. What about you? What did you like, as a child?

Kenneth tips his head up, thinking, and bites his lower lip. Under the lights his teeth gleam large and yellow and perfectly even.

Let me see. Um, jazz, something with a bit of *combustion* in it.

He does a little sideways feint, like an old boxer, as he says it.

My father used to play Cab Calloway, and there was Dizzy Gillespie, Satchmo, Earl Bostic . . .

No relation? asks Maggie.

What? Ah, very good, yes. I mean no.

He smiles, enjoying her teasing, but not the feeling it produces in him. Maggie raises her eyebrows, nods her head towards the stove.

Something might be combusting right now, she says.

Kenneth grabs the pan off the gas, quickly swapping from one hand to the other until she passes him a tea towel to wrap around the handle.

What do you think? he says, tilting it towards her. She stares into the volcanic mass of bubbling brown, feeling a wet heat on her face.

Caught it just in time. What's in it?

Top secret. But this beef will need a while longer. Could you pass me the wine?

Maggie fetches him a half-full bottle of red, from which he takes a long swig.

That'll make it taste better, he says, smacking his lips.

She reaches out and cuffs him lightly on the arm.

Oh, all right then, he says, pouring the wine into the pan. The light drops suddenly as the sun outside the kitchen window slips behind the trees.

So, what did you write about the hymn? he asks, In the end?

Maggie decides she will answer him truthfully.

Just two lines. But very fitting. I thought it might be an idea to save them up.

Once the stew is bubbling again, Kenneth stirs it, scrapes the gunge from the sides and turns the heat off. He seems not to be listening, until he looks at her.

Why don't I pour us a G&T, Maggie, this'll need half an hour to meld. Save them up how, exactly? he says, crossing to the fridge and fetching a tray of ice.

Again, they take their drinks out under the cover of the

terrace and sit side by side on the wrought-iron bench. The sun has sunk away completely now, but the sky is pink and blue and shimmering, like the skin of a rainbow trout. The river below it is a lash of fractured purple. Kenneth sits so near, Maggie can see the small bobbled graze of a shaving cut on the line of his jaw; she can smell his cologne, cedarwood and spice. So, he's taken trouble for her, too. She glances at him from the corner of her eye as she explains.

I thought – you'll say if you don't like the idea – that we could record your music story chronologically, from childhood to now. That way, you could read what I've written at the very end. I'll still type it up. It'll be like a . . . musical memoir.
He lifts his glass and takes a long drink. She wants him to look at her now; she could easily bear it.

Like *This is Your Life*, she says finally, with an anxious smile. Kenneth nods, gently swirling his tumbler, making the ice clatter. She clutches her drink, feeling the beads of moisture sliding under her fingers, the crisp scent rising up. She hasn't tasted it yet. When he smiles too, she takes a quick, choking gulp. The chill and burn of the gin on her tongue is wonderful.

That wasn't the plan, Maggie. The plan was to be random, to have one piece of music trigger off another. Spontaneous, indirect. Like the way memories flood in and out.

Not much flooding today, she says, My fault.
They are silent for a moment. In her head, Maggie hears the hymn again, the sad wheeze of the organ before the children's voices cut in.

But, d'you know what? I think it's a rather good plan, he says at last, We don't have to work in sections, but maybe you could organize them later? Childhood, adolescence, young adulthood—

It was a very good year, she says, swaying into him and laughing. Kenneth looks askance for a moment, then his face lights up.

Ah, yes, A Very Good Year. Well done, you clever girl. *When*

I was twenty-one, it was a very good year, he sings, *For something girls who lived up the stair, with all that beautiful hair . . .*

And it came undone, says Maggie, blushing. Kenneth blushes too, putting his mouth to his glass and finding it empty.

If only I was twenty-one again, he says.

Me too.

She expects him to say the usual stuff, about how she has her whole life ahead of her, but he slaps his leg, lifting himself up from the bench with a groan.

Which reminds me. Wine. Come and help me choose a bottle, he says, holding out his hand for hers. She doesn't think it strange or unusual to slip her fingers into his. Kenneth leads her through the kitchen, pausing at a narrow door in the far wall. It has an ancient calendar hanging on it, a sepia-tone picture of a horse and plough.

The years turn over fast, says Maggie, giving him a look. He raises his finger,

Don't tempt me, he says, A gentleman never asks a lady her age.

If you must know, she says, I'm thirty-several.

How excellent, he says, tracing the top of the door frame with his fingertips and fetching down a rusted iron key, And that makes me sixty-several. You know, I feel younger already!

It takes Kenneth only two attempts to feed the key into the housing. He stands aside and pulls open the door with a flourish, as if he's performing a conjuring trick. And it *is* a sort of illusion, this dark, constricted entrance into the bowels of the house. Maggie tracks him single file along a corridor of sweating brick, ducking through an archway and almost stumbling down the steps into the wine cellar. They pass banks of wooden shelves, stopping when they reach the far corner. The only light is from a square grille of window cut into the outside wall. The smell is damp dog, mushroom.

I keep the decent stuff back here, out of reach. Would you like to choose something? he asks, Something special?

I'd have no clue, says Maggie, squinting in the near-darkness, Unless you've laid down a stash of supermarket plonk. She puts out her hand, gingerly, fearing spiders, or mice, and lifts a random bottle from a rack.

Let me see, he says, taking it from her and holding it at arm's length, Haven't got my glasses. Maggie, would you?
He passes the bottle back.

Margaux, she reads, wiping off a skin of dust with her thumb, 1968.

Lovely. That'll do me, he says, But the question is, will it do my son?
Maggie doesn't feel the smooth glide as the bottle slips from her grasp, doesn't hear it explode onto the flags. Doesn't feel the splash of vintage red spatter her legs and dress. Such is the shock of it. The seconds replay themselves in slow motion.

Your son, she's saying, as the bottle falls, and her voice is cool and close, and then there is a moment, in the near-darkness, when their eyes meet and a recognition passes between them – of sadness, disappointment – before Kenneth jumps back from the flying glass.

Oh, my dear, he says, Never mind, never mind— drawing her away from the centre of the smash – I should get the light fixed in here, Will's always saying so. There'll be another bottle somewhere now, let me see.
Maggie stands appalled, hands on her face, peering down into the spreading shining wet.

But was it really expensive? she cries, I bet it was.

Come away, Kenneth says, ducking through the archway, You'll cut yourself. Look, I'll fetch another. Come now. Will should be here quite soon.
At the door to the kitchen, she touches his elbow.

Could he not come over tonight, she asks, Could you put him off?
She's about to say something else, but then, as if stung, she turns a circle on the threshold, her hands flying around her head. A

long grey cobweb hangs from her hair, wafting on the breeze from the cellar.

Get it off! she yells, spinning again, and Kenneth catches her arm to still her, turning her round so he's looking at the pale nape of her neck, the scatter of freckles there making his stomach lurch. He would not have believed it. Here he is, remembering the straw caught in her curls and putting his hands on her now, removing the tortoiseshell clip with a sudden click, watching the hair fall onto his fingers. He brushes his palm over her head, smooth and quick, catching the web. It feels sticky as glue. And he turns her again.

It came undone, she says, her face flushed this time with relief. The way she says it, it's an invitation, Kenneth thinks, and she makes it easy, smiling in the dusty light of the doorway, for him to pull her near. Like a kite being wound in. But when she puts her palm up to his chest he understands it's to stop him getting any closer. Her other hand catches him by the wrist. He feels her grip, tender but insistent.

Maggie, I do apologize, he says.

You don't know what came over you, she says. She sounds scornful, but she doesn't remove her hand from his chest, and still she holds his wrist in her grip, and both places are unbearably hot for Kenneth, as if she's transmitting fire through her skin.

I do know what came over me, he admits, You're very—

He pauses, searching for the word. *Bounteous* was what came into his head; he knows it's not right but can find no substitute. She fills the space for him.

Very clumsy, she says, I did warn you.

No, no, you are all grace. And I'm a silly old fool.

Not so old, she says, loosing her hold on him, But I can't comment on the rest.

He's thankful for the joke, glances away as she brushes a remnant of web from the front of her skirt. She lifts the hem to inspect the zigzag splashes of wine, and as he looks back,

Kenneth catches sight of her knees, so awkward, so vulnerable, and has to look away again.

I'll clear up that mess and then cancel my son, he says, As we've completely ruined your dress.

And disposed of the wine, she says.

He starts to say, I'll fetch another, when she nods at the fridge.

I'd quite like some white, really, she says, Nothing fancy.

Kenneth turns the key in the lock and places it back on the top of the door frame. His expression when he faces her is severe again.

Now, Maggie, he says, in a scolding voice, A wine can be unassuming, it can be modest. Sometimes, we say it's a friendly wine. *Fancy* is not, as far as I'm aware, a technical term. I can see you have much to learn.

Shall we start with where the glasses are kept? she says, A girl could die of thirst round here.

Patience, my dear, he says, pulling open one drawer after another, It's here somewhere. I may be forgetful, and silly— he breaks off, brandishing a horn-handled waiter's friend – But there are some things a fellow never forgets. You have to open the bottle first, he says, And release the genie!

She doesn't remind him about the broken glass in the cellar. She'll clear it up herself tomorrow; she knows where he keeps the key.

But now it is today: yesterday's tomorrow. Maggie shivers as she creeps down the stairs; despite the promise of another warm morning, the house at this early hour is chill. Only the tick of the grandfather clock breaks the silence. She walks in time with it, through the hall and into the kitchen, fumbling along the top of the cellar door for the key until she finds it. Inside, she gets only as far as the archway: a waft of cold air blows on her face, stalling her, making her blink. The grille at the far end casts a square of dismal light onto the floor, showing where the wine has soaked into the concrete. All that remains is a flat black stain and a jagged crescent of glass, surrounded by a halo of glittering splinters. Maggie retraces her steps and puts the key back where she found it.

Outside, the morning sky is a soft pearl grey, a score of red slashes marking east. She'd slept badly again: her recurrent nightmare – of a flash of white light burning into her eye – seemed to repeat itself on an endless loop. She was woken by the sound of a dog barking, but couldn't tell whether it was real or part of her dream.

Her plan is to walk off the noises in her head, the dull ache behind her eyes; both the result, she thinks, of too much wine. She has hours before work – before Kenneth plays her more of his memories. She chooses not to think about what he will say, what piece of history he will attempt to resurrect. Instead, she aims directly east, moving swiftly now through the middle of the rhododendrons and down the lane, entering a dewy copse. It's lush inside; full of waist-high nettles and bindweed, overhanging branches strung with silver spiderlines. She hears a woodpecker drumming a tree, distant traffic on the motorway. Maggie sinks further into the thick silence of the copse, feeling a change in the air on her arms. She follows the descent of a narrow track this way and that, scenting out the river.

The mooring on the far side is home to two boats; a rackety narrowboat and a sleek white pleasure cruiser. She scans them both for signs of life, and finding none – it's early still – turns her eyes to the water. The willows at the river's edge chop the surface into black strips; further into the middle, the reflected sky lies flat as a pan. It's impossible to judge the depth. Maggie takes off her boots and socks and slips quickly down the bank, her fingers finding purchase in the gritty mud and small stones, until her feet are in the water. It is burning, numbing cold. She moves slowly forwards until she feels the ledge begin to fall away, then she stops. Her skirt rises up around her like a water lily.

Standing quite still, feeling the slow drift of the current

nudging her body, Maggie watches the way the growing daylight is mirrored on the water. She thinks of her mother, of the river, and of how the two will always be connected. It would be the last thing Nell would want, to be bonded to her fear. But she never moved far. Maggie considers it again; how Nell ended up in Field Cottage, only fifteen miles from Weaver's and still in plain sight of the river.

As if I have a choice, she'd said, shrugging, I just go where they put me. They have all the power round here and don't you forget it. They don't just uphold the law, they make it.

And then, a second reason, as if the first one wasn't enough:

Keep your friends close, and your enemies closer.

Maggie understood her mother's anger over the Cranes and their kind; her father had abandoned them, with hardly a look backwards, but Nell never forgot that Maggie was Ed's child too: she was a Crane. Nell would live on the moon if it meant she could keep her daughter. Maggie knows it now, what an enemy fear can be, what a bully; waiting round the corner, spying, turning up when you least expect it, when your defences are down. Far better to keep it in plain sight. But the river isn't Maggie's enemy: she loves it, her only rebellion against the force that was Nell. And Kenneth loves it too, she knows he does. The way he sits there, watching it, breathing it in. The certainty is oddly pleasing to her; the thought that they should be so different, but share something ordinary. She was grateful that he told William not to come. And the evening had been enjoyable, despite the awkwardness of the pass he'd made, despite the burnt stew. She tells herself not to think about him, but like the current, he tugs her back. If she is to stay, she must prepare: she has to be ready to meet his son. She knows there is a right moment, but that it isn't now. Today she will be cheerful, she won't try to lead Kenneth anywhere in particular, and it'll be easy, he makes her feel easy. Easy, she says, pulling herself up onto the bank. Her skirt clings like river weed to her legs, black spots of mud freckle her shins and feet.

It's then she hears the sound: a low, rumbling growl behind her. She turns to see a man standing on the deck of the narrow-boat, with a face so tanned and lined it looks like a mask. His eyes are squinting at her, the fingers of his left hand are buried deep in the scruff of a large red dog. In her ribs a quick, intense stitch of pain: the spiteful poking of the fear.

seven

Skiffle, Maggie! cries Kenneth, as she enters the library, Can't beat it to get the blood flowing!

He's bending from side to side, shaking a pair of imaginary maracas. He looks ridiculous. Clearly, the wine they drank last night has had no effect on him. She perches on the edge of the armchair, opening the notebook slowly and emphatically, hoping he'll take the hint; but he merely circles her, smiling, and leans over the wing of the chair.

It's a very fine morning, don't you think?

And you are very fine, he says, in his head.

It's a lovely day all right, she agrees, But all that drink last night; I'm just not used to it.

Maggie expects this statement to be met with solicitous dismay by Kenneth, but he surprises her.

What you need is a bit of something to pep you up, he says, raising his arms again and twisting his wrists, Something . . . life-affirming.

He follows Lonnie Donegan with Buddy Holly with someone she thinks is called Tubby Hairs; but when she asks, Kenneth shouts over the frenetic sound,

Never mind that now, just listen. That sax. Miraculous!

Despite herself, Maggie is transfixed by Kenneth: by the sight of him, his pure joy. He dances round the room like a child.

Possessed, she thinks, that's what he is: he's been taken over. He announces an Alvin Robinson song, following it with another three or four bursts of music, half-played and snatched from the turntable before she can find out what they are.

Kenneth, I need some help here, she says, What should I be writing?

Robert Johnson, he cries, Just listen to this.

A sound of thin wailing, dry and dusty guitar, as if the man is locked inside an old tin can. Maggie writes down the name and asks Kenneth for the title.

The devil himself, he says, not hearing her.

He pauses, his face questioning hers.

Maybe something a little more upbeat? Maybe the devil isn't for you. Rusty never liked him either.

He ducks down beneath the stereo and brings up a battered LP with no outer sleeve.

How about this? he says, You gotta like Ike.

Maggie watches as he stares into space, begins to dance, then stops, then starts again, like a robot with a faulty circuit. She can't help but smile, even if he is in perfect time with the guitar, even if it makes sense. He catches her eye, smiles with her.

C'mon, Maggie, twist those strings.

And he pulls her out of her chair.

The silences are important, he says, stopping with one finger in the air and then jumping about when the music kicks in again, It's the spaces in between things that count. Listen to the gaps. They're music too.

She tries a self-conscious hop from one foot to the other, until he takes both of her hands in his and swings her round, and round again, round and round, until the room is turning too and she's in free fall, and the feeling is like sherbet fizzing on her tongue; it makes her laugh out loud with delight. Then the music ends and Kenneth drops her hands and slumps, sweating, into the window seat. Still weightless and elated, Maggie sits down too.

Better than a workup at the gym, he says, wiping his fore-head with his arm, Haven't boogied like that in years.

You were good, Kenneth, perfect timing.

Oh, that's me, he says, tapping his brow, Upstairs for thinking, downstairs for dancing.

When, she says, When was the last time you danced?
She picks up her notebook, feels her hands trembling. Kenneth scratches at a bead of sweat on his nose.

They have ceilidhs in the village sometimes. Probably a few years back.

And they dance to jazz? she asks.
He leans across the seat and pushes the window open; cool air fills the room.

They dance to violins – fiddles – you know what a ceilidh is, surely?

It's a barn dance, she says, I'm just asking.
And then she releases a truth.

I used to go to festivals in Charmouth. You know, free festi-vals, like raves. Didn't matter if you couldn't dance so well, nobody minded.
Kenneth frowns at her.

Raves. They're a nuisance, all that noise and litter. All that destruction. Can't say I see you enjoying *that*.

They weren't illegal. It was folky, Kenneth, like, um, like an outdoor barn dance. It was very peaceful. Lots of tree hugging. She has his attention again.

You've actually hugged a tree?

Don't knock it until you try it, she says, It's quite soothing. But not with that monster in the courtyard – the one with the scary eyes.
She's about to ask him about it when Kenneth swipes the note-book from her hands. A leap of panic as he takes the pen. He bends away from her, shielding it with his arm like a schoolboy as she tries to snatch it back. On the cover he writes, in broad

57

capitals, THIS BOOK BELONGS TO MAGGIE. IF FOUND, PLEASE RETURN TO—

Where? Bilbo Baggins at Bag End?

Har har. Give it back. You're not allowed to see it until we're finished. And we'll never get finished if we don't get on.

Relax, he says, waving her away, We've got all day. We've got all summer. Haven't we, Maggie, the whole lovely summer ahead.

When she doesn't reply, he scrawls two more words on the book and makes to give it back, holding the edge so it's trapped between them. EARL HOUSE is written beneath her name.

You will stay, won't you? The Fates have ordained it. Or the fairies, if you prefer.

Where were we? she says, finally gaining possession, the book safe again. She won't be sidetracked by his teasing.

We were dancing.

You said something about Dusty, she says, and guesses, Dusty Springfield?

Rusty, he says, First met her in the Sunset Strip. He raises his eyebrows, Soho.

Was she a performer? asks Maggie.

Kenneth smiles, puts his head on one side in what looks like a gesture of forgiveness,

Not exactly, he says, Dear old Rusty. She was my wife.

eight

Every time she touches the keys, the noise of the machine drills into her head. Maggie works quickly, not checking what she types, keen to be out of Kenneth's memories and back into her own.

```
Lonnie Donegan
My Old Man's a Dustman, but he wasn't was
he, Kenneth? Your old man was a high court
judge, and he knew my grandfather. They're
both dead now; presiding in Heaven.

Alvin Robinson
A  sound  that  smells  like  a  swamp,  says
Kenneth. RIP Alvin, lie deep.

Robert Johnson
Not much of a name for the devil. You don't
scare me. Dead and gone, dead and gone.

Ike Turner
You're  dead  too  but  you  don't  sound  it.
Kenneth likes dancing to you. He says the
spaces in between are as important as the
```

```
sounds. Listen to the gaps, he says, They
are music too.
I'm doing that, Kenneth, I'm listening to
the gaps and I'm trying to fill the spaces.
Not dead yet.
```

Upstairs, Kenneth sits at the desk in his office, his ear cocked
to the open door. He can hear, with bright satisfaction, the
stabbing sound of the typewriter keys, amplified and hollowed
by the wooden staircase. From the irregular stops and starts of
noise that Maggie makes, he can tell that she's a far from expert
typist. And he has looked over her shoulder in the library:
despite her claim to have shorthand, her notes could be read
by anyone. So, she is a fraud. So what? He's a fraud too. And
none of that matters to him now, if it ever did. From his first
glimpse of her, he knew that she belonged here, with him.
There is a pause, a vast, empty stretch of silence, where nothing
seems to happen and Kenneth wonders if she's finished for the
day. He presses the nib of his fountain pen onto the blotter
and marks out his shortcomings in furry blue blobs: his age;
varicose vein like an elver climbing up his leg; hair falling out
where it should be growing and growing where it shouldn't.
How big his earlobes are. The terrible, irrevocable whiteness
of his pubes. Spreading his hands in front of him, he studies
the familiar tremor. If he could remember where he'd stashed
that half of whisky, he'd have a steadier now. He rummages
through the desk drawer, scrabbling beneath the piles of CDs
and abandoned papers to the very bottom. He put the photographs in here. It was almost the first thing he did after he saw
Maggie down in the field: crossed the room, straightened his
tie in the reflected glass of the painting on the wall, then had
second thoughts and removed it altogether. He took the two
silver-framed pictures from his desk and hid them away in the
back of the drawer. Slung his tie in there after them. He is
meticulous in his vanity: he didn't want her to see him as he

used to be; young, with Will hanging off his neck, like a proper doting dad. And he didn't want her to see the *Vogue* portrait of Rusty in her off-the-shoulder wedding gown.

He would like – he thinks it through carefully, feeling the words slip away from him even as they're forming in his head – he would prefer Maggie to love him for who he is now. For what he is now.

The sound of her fingers on the typewriter keys, like Morse code, comes up the stairs. He tells himself again: what he is now is an old fool. He doesn't care a bit.

Maggie rips the page from the machine and puts it with the others in a box file on the desk. She will have to be more careful; he could find any of this. She will take the file to her rooms each day, and be vigilant when writing down his notes. He was playing a game this morning, but she knows he is more than capable of spying on her. She stretches across to open the window, pushing it as wide as possible to let in the light. The air that greets her is green and fresh, blowing up from the river.

★

September has always been my mother's favourite month. She used to say it was the last gift of summer. And of course, I was conceived in September. The best gift of all, she used to say, although at the time she felt it was more like a hex.

Nell's pregnancy isn't the sort they tell you about in maternity classes. She is violently sick, almost from the first week. She staggers from toilet to bedroom and back again, resting one hand on the mossy brick of the lean-to while she pours the slop of bile from the bucket with the other. She thinks it's the vegetables they're growing. She's seen the farmer spray his land; perhaps the chemicals have carried on the wind. Or it's too much local cider. She's heard it said that anything goes into the mash – rotten apples, unfortunate rats. She thinks if she doesn't eat, doesn't drink, there'll be nothing to throw up, but she couldn't be more wrong; the sickness gets worse and my mother gets thinner. She's so dizzy, she has to lie down to stop falling over. Even Ed starts to worry. He enlists Cindy to come and help; one look at Nell, and she diagnoses pregnancy.

Despite the women's movement, or maybe because of it, Ed thinks these matters are strictly female. My mother never had these problems, he brags to Cindy, And this— he gestures to the empty pantry and the dirty plates – It's, y'know, a bit of a drag.

When Cindy relates this anecdote to Nell, my mother lifts her sweated head from the bed and cries,

Poor Ed, it's a drag is it? Should have kept his cock to himself!

Leon is kinder. He fetches spine-cracked novels from the charity shop, bunches of fireweed picked from the meadow; or he'll sit on the end of her bed and play her their latest composition. Nell could do without the singing; to her ears, their songs always seem to be about a dark lady and a river, and even the raindrop sounds of the tabla give her a headache. She has more pressing matters to worry about than whether Misty Lure, as Ed and Leon have called themselves, will have enough material to go on the road.

At night, Nell hears them in the kitchen below, their quick laughter rattling like gunshot off the ceiling. Cindy sings harmonies in a West Country burr, her eyes closed, her hand cupped over her ear. She has grown her hair, she wears long gypsy skirts with a petticoat below the hem, tie-dyed blouses revealing her shadowy cleavage; bangles up to her elbow. Ed remarks that she sounds like Sandy Denny; that their duo could be a trio. When Nell does venture downstairs, clinging to the narrow rail, afraid of falling, splitting her belly open on the stone floor, she finds the kitchen table awash with empty cider flagons, sticky glasses of pale liquor, nests of newspaper holding the savaged remnants of fish and chips, sausage in batter. She doesn't have to see the food; even thinking of the words makes her retch.

At other times she might find them blissful and out of it, a sheet of blue smoke above their heads, and then she'll notice Cindy is sitting on Ed's lap, a jingling arm snaked round his neck. Nell doesn't mind this at first, because she has her own private duo now: me and her. Let Ed do as he pleases, she thinks; it's a free country. But one night, after she has endured hours of churning nausea, Ed comes to bed late. A hint of patchouli oil on his skin; a flush of red at his throat. Lifting his hand to her face, Nell finds the rare damp earth of another woman's smell on his fingers. She dreams, sleeping and waking, of a terrible accident; Cindy floating like the Lady of Shallot through the river weeds, Cindy diving down and smashing her head on a rock. Cindy, drunk on elderflower wine, wading to her death, the water lapping around her legs, waist, chest, until she is vanished from sight. Nell gives a good deal of thought to consequences these days; of what will become of her, what will become of us.

★

Kenneth knows by her scent that's she's been in the library. He stands quite still in the afternoon heat, filling his lungs with her, breathing her in. A sound from the far end of the room makes his heart bang in his chest. Through the gloom he sees Maggie straighten up from behind the stereo. She too takes fright when she notices him, half-jumping sideways, hands flying to her face.

I saw this earlier, she says, with a voice like water, And I just wanted to hear it again. I hope you don't mind.
He shakes his head.

Never, for you, he tries to say, but the shock of finding her steals his words.

Maggie moves slowly towards him through the semi-dark, just as the music starts. Time beaten out like a drum, a medieval rhythm, slow insistence. The peculiar feeling he has, watching her faltering steps: as if he's invisible. No: as if she is blind. He almost puts out his hand to guide her, but is stopped by a pure voice rising up into the coffered ceiling of the library. They listen together, Maggie smiling, Kenneth shivering slightly despite the heat. She's looking at him but her eyes are remote. She's seeing a memory. Kenneth understands perfectly how that is, and is jealous of it. The words of the song are spun out, slow and careful and full of dread, and even though he would rather not listen any more – such is the awful feeling he gets from the sound – Maggie is close enough to touch: he wouldn't break the moment for the world. Kenneth doesn't recognize the song, or that he is panting slightly with the heat, with her proximity, with the strange cast of light in the room. He watches her open mouth, her lips shaping the words, and feels his breath desert him.

> *And then she went onward, just one star awake*
> *Like the swan in the evening*
> *Moves over the lake.*

It's hard to look at her and impossible not to. It should be awkward, and he checks her face for any sign of embarrassment, or irony, something that would tell him how to react. But her eyes are fixed on his and he is unable to feel anything, now, only a wretched and hollow longing, rising like a sickness, for this woman and the faint sounds coming from her lips.

When the song is over and the next one begins, Maggie moves swiftly back to the stereo and lifts the needle off the record.

Not this one, she says.

I didn't even know I had that, says Kenneth, Who is it?

Fairport Convention. Their first album with Sandy Denny. Maggie turns to the wall, searching out another record.

Oh. And she's dead, she says, matter-of-fact.

That's sad, he says, sensing a sudden awkwardness between them. Maggie slides an album from the shelf, turns it over to read the sleeve notes. When she speaks again, his suspicions are realized.

My mother used to love Sandy Denny. Then she hated her. Here's another dead one, look. It's like a morgue in here, Kenneth.

A minute ago she sang to him, now she's accusing him of something. The cellophane cover glitters darkly in her hands. Ordinarily, he'd fight back. What business is it of hers? Ordinarily, and he feels the knowledge like a pinch, he'd tell her to go to hell, that most of the great music, like art, like literature, like everything, belongs to the dead. And she's an employee, and her opinion counts for nothing. But here she is, and he's buried in her hand, in that unnerving look of scorn she wears. And he says,

Well, they're immortal really, aren't they? And they'll always be alive in here.

Maggie swings round to see him pressing his chest. He raises his chin, peering over at the record.

Who is that?

Otis Redding. Also unplayed by the look of it.

Shall we hear it now? he asks, moving slowly closer, You could play me the good tunes.

They're all *good tunes*, Kenneth, she says, curling her tongue over her lip, This is Otis we're talking about, not Cliff Richard. But no, she says, her eyes scanning the room, It's not the right weather.

Not the right . . .?

Maggie turns away to search again, her fingers tripping along the spines.

It's not just alphabetical, he says, It's alphabetical by genre.

I know, she says, dipping down into a crouch, so that he can only see the top of her head.

What do you mean, 'not the right weather'?

Otis is rainy day music.

Kenneth draws closer, staring down at the shadowy curve of her cheek as she bends her head this way and that.

Oh yes, he says, I see. Like my spring morning, my Poulenc. So, something we both know? he offers, confident that they're on easy terms again. Maggie straightens up and faces him, sucks air through her teeth.

Well, it's not quite that simple, she says, There are all sorts of variables. Time of year, time of day, place, mood, of course—

Company, offers Kenneth.

Good, yes, we must always consider company.

Maggie, are you making fun of me again? Because as you know, I take my music very seriously.

She ignores him, crossing to the nearest window and un-clasping the shutter. She lets in a long finger of sunlight.

For example, what's the most perfect music for this moment? This one right here, she says, pointing at the floor. Kenneth swallows hard. His mouth is dry. He looks about him, at the woody softness split by the light, and the heat it brings in. There's the buzz of summer outside the window, and Maggie in shadow, but smiling again. He feels he's being tested.

One song, Kenneth, she says, Just one. I'm not asking for the world here. Don't knock yourself out.

Oh, but she is asking for the world, and Kenneth would easily give it to her. His mind races through all the romantic summers he's known or dreamt of, all the times he's sat alone and daydreamed of such a moment, with a faceless woman who now has a face and is asking a small price for him to pay. No, a love song is too obvious: he veers into neutral: simple music for a hot day; Tailleferre, or Schubert's 'Nachtviolen'. But he doesn't want to bore her, that would be a mistake. A song, she said; it should have meaning. Bound to be someone dead, but he can't help that. Then he hits on just the thing, just the perfect thing, for this mellowness and promise. The perfect thing for him. But would she agree? He crosses to the wall and finds it immediately: his Nat King Cole collection. There are four blasted records! He removes the one he's looking for, angling it to the window, squinting at the tiny words on the label. Maggie waits, dancing her sandalled foot in and out of the light, like a cat teasing a sunbeam. In the silence Kenneth fumbles, tries to steady his hands; she must surely hear his breathing, cutting the air like a bellows. The violins save him, the violins and then a voice pouring out like cream. 'Stardust' fills the room. Maggie listens carefully, her eyes on him, but he disguises the flash of alarm on his face with a raised eyebrow, a practised smile: he's got the wrong track. He meant to play her 'Unforgettable'.

It's very sad, she says, So much loneliness. So haunted by memories.

Kenneth bends his head. He'd wanted to woo her, and be plain about it, he'll admit that; he was going for a definite message. He's made a mistake after all: now she'll think he's maudlin, stuck in the past; an old man.

Would you like to choose something? he asks, turning away.

Nope, she says, turning him back to her, tugging on the sleeve of his shirt so that he almost stumbles over her feet, I think this is pretty near perfect. Pretty much right for now.

nine

The summer mornings were the worst: endless hours, the endless day, drinks ticked out by the clock. No alcohol before eleven, that was his rule, but eleven seemed an eternity away when you were awake at 4 a.m. In the wintertime, Kenneth could put on his bedside lamp, take up his book, and read. Or he'd find the World Service, some tedious discussion about global warming, and fall back to sleep again. But as soon as the clocks went forward, he'd be sharp awake; the blackbirds startling him with their police sirens, and the wood pigeons mocking: *get up you fool, get up you fool.* It hurt the most then, when he'd forgotten how old he was, only to be reminded too quickly, staggering from his bed with a dead leg, bursting for the lavatory. Then there were simply too many hours to wait until the clock struck eleven.

Since Maggie has arrived, Kenneth hears the dawn chorus differently. These days the blackbirds sing fabulous, intricate jewellery songs; a shower of emeralds, a cascade of silver. The pigeons in the trees woo each other with throbbing purrs. He lies in his bed, fondling the sleepy damp nest of his penis, and thinks of the day ahead: what he will play her, what he might cook for supper. The air tingling, the light so fresh he could bite it. He takes his time showering: hot, a bit hotter, then cool, cooler; and he shaves carefully, using the magnifying mirror

Will bought him one birthday, the one that shows him how hideous he is close up, but minimizes the nicks and rough estimates that result from shaving blurred. A dab of cologne on his jaw and wrists – another gift from his son, another birthday ago. Kenneth cleans his teeth twice over, first with paste, and then with bicarbonate of soda, dabbing the toothbrush in the powder and trying not to taste the grit of it. He would like to gleam as bright as the birdsong.

That's why, Maggie, it's incredible, that you something unforgettable, something something unforgettable too.

She hears him singing; she hears him forgetting the words. Maggie pauses in the slatted shadowlight of the wrought-iron stairway, waiting for his footsteps on the other staircase to recede; imagines him walking through the hallway, jaunty, a pocket of cologne trapped on the still air. She sees it start to move, slowly, like a vapour, then more urgently, wending its way up the stairs, seeking her out. Come and find me, it says, Come and be with me.

Nine-thirty. Another hot promise of a day. She finds Kenneth with his eyes closed, his head nodding faintly in time to the music: solo piano, a tune she doesn't know. He looks quite relaxed, sitting in his wing-backed chair near the stereo, hands in his lap. The scent of him, like a bridge, carries her over to his side.

Maggie, he smiles, You slept well?

Yes, she says, taking her seat.

Another beautiful you, he says, so she looks up sharp and checks him.

Another beautiful *day*.

Is there an echo in here? he asks, cupping his hand round his ear and opening his mouth in a silent laugh. And so, they resume. Kenneth takes the record off the turntable and replaces it with another: again the click, again, the hiss.

It begins with a single sustained note, like an idea being formed, gradually developing into a certainty. Over the sound, a distant horn, calling. Then a darker note: the reply, weaving through the forest. Maggie sees two people climbing down a steep set of stairs, hesitant and careful, as if they don't know what they will find at the bottom. One person drawing the other on, telling her to be careful and – Shh! Be quiet! – then a sound like a door opening. They are moving through the garden now, past the dead bonfire and the shed, through the long grass at the river's edge. A plucked violin string, like rain-drops falling from the trees. It is very early in the morning. On the record, a cuckoo cries. Maggie sees the black earth, spongy underfoot, sees her slippers soaking up the moisture. She would like to tell the boy about it but she's afraid he'll shout at her again. Her legs are cold, her feet are getting wet.

Kenneth throws his head back as the first movement ends, as if to drink the air.

Fifteen minutes of wonder. Don't you think, Maggie? Spring and no end to it, Mahler said. Can't you just smell that morning dew?

Her body jerks in shock.

How did you know? she cries, How did you know that?

He opens his eyes, smiling, but stops when he sees the stricken look on her face.

Maggie, the First . . . it's a symphony about the glory of nature. This movement is the awakening. Everybody knows that.

Not everybody, she says, Would you like me to get that down, about nature and all its glories? About *awakening*?

He hears rage in her tone, can't imagine where it's come from. Getting up, Kenneth takes the needle from the record, and moves to the window.

Let's just have a minute to reflect, shall we? he says, over his shoulder. And he thought they were getting on so well.

He'd spent yesterday evening alone, had deliberately left her alone – kept out of her way, in fact, after the strange intimacy of the afternoon. He was conscious of his desire to spend time with her, more conscious still of the position she was in: he must let her have some privacy. Trying to find a distraction, he took refuge in the garage. He would polish the car; it would occupy an hour. With Borodin on the stereo, in the soft, dusty light, he could imagine he was driving through the open coun- tryside, top down, greenery shooting past him and the glide of the steering wheel under his fingers. Not Maggie's hair falling into his palm, not tracing the smooth line of her jaw with his knuckle, not looking to his left and seeing her sitting next to him, one arm bent across her head, trying to keep her fringe out of her eyes.

I said you should have brought a scarf, he shouts, turning his face back to the road. And in this fantasy, his voice is young and full of strength, his hands on the steering wheel are firm. She pulls at a strand of hair caught on her lips, she laughs, and leans in – he's noticed how she does that, as if to whisper a secret – Can we get one in Winchester? she asks, Will there be time? and he nods, yes, because in this life there will always be time.

He'd worked the wax into the bonnet and buffed with the chamois until he was coated in a melting sweat. He didn't notice her at first, over the swoon and thunder of the Dances, but as the finale reached its crescendo, he heard his name called, once, twice. She was standing at the door.

Come in, he'd said, wiping his forehead with his wrist. But she just stood there. He couldn't read her face in silhouette.

Why don't you come out?

The sun was low, but the air was warm; fresh sweat broke open on his brow.

Just polishing the car, he said.

Obviously, she said, and he saw her trying to hide a smile, It's beautiful, what is it?

Kenneth stared at the cloth, saw himself folding and unfolding it; felt the greasiness of wax on his fingers.

It's a Mercedes.

He was going to elaborate, but then she surprised him. Crouching slightly, she peered into the shade of the lock-up.

Would you let me have a go? she asked.

She hadn't struck him as the type of person who would ask that. It baffled him; for a moment, he felt insulted.

Of course not, he said, What an idea!

Just round here, on the estate. I do have a driving licence, you know.

He had never let anyone else drive his car; not Rusty, certainly not Will. He wanted to say so, and heard how he would sound: like an *old fart*. Will had called him that when he flatly refused to loan him the car; it was how he'd felt seeing Maggie's face, her eyes full of hurt.

I'm sorry, I didn't realize it meant so much to you, she said, Or I wouldn't have asked.

And that was how he'd got behind the wheel again. He drove her only a short distance, past the rhododendrons, turning round at the top of the drive and falling back down through it, getting some speed up, just enough of a breeze to trouble her hair. And it made her laugh: he knew it would. Afterwards, he'd retreated to the garage on the pretence of fixing a rear light, but he couldn't remove the image of her from his mind. The canopy of leaves above them, her luminous face, her hand in his as he helped her out of the passenger seat. It had taken all his willpower not to try to kiss her again. Later, sitting on the terrace, he felt his blood quicken when he thought of her; pictured her lying in the field. Pictured her lying in his arms.

Well? Have you reflected? she says now, pen held like a scalpel over the page.

Maggie, have I upset you? he says, Was it something I said?

She shakes her head, and shakes it again more emphatically, as if the first attempt to clear it didn't work.

No, Kenneth, of course not. Come on. When did you first hear this piece? Maybe we can make some notes before the next bit.

I would have been about fourteen. All the boys at school were into jazz and some rather arcane music – Delta blues, Stockhausen – it was deemed very *radical* to find the most esoteric stuff and pretend to like it – except for this one boy. He had a funny way of talking, sort of whistled when he spoke, made odd tweeting sounds.

Tell me his name, says Maggie, writing quickly.

His name was Philip, but of course, we called him Trill.

How very sympathetic, she says, under her breath.

And this boy Trill had tickets for the Mahler concert at the Philharmonic, but he was such a strange little cove, no one would go with him.

And you felt sorry for him? Maggie interjects.

Yes I did, says Kenneth, matter-of-fact, And I said I'd be happy to go with him. Turns out it was the Philharmonic in Liverpool. Ha-ha. Had to spend hours on the train listening to Trill tweeting and whistling. In those days, you had separate compartments, which was always a mixed blessing. No one sat in ours for too long.

And the concert?

Divine. It's not often you feel your pulse racing these days, he says, looking at her bent head with appreciation, But when you find something special, something seemingly simple and yet difficult, intricate – he pauses, enjoying the sound of the words flowing so easily from his lips – When you discover something for the first time and you think you're the *only* being on earth to truly understand it, that no one else can possibly feel the way you do . . . it's – Maggie – it's divine.

★

In the afternoon, in the quiet semi-darkness of the prefect's office, Maggie is struggling.

It's not enough, Kenneth, she says, ripping out a page from the typewriter and balling it up, Divine is not enough. Divine will not do for this spring awakening. No – bloody – end – to – it, she says, snatching up her pen.

★

Here's me and my mother in the lane outside our house. This is what I know: I'm wearing a red raincoat with a woolly collar, and a pair of wellies because it's been so wet. It's 1975, and the first Christmas I can remember, although I have recollections of other things around this time: an orange and white dog that swims in the river, Geoffrey and Bungle, Leon and Nell teaching me how to do the Bump. I'm only three and a half, but I know it's dangerous to go too near to the fire and that the stairs in the cottage are very steep and that I'm a lucky girl because I can play with nearly anything I want, even Leon's drums. This is because I am a wise head on little shoulders. What I don't know is that people will want things that don't belong to them, or that they will take those things without asking. In our house, everything is free and everyone is happy.

I'm holding the bag for my mother to drop the holly into. I mustn't touch it because it will prick me. I'm calling her now, Nell! Nell! because she's gone round the back of the hedge and there's a car coming. I always have to shout if there's a car. She pulls me to the side of the road, but the car stops anyway and the river man sticks his head out of the window. There's the orange and white dog sitting next to him, and in the back is the boy. He's wearing a tartan hat with a bobble on it like Woody wears on *Top of the Pops*. My mother says hello to the river man and wishes him a Merry Christmas.

Have you got your tree yet? he asks, and my mother says,

No, Ed says we aren't Christians, so why go to all that bother?

The man laughs, and my mother does too, although I can tell she thinks she's done something wrong because she goes red when the man points his thumb behind him.

Or maybe it's because there's nothing left to stick a fairy on, he says, and then he drives away.

My mother is going: *Fuck off, Fuck off,* shouting down the lane.

Ed has cut down all the trees around our house, for firewood. Nell always says there's no privacy any more but then he says,

What's your problem? Who do we ever see up here?

Or sometimes he'll smash his hand on the kitchen table and make all the cups jump, yelling,

If we had bloody trees, no one could see us freezing to death. Is that what you want?

Any of these things can make Nell's lips go white. Later, when she tells him about what the river man said, Ed says,

Fucking water bailiff, he should learn to mind his own fucking business.

Then he says he'll speak to his father about it. That's my grandfather, who we hardly ever see. You can tell when he's about to pay a visit because Nell cleans the whole house and the toilet and everything smells of bleach. My grandmother has never come to see us; she lives in Chelsea.

We did have a Christmas tree in the end. We went to sleep one night and when we got up in the morning it was there in the living room standing in a bucket. The whole place smelled like frost. Leon said the fairies had brought it, but then Nell laughed and said,

Thank you, Baby,

and kissed him, so I knew it was Leon, really.

There are no such things as fairies and ghosts: there are only people; nice people, friendly people.

I have always slept in the big bed with Nell. Leon has always slept on the sofa downstairs. Ed has always slept in the back room, which they call the Spare, because Nell says his snoring keeps us awake, even though Cindy doesn't seem to mind it. Cindy is like a cat; she will sleep anywhere. Sometimes she comes in with me and Nell, sometimes she'll curl up next to Leon downstairs, or else she goes in the Spare. Nell tells me it's because Cindy's a gyppo. I think the way of things is fixed; I think people are fixed. I can find them in their beds, I can find me in mine. But then Ed goes with Cindy to London to make his fortune, and his bed is empty. I want to tell Nell I don't like it. I should be the singer, not Cindy. He promised me. But Nell doesn't want to talk about him any more. Sometimes in the afternoons I lie on his bed and smell his smell and think about him moving around and laughing.

My mother says, Who knows where the time goes? and cries a bit but she still won't talk, and if I try to cheer her up with a song she'll say, Shut it, you're doing my nut.

It's February and spitting solid rain when Ed and Cindy leave for London. Nell rages when she finds out that Cindy has taken her fur hat, but Leon says, What does it matter, I'll make you one. Leon catches rabbits and cooks them on the fire. He makes my mother a rabbit-fur hat but we have to leave it in the shed to cure, he says, which is to make it not smell of death.

March is snowing when the postman comes, sliding up to the door and banging on it. There used to be a bell on a rope outside but it went missing one day and no one knows where. Nell jumps with fright when the postman does that. She says, Why does he have to bang so loud? And, He should be a debt collector with that gift.

This time it's a telegram for Leon, from someone called Athame, telling him they are going to make a record – Come up. Stop. Paved with Gold. Stop – it says at the end. Nell says Athame is a bad word and will bring us bad luck, but Leon says it's the new band name and is quite cool, really. My mother cries again. When I ask her why, she says the postman has wanton eyes and what will she do if Leon goes to London as well?

On Walpurgis night, Leon and Nell drink wine and make a sacrifice to the god of Mammon. They burn Leon's drums on the bonfire. My mother takes down the sketch that Ed drew of her with me in her belly, and burns that as well.

Shame, says Leon, I liked looking at your big belly.

The days start burning too. May has not a speck of rain, and the river man comes over and says we're not to draw water from the river on account of depriving the fish. He says there'll be trouble at this rate. Nell says, As if I would, to his face, and, What bloody fish? when he's gone away again. She tells me that this is the hottest summer in history. We try to fry an egg on the ground, but it doesn't work, even though they did it on the telly. It just sits there on the path looking sticky. Later, the birds come down and peck it all up and Nell goes, Look at that, filthy cannibals.

Nell says you can't be too careful in the sun. She buys me a straw hat and puts oil and vinegar on my skin whenever I go out playing, but she wraps a piece of tinfoil under her chin when she sits in the garden so that she'll catch the rays. Leon builds a greenhouse out of some old window frames and grows tomatoes and weed. He sells the tomatoes on the road at the top of our lane, and the weed to the lads in the Market Tavern. For my fourth birthday, he buys me a *Wombles* annual, and Ed sends me the Joni Mitchell songbook from London. When Leon sees it, he says, It's way beyond, and shakes his head. I don't know what the Wombles are, except hideous, with their beady eyes and their pointy snouts. I have to hide the annual under the bed to stop them looking at me. Nell teaches me to read using the songbook. We start to sing again. We learn 'Blue', and make loveheart tattoos on our skin using cochineal out of a tiny bottle, but when we get to 'Cold Blue Steel and

Sweet Fire', Nell always skips the page. She says I'm not ready for those words, or the ones in 'Banquet', but I've seen them and they're easy enough. Everyone says I'm an exceptional reader. I've got my own library tickets and everything, even though the lady in the library said it wasn't allowed. Nell said, She can read, you show her, my Bird, and lifted me onto the counter. I read a whole *Janet and John* and then the lady said, I suppose we can make an exception for such an exceptional little person. I think words are songs waiting to happen. I think talking is singing: I don't ever separate the two. When the *Newbury Advertiser* gets delivered on Fridays, I sing the articles out over breakfast. I think this is how everybody reads. Leon says I sing like a bird and calls me Birdie all the time. Nell calls me Birdie too, and My Little Bird, My Dove.

Nell says I'm old enough now to know what's right, and to be careful, and although I'm not allowed to go in the river – Never go in the river, she warns – sometimes she lets me sit by the bank. That's when I first see him, hiding on the opposite side. He likes to watch. Sometimes he's in the boat, sunk low down so only his head is poking up; sometimes he's sitting really still like a squirrel on a branch. Once I waved at him, and he waved back, but last time, I shouted, Hello! and he ran away in a mad rustle. Now I have to look really hard to see him; I can't always tell if he's there. Nell's more relaxed about the river, but always says, Don't go in, Bird, a person can drown in an inch of water, and Leon asks her what planet she's on. Planet Leon, she says, crinkling her nose and smiling so wide you can see right through the gap in her front teeth.

One afternoon, I come in from the garden and see Leon in my bed with Nell. He says, It's cool, come 'ere, kid, and Nell is smiling and she looks shiny-faced and sleepy. We were just having a snooze, she says, throwing back the covers, Want to cooch up?

It's funny having Leon in the bed. There's less room, for

starters, and his legs are hairy and rough. The bed smells different as well, bleachy, like the toilet. I don't quite like it. I suppose that's why I end up sleeping in Ed's bed. I end up in the Spare.

ten

Maggie comes down in the late afternoon, the Mahler symphony still circling in her head. She'd fallen into a fitful doze, lying on her bed with the curtains drawn, and dreamed of taking a train. The whistle of the boy Trill became the high clarinet of a cuckoo in the chestnut tree, then the tree began to weave in time to the music, and its eyes slid sideways, beckoning her. The branches parted to reveal a cobbled yard, a wooden door set low in the wall. The sun, beating down through her bedroom window, found the gap between the curtains and fell on her in a long bright strike. It was in this half-waking state that she realized: she wasn't looking *at* the door, but from behind it. Her eye to the slat; a single white line of arid heat.

She woke with a terrible thirst, her tongue stuck to the roof of her mouth and her head pounding. A sliver of light in the darkness, the feel of rough wood under her fingertips. What else was there? A smell of leather, and something else. She licked her lips and at once could taste the smell. Spearmint. Leather and spearmint, and the roughness of the door, how pulling at it gave her splinters, how blinding the light was.

She'd made the decision, sitting up in the sweated air of the bedroom, to talk to Kenneth directly. She wouldn't have to give too much away; she would be discreet. Maggie knows how tight-lipped people can get when she starts to ask questions. A few weeks after her mother died, she had gone to visit Thomas Bryce, the water bailiff, long since retired, with the hope that he might be able to remember some details about that time. She didn't know what she expected, but Bryce was in no mood for answering questions. The mere sight of her seemed to frighten him. Even if she could find the words, she would need to be very careful about what she asked Kenneth.

Instead of music playing, and Kenneth's wide smile to greet her, she finds the kitchen empty. A dusting of soft light across the room, the back door closed and bolted. A single sheet of paper is stuck with a magnet to the door of the fridge.

Dearest Maggie,
I am in London. Wretched business meeting. Back in a few hours. Explore!
xK
ps. If you would like to cook for us tonight, there's something in here to give you inspiration.

Wretched business meeting, indeed. She knows Kenneth is retired; knows – as anyone would who'd read the local press – the size of his golden handshake from Newton and Crane. She intuits that he spends most of his time upstairs in his office with his feet on the desk and his headphones clamped over his ears, listening to Mozart. Or in his den, trying to decipher his wild hieroglyphics.

Maggie looks in the fridge. Amongst the jars and yoghurt pots he has laid two Dover sole on a plate, covered with cling film. On the shelf below is a bottle wrapped in tissue. She can feel by its weight and shape that it's champagne, but rips the paper off anyway. After she's shut the fridge, she considers for a moment, then goes back to take an opened bottle of Chablis from the door. She carries it to the prefect's office. Her notebook is still in her room, hidden under the mattress like a schoolgirl's diary. Cradling the bottle of wine, she makes her way up to the first floor. If Kenneth's not here, she thinks, there's no reason for her to be stuffed under the stairs like a pair of old boots.

Passing the landing and Kenneth's office, she pauses. *Explore*, he'd written, but when she tries the door, it won't open. Maggie feels a surge of fury; apart from the cleaning lady, they are the only two people in this house. So why lock her out? She stalks the long corridor. A room on the right overlooks the staircase; this door at least is unlocked, but when she throws it open, she sees why. It's a bedroom – a guest room, she supposes – furnished with polished antiques. She lies on the bed for a while. The quilt smells freshly laundered, the pillows plumped and smooth, as if awaiting the imminent arrival of a visitor. She listens to the ticking of the grandfather clock in the hall downstairs, stares at the ceiling. Tilting the neck of the bottle, she takes a couple of deep swigs. The wine tastes clean and sharp: immediately, she feels better, and takes another long drink. Maggie tries to work out how many rooms are on this floor. Five on this corridor, she guesses, and then at the very end there's another locked door, just beyond the steep staircase leading to her bedsit. Which would put her in the servant's quarters. She gets up, angry again, and swings open the door to the next room. It is almost exactly the same as the first, made up for immediate occupation. She searches the drawers of the dressing table; all unlined and empty. Perhaps this was Rusty's room. But no, there's nothing here to suggest a feminine presence, not a hairgrip, not a hair.

The next room is a shock, seemingly out of place: Kenneth's bathroom. It's enormous inside, high-ceilinged and hollow sounding. Maggie stands for a moment and breathes the scent of him. Gazing up to where the cornice at the far end of the ceiling disappears, she realizes that the room has been modified; that the door at the other end must lead into his bedroom. She closes the toilet seat and sits on it, takes another swig of wine. She hardly knows what she's doing. Opposite the bath is a chaise longue with a velvet footstool beside it; on either side are two large potted palms in gilded bowls. The Victorian toilet with its high-level cistern and brass chain; the claw-foot bath; the chrome towel rail – all are spectacularly clean and shiny, just like new. But the washbasin has a residue of soap around the inside edge, and the mirrored cabinet above it is dappled with opaque white spots that come away when she rubs them and smell faintly of mint. Inside the cabinet, she finds a stockpile of lotions and pills and ointments. She tries not to feel the shame creeping up under her skin, and pulls out a bottle at random. It takes her a second before she realizes: he dyes his hair. Of course he does, she should know that. No man in his sixties would naturally have hair that dark. But his eyelashes? She sees his eyes again, the lucent blue of them, his direct, trusting gaze on her. Behind the gummy, misshapen tubes is a plastic bottle with a picture of fruit on the front: Think Well! Wild Blueberry Supplement, she reads. And then there is the Nytol, and a bottle of Sleep Tite, which, when she rattles it, feels almost empty. She catches a look at herself in the mirror, at her guilty face. It's enough; she doesn't want to see Kenneth's bedroom now. She is fearful of the idea: leather slippers placed neatly at the side of the bed, a plaid dressing gown hanging on a hook behind the door. She doesn't want to know if he has a magnifying glass on the bedside table or a reading light clipped to the headboard. She doesn't want him to dye his hair, have sleepless nights. She wishes she didn't care, because all of this is getting in the way. What she wants to find is arrogance, contempt for others, self-regard. And here, instead, is Kenneth; gentle and foolish, staving off the years with pills and lotions.

She sits on the edge of the bath and traces her hand along the wall, feeling beneath the paint and the lining paper a wide, ridged band, and it gives her an odd sensation when she touches it, as if her fingers are reading Braille. A revelation sparkles through her: the wall is a palimpsest of another room and another time. This bathroom *is* new – pretend old – and so are all the other rooms. The atrium downstairs with its pristine cushion covers and architectural greenery; the cold sitting room on the other side of the library with its smell of furniture polish; the barely used dining room – all fake. Whatever really went on in them, whatever lives were led, have been eradicated. No photographs. No personal items. No one lives here. These rooms don't stand for anything, and they don't signify anything, except the determination to wipe out what went before. All that is left of Kenneth's past is the stuff he hoards in his den. And his music. He has retreated, she thinks, he has withdrawn himself from all of this. That's why he wants to bottle up the good memories, because, despite his best efforts to cleanse his past, it's all still here underneath: the odour of despair, the stink of loss. It makes her sorry; not for Kenneth's family, and not for herself, but for him. Of course, he isn't to blame; he's an innocent, just as she was.

Like a ghost she retraces her steps, back down to the prefect's office, to the empty page.

MAHLER, SYMPHONY NO.1 first movement.
You were fourteen, Kenneth, when you first
heard this piece. Not much older than your
son was when he stole me from my mother.

the river man

Thomas Bryce is sleeping, his chin on his chest, one arm hanging down the side of the chair. In his lap, his glasses rest on top of the newspaper, magnifying a corner of the racing page. The television in the corner of the room is flat-screened and massive. He keeps it switched on most of the time, and a cookery programme is starting now; the title sequence, of a brash fanfare followed by angry shouting, doesn't disturb him. On the shelf behind Thomas the radio is turned down low; he keeps that on too, just in case. A fat spaniel lies stretched out in front of the dead fire. On the floor by his side, Thomas has left his dinner plate. A short while after he fell asleep, the dog bent over and licked it clean, before flopping herself back onto the rug.

Sometimes, when Thomas wakes up in the middle of the night, he'll see nearly naked women on the television screen with their fingers in their knickers or sticking their thin buttocks in the air and pumping them up and down or pinching their nipples really hard. They want him to call or text; there's writing at the bottom of the screen that Thomas now knows are messages from men, asking the girls to do things to themselves or each other. He doesn't bother trying to decipher the messages any more, and he isn't remotely stirred by what they get up to with their bodies. Their faces interest him. He likes the plumper ones, and the ones who look like they need a wash, and he likes to see the barely disguised boredom in their eyes. He wonders about how old they are, whether their boyfriends are sitting at home watching them and wanking off. Occasionally he'll lean forward out of his chair, worrying that he's seen a bruise or an insect crawling on them, satisfied that in the end, it's just another tattoo. Often he'll fall back into a restless sleep and won't wake properly again until he hears the early morning shipping forecast on the radio.

Thomas doesn't go to bed these days; there's no point: his bladder wakes him frequently, the sharp urgency coming with no warning, or not enough warning to get downstairs to the toilet. He uses the bedroom only to change his clothes, which he does rather less often than the woman in the shop would like, standing there behind the counter with her can of Glade at the ready. No shame to her. He'd like to tell her what he thinks of her, so concerned with herself, worrying about a smell, frightened by the idea of germs. He'd like to tell her how everything dies in the end, how it all goes bad; he's only reminding her of a natural process. And the landlord at the Winterbourne never makes any objection when he turns up there for his two pints of bitter. Thomas remembers the place when it used to be the New Inn and you could sit at any of the tables and pass the evening, having a drink and a smoke. Then it had a refit and started doing food and all that was left of the old pub was a long bench opposite the bar. The rest of the space was for diners. The landlord never said don't sit there, he just got a waitress to put place mats out on all the tables and a reserved marker in the middle. Thomas would squash up on the bench with his pals, all in a line, and they'd watch people from town turn up in their cars and order from the menu and sit at the tables, candles glowing between them like a secret. Then the landlord asked would it be all right if he left Bramble at home. It wasn't all right, and he told him so, and they boycotted the pub, him and Freddy Peel and Flynn and Flynn's cousin Raymond. But they crept back, eventually, Thomas as well. These days, when the landlord isn't looking, he sneaks Bramble under the bench where she's happy to lie with everyone's feet on her. These days, Thomas isn't allowed to smoke in the pub any more. He wonders how long it will be before he isn't allowed to drink.

Bramble's not a bad dog, but she's lazy. Her problem is she thinks she's a pet. Thomas has had a few dogs in his lifetime, all working stock. He can tell that Bramble hasn't ever been worked. Her previous owner put her in a rescue centre because he was too old to care for her. When the girl at the centre told him that, Thomas wondered if she thought that he was too old, too, at seventy-eight. He's taught Bramble a few things, but she hasn't got the nose for field work. Her retrieval is aimless at the best of times, and her delivery is poor: she drops the dummy anywhere. And she eats too much, foraging in the bins at the back of the lane when he tries to reduce her portions. Her breath is on him now, a happy, panting stink.

When morning comes, regardless of what kind of night he's had, Thomas will go through his regime: turning off the sidelight to watch the dawn come up, quiet and steady, or quick and rash, through the window. Different day, different dawn, same routine. At seven-thirty, he'll make some tea and toast, and take Bramble out for a stroll along the river. It's what he does every day, and he walks the same route, never deviates. It was difficult to keep to it for the first few years, he'll admit that. Despite his resolution to go on as before − to take the river path, track left down the far field and into the copse − by the time he'd re-emerged at the other end of the wood, Thomas would find himself half a mile off course. Sometimes he'd be knee-deep in a farmer's crop; sometimes he'd be at the lane at the top of the village. Once, he was back at his own front door. As if his feet were wandering of their own accord, he thinks, As if they had a mind of their own. He'd had to steel himself, then. Whichever particular dog was at his heels,

Thomas would retrace his steps, find the footpath, and continue the way he always did when he used to work the river: past the Earls' place and along the bowl barrow field.

He pushes Bramble to one side, and shifts in his seat, testing the heaviness in his groin. There's a politician on the radio answering questions, a man on the television is having an argument with another man. Thomas stumbles through to the kitchen and urinates into the sink, thin stop-start spurts, running the cold tap to help him. Through the window, the view is of the lane and the sinking sun, a greasy smear of amber hovering in the distant trees. He squints at it, willing the pressure in his bladder to subside, trying to concentrate.

He beat his problem eventually, although in a funny way the Earls helped: after the business had died down, they turned the field over to wheat. But then someone decided it was the site of an ancient monument and had to be protected. They could grow the wheat, they could reposition the culvert, but they couldn't disturb the barrow. Now you wouldn't know it was there, unless you were looking for it. Thomas tries not to think of what happened; there's no point. He knows he will only relive it again in the morning, as he does every day when he passes the spot, passes the Earl place, passes the barrow where all those years ago he found the girl. He has beaten his problem, is what he always tells himself. It was Sonny that unearthed her. Now, Sonny, he was an exceptional hound.

part two

small hours

eleven

Kenneth tries to stop himself from checking his watch; time won't move any faster just because he's looking at it. Through the tinted window of the train, the lights of the tower blocks flee back to London, leaving only his reflection, staring uneasily in at him. He thinks about the number of times he's made this trip in his life; countless occasions when he was a young boy coming home from school, then a hiatus of forty years or more, when he drove everywhere. Can't do that now, wouldn't trust himself now. Not after that last episode, cruising at speed the wrong way up the motorway, car headlights flashing like sparks in front of his eyes. He knew something was amiss; the central reservation was over on the passenger side, the one-way became inexplicably two-way. Too late, Kenneth realized that it was him going against the flow and not everyone else: by then, the sparks of those oncoming headlights had turned into the blue scroll of a squad car beacon.

A caution, and his licence revoked: he was told that he'd been lucky, but he didn't feel lucky; he felt as though he'd had an arm cut off. Will suggested a chauffeur, not understanding, or choosing to ignore, the simple pleasure of driving, with only *The Pearl Fishers* or *La Bohème* for company.

Oh Mimi, he says, thinking of Maggie, You will love Jussi Björling, I just know it.

Kenneth decides he will play her some opera on his return. He checks his watch again.

Maggie is burning dinner. After she'd written up the song notes, she'd laid her head on the desk and closed her eyes: only the stained-glass woman in the window to watch over her, the light in the room gradually softening to caramel brown. She felt unable to move; couldn't even reach up for the latch when the cool draught of river air rose up and scattered the pages. When she roused herself, it was to a dusk-filled room, the beam of a car playing over the walls as it swung up the drive. Maggie thought it would have to be William. Remembering Kenneth's bathroom, she bolted up the stairs and checked herself in the mirror. Her face bore a long pink crease where she'd been lying on her sleeve, an imprint of mottled dots on her cheek. She filled the washbasin, smelling again Kenneth's shaving soap, and splashed her face with water. As she was making her way back down, the doorbell rang twice, two short peremptory bursts, followed by an expectant silence. She wiped her hands along her dress, breathed in and out slowly, pulled the heavy door open. It was not William. Standing before her was a woman in a pale-blue trouser suit, her hair carefully coiffed, a diaphanous scarf around her neck. Maggie felt faint with relief. The woman barely glanced at her before pushing her way inside.

Can you tell Mr Earl that Mrs Taylor is here, she said, making a statement of the question, Where is he? In his *den*, I suppose. She set off so fast along the hallway, Maggie had to half-trot to keep up. She was oddly satisfied to see that the woman had a chalky white teardrop of bird excrement on the back of her jacket.

He's not here, said Maggie, catching her up at the kitchen door.

The woman turned.

What do you mean, he's not here? Of course he's here, she said, peering into the kitchen, He's always here.

He's gone to London – on business, said Maggie. Even she thought it sounded like a lie. The woman looked at her directly for the first time.

I do apologize, you must think me very rude. I'm Alison Taylor, she said, holding out her hand, A friend of Kenneth's. And you are?

Maggie, she said, shaking the offered hand. She felt the cold lump of a diamond on the other woman's finger, the bones beneath the gliss of hand cream.

And are you a guest, Maggie? she asked, and not waiting for a response, added, It seems rude to leave a guest all alone, don't you think?

Maggie didn't reply immediately. She was thinking that this was the woman who had styled the atrium, and probably all the other rooms too; could see right through the woman's eyes and into her skull: friend of Kenneth or not, she wanted this house and her place in it.

I work for him, Maggie said, at last, And he'll be back later this evening. Would you like to leave a message?

Alison Taylor turned her wrist over, sliding a gold bracelet around to reveal a small watch-face, which she studied, tapped with her fingernail, and jangled away again up her sleeve.

I don't think so, she said, through a bleached smile, He's clearly forgotten.

Maggie followed her out into the hall.

Was he supposed to meet you? she asked, unable to help herself, Only, he didn't mention it.

Ah, and why would he? Are you his secretary?

Even though the smile was still in place, the woman's tone was hostile.

I'm . . . we're compiling an archive.

An archive. How fascinating. And what kind of archive are we compiling?

Maggie opened the door.

I think maybe Kenneth will want to tell you that, she said, marvelling at how smooth she sounded.

The older woman narrowed her eyes into two crystallized beads.

He might, she said, But he's very forgetful. He might not even remember why you're here. Come suppertime, he might not even know who you *are*!

Maggie leaned against the heavy wood, listened to the thunk of the car door, the thick roar of the engine. The exchange had left her feeling grimy, impoverished in a way she couldn't define. Anything but smooth. Catching her reflection in the long glass casing of the grandfather clock, she saw what Alison Taylor would have seen: a blurred person, frayed, someone incomplete. She threw the tray of Dover sole into the oven and went to take a shower; stood for an age under the scalding needles of water, imagining herself rinsed, brand new.

She lifts the tray out and wafts a tea towel over it. The sole are scorched black, and the olive oil dressing has solidified into a sticky brown stain, as though the fish have bled tar. She kicks the oven door shut, and studies the recipe book. The timing was right, nearly; perhaps the temperature was wrong. Maggie stares at the stove as if it's to blame, and then remembers the tinned tuna in her kitchen upstairs. She can make something with that. Tuna pasta salad, she thinks. If what Alison Taylor says is true, maybe Kenneth won't remember about the sole. Standing at the back door and breathing in the silky night air, she considers what it would be like if he were to come home and not remember her.

The train fills up at Reading. The man who sits opposite Kenneth makes a great fuss of unpacking his bag, claiming the table with a bottle of water, a cellophane-wrapped volcano of muffin, his mobile phone. He slides his laptop out in front of him and flips open the lid. Now Kenneth can't see him any more, unless he looks in the window, where he watches the man's reflection, face lit up, eyes fixed on the screen, fingers flying. Kenneth runs a hand over the front of his suit, tracing the outline of the package in his inside pocket. He has bought a gift for Maggie: a Montblanc fountain pen. The cap is finished with an emerald, nearly the same colour as her eyes. But now he's uncertain: perhaps he should have got her a laptop to make her notes on. He wonders what she writes about, finds it marvellous that he trusts her. Thinking back to only a week ago – his firm belief that he wanted no interference in his plan, no one making a suggestion, not even a noise – he can hardly credit the person he was. Kenneth stretches his legs out, knocking his foot against that of the man opposite. They both apologize and renegotiate the space beneath the table. Kenneth looks at his watch again.

Alison waits until she gets home before phoning William. He answers on the third ring, sounding brusque and very like his father. She tells him what she found at the house: who she found. William professes no interest, until she adds that Kenneth had forgotten that they were going to the theatre this evening, and then his voice takes on a new timbre. Now he has questions. She delights in her answers; she has thought them through carefully on the drive home.

She's thirtyish, a bit bedraggled-looking, she says, Slightly gauche, but that's clearly an act. You say he cancelled *you* a few days ago?

She pulls the scarf from her neck as she listens, slowly drawing the silk away like a shed skin.

Well, perhaps you should go and meet the ingénue, she says, Make sure your father isn't getting out of his depth.

When she replaces the receiver, she feels a spreading pressure between her ribs, a sudden stab of indigestion.

twelve

Maggie is nowhere. The dining room, the kitchen, the library, all are empty. The door to the prefect's office is open. Inside, Kenneth sees the window is thrown wide. He pulls it shut, resting his hand on the papers as he reaches across the desk. He resists the urge to look. Instead, he removes the pen from his pocket and leaves it there for her to find. Imagines the delight on her face. He thinks she must have gone to bed; it's after midnight.

There had been a long delay just before Reading, then an unscheduled stop at Thatcham station, where the train sat motionless on the track for a full half-hour before grinding to life again. Kenneth had looked longingly at the man with the laptop as he phoned his wife, wishing he'd taken Will's advice and got a mobile himself. Bring you into the twenty-first century, his son had said, which made Kenneth all the more resolute not to give in. But the waiting – the dismal thicket of bushes outside the window and the way that time sat like sweat on his skin – made Kenneth do something extraordinary. He'd seen others do it, before everyone had their own phone: he'd asked the man if he could borrow his. The handset was warm, and the square screen too small to read. And Kenneth couldn't remember his own number.

Now he consoles himself with the thought that Maggie

probably wouldn't have answered the phone, anyway. In the kitchen, he goes to the fridge and sees the champagne is untouched. He pours a large glass of wine to take to his den, thinks again, and opens the back door; he will drink it in his usual spot. Then he sees her. She's lying on a blanket on the grass, her legs bent up under her skirt and her bare feet white as chalk, her head resting on her arm. He continues as planned, sits quietly on the iron bench and lets his eyes wander over the sweep of lawn shining in the moonlight, the silhouette of trees beyond. He's completely at a loss; worse, he doesn't know why. He *wanted* to find her still awake, would have liked to talk with her, hear her low voice mocking or scolding or just asking a plain question. He doesn't know why the sight of her alone out there in the darkness fills him with such sorrow.

I'm not asleep, she says, I'm watching.

She gets up onto her knees and turns around to look at him. Her hair swings low over her shoulder.

What are you watching? he asks, trying to keep his voice steady.

Come and see, she says.

Kenneth goes and sits with her on the blanket, noticing the empty plate on the grass, her half-full glass balanced on top.

You have to lie down flat, she says, sinking back onto the blanket. It takes Kenneth a little while to accomplish the manoeuvre, holding his wine aloft, feeling the night air on the exposed skin between his trouser-bottoms and his socks. Maggie's arm glides across him as she takes his wine glass and puts it with hers.

Hope you don't mind, she says, I finished the Chablis.

Of course not, he says.

His face feels constricted with blood, as if he's lying on a downhill slope.

And then I opened another one, she says.

Good girl, he says, That's what I would have done.

He can feel Maggie's body quivering beside him. He turns his head; watches a silver tear run down the side of her face and around the curve of her ear. It takes him a second or two before he realizes she's laughing, and it's such a relief, he laughs too.

I burnt the fish! she cries, wiping her eyes with the heel of her hand, And then I thought I'd make us some pasta, and I came out here to sit until it was done and then I forgot all about it. Burnt the pasta.

Was it tasty? he asks, which makes her roll sideways and beat her hand on the ground between them. She is very close to him now.

Uh—

She's trying and failing to speak. Her face is creased with effort.

I'm sorry I'm so late, he begins.

Shh-shh, she says, Now, we have to concentrate. Look up, she says, and he does as he's told. She clears her throat, lifts something from her side and holds it high in the air between them. Kenneth sees it's a wooden spoon.

Is this some sort of magic, Maggie? Are we dowsing for soup?

He's delighted when he feels her trembling again.

Watch, she whispers.

They lie quite still together, Maggie subduing a hiccup, offering the spoon to the sky. First there's one, then another, and a third, spiralling above their heads before winging into the black.

Bats! says Kenneth, Maggie, you're a witch.

The bats flicker in and out of the space; they weave, dive, and drift away like cinders of night.

Aren't they incredible, she says.

Who taught you that? he asks, when finally she drops her arm.

My mother. They'll home in on any vertical object.

Home in, sighs Kenneth, And fly away again.

Sometimes they come back, she says.

Can you make them come back?

She passes over the wooden spoon for him to take, and he

looks at her steadily for a moment, sees how pale and delicate her hand is in the light from the kitchen door, and how dark her eyes, before accepting it from her. He holds it up as she did, and they wait again. It's not long before the bats return, a sudden swoop of one, two black flashes, circling above the spoon and vanishing again into the night.

Wonderful thing, radar, says Kenneth.

Echolocation, says Maggie.

Kenneth shifts himself up onto his elbow.

Do you think you could echolocate my wine, my dear? All this excitement has made me quite parched.

The touch of their glasses chimes on the night air.

To bats? she offers.

To the grape outdoors, says Kenneth, waiting for her laugh. But she doesn't laugh, she keeps her eyes fixed on his, puts the glass to her nose and sniffs into it.

See, she says, I have been paying attention.

You should use just one nostril, he says, showing her, But I don't think it counts if you've already had half a bottle.

True. It all tastes the same to me.

The palate must be educated to notice the difference. The bouquet is critical.

He makes a pretence of sniffing, swirling, and sipping. He'll go to any lengths to amuse her, and finally he gets his laugh, followed, as seems to be the pattern with her, with a rebuttal.

I'm not doing all that slooshing.

He looks over the rim of his glass.

What does it remind you of? he asks, with the voice of a schoolmaster.

Kenneth sees her open mouth, and the rim of her glass catch the moonlight as she tilts it, and has to look away.

Vanilla? she offers, her tongue on her lip. She smiles at him, a flicker of comprehension in her eyes.

OK. It reminds me of when . . . when you're down at the beach and you pick up a pebble and you lick it, she says.

Water over stones, he says, with a small nod of assent, Quite so.

And you, she says, It will remind me of you, one day.
Kenneth can't read what she means; it sounds like a goodbye. Her eyes are distant, now, as if she's hunting out words in the dark.

Do you ever swim in there? she says, flicking her gaze to the trees.

In the river? No!

Nor me. I was never allowed, as a child. And when you're grown up . . well, it's just not something you do.

Isn't it? says Kenneth, Why not?
Suddenly he can think of nothing more wonderful than to swim in the moonlight with Maggie. He gets up, holds out his hand.

I will if you will, he says.

Not at night, that's daft. And I've been drinking.
And now he feels ridiculous, and as if he hasn't been drinking nearly enough.

Of course it is, he says, and just as he leans forward to retrieve his glass, Maggie takes his hand and pulls herself up.

I quite like daft, she says.

I adore it, he says.

Shall we?
From inside the house comes the sound of the telephone: seven rings, and they wait, listening, looking at each other.

It's been ringing all night, she says, Ever since – oh, I should tell you, Mrs Taylor dropped by.
Kenneth keeps his face.

Did she? What did she want?

She wanted you, Kenneth, says Maggie, drilling a finger into his chest, And she wouldn't leave a message. She looked a bit put out to find you'd gone away on a secret mission.

That's her usual expression, says Kenneth, then, feeling he's betrayed his old friend, Actually, she's all right. Did Ali say that? About a secret mission?

No, I did, says Maggie, grinning, And I couldn't find the answerphone. I presume it's in your office. Your *locked* office.

I'll call her tomorrow, he says, It's too late now.

Too late now, echoes Maggie, her voice ghostly.

I believe you are in your cups, says Kenneth, A man could take advantage of a lady in such a state.

But a *gentleman* would not take advantage of a lady, she counters, lifting her chin high and looking up into the sky. She blinks, leans in a fraction so her shoulder butts against his.

You know, I think I must be a bit drunk, she says, Because that moon looks three-dimensional.

Kenneth gazes up with her.

That's earthshine, he says, Also known as the ashen glow.

You're making it up, she cries, trying to stand straight, Not very romantic is it, 'By the light of the ashen glow'?

Kenneth finally gives in to his thoughts. He tries to make his voice sound bluff and cynical.

Well now, if you want romantic, he says, which makes Maggie lean in to him again, If you *want* . . .

But he won't finish. Maggie puts her hand on his.

Go on, she says, If I *want* romantic . . . ?

Kenneth closes his eyes, defeated, and lets out a small puff of breath,

They also call it, 'the old moon in the new moon's arms'.

He feels the lightest brush against his lips. When he opens his eyes, she is just as she was, looking at him intently. He must have imagined it.

Later, he will think it felt like the flutter of a bat's wing, or a stray lock of her hair as she turned her head, or a faint breeze carried on the night. He is willing to believe anything but the kiss, which is, to him, beyond belief.

thirteen

I spy, with my little eye, something beginning with D.
Dark!
The answer is always the same. I'm playing on my own, and
that's all I can see. D for dark. And black: B for black. It's not
cold, it's stuffy, and I have to wipe my nose on my pyjamas
because it keeps going wet. My eye is wet too, like crying, but
I'm not crying. Leon says only babies cry. M for mouse, which
I can only hear so it doesn't count. I can't tell what time it is.
At home we have a clock on the wall in the kitchen but it
only has one hand on it because Nell tried to move them back
for winter and the little hand snapped off. Leon says, Oh look,
it's twenty past something, I'll be late! about six times a day.
There's another clock next to Nell's bed. The numbers go green
at night, so no matter how much dark there is, you can always
tell the time, if you know how to do it. And you can see Nell's
face in the light when her head is near the edge of the pillow,
green like Kermit the Frog. I'm not crying. The boy said I
must wait until the Time is Right. He said he will fetch me
when the Time is Right and I mustn't be sad about anything.
But I am sad. I want Nell and Leon. I don't know how to do
the time yet. I don't know when it will be right. He said, Don't
cry, you'll meet your mummy, and I said, My mummy's Nell,

I've already met her. He said, Not that whore, I mean your proper mummy.

★

Maggie pauses, raises her head; in a corner of the window, a pale-blue dawn is breaking: she is thankful for this. She sits up straight at the long desk and breathes deeply, mouth open, listening for any sign of movement above her. Earlier, she had tracked Kenneth's footsteps on the staircase, slow and steady, a door opening and closing; listened to the rush of water in his bathroom, his happy tuneless humming. Nothing now, no sound except the quick low rustle of a breeze in the bushes outside. She pushes away the dark, pushes away that child in the dark, and immediately feels a wrench of guilt: she's only just found her and already she wants to forget again, wants to put her away in the dark again. She's no better than him. Maggie clenches her jaw, holds out her left arm in the half-light, twisting it, bending the wrist backwards and forwards. Her skin looks as blue as the sky. Getting up from the desk, she closes the notebook and picks up the fountain pen, exposing the pale soft flesh of her upper arm, offering the skin, like a sacrifice, to the morning. She feels a chill air blowing off the river. She stabs the tip of the pen, once, twice, into the soft underside of her flesh. And then again, again, the point jabbing, black, black, pockmarks of black surrounded by fresh pink haloes of trauma, and quickly now, black, black, blocking out the thought of the child, burying the thought of the child, pushing her deeper and further in, until finally, she is without thought. A rush of saliva fills her mouth. It's a glorious taste. Like Chablis. Like water over stones.

fourteen

Today, Kenneth plays her what he calls cool jazz: Chet Baker, Gerry Mulligan, Miles Davis, moving not quite seamlessly from Dave Brubeck to the Alan Price Set. The sounds are interesting, but his reminiscences involve a detailed, lengthy and, to Maggie, stultifying potted history of the music. But he speaks and she takes notes; lets him ramble on. Neither of them has referred to last night, although she can see in his eyes that he thinks they have moved beyond friendship. He is quieter this morning, looks tired and elated. He talks about London clubs, and fast cars, and his college friends and business associates, buying his first house and the view of the park and painting one room entirely purple; about driving a Bugatti down to the south of France, being propositioned by a princess in Cap Ferrat, meeting Jimmy Stewart in Nice. He's making it up, she thinks, he's creating a fantasy. Not once does he mention Rusty or William; the avoidance hangs like a stink in the air between them. When he starts another long monologue about cars, she interrupts.

You can tell the truth, Kenneth, she says, These notes are for you, remember?

He looks directly at her as she says this, gives her a tense smile.

Am I so transparent?

'Fraid so. Why don't you tell me about meeting Rusty? She was a performer, wasn't she?

Kenneth retreats to the chair in the corner. He would like to say that he doesn't want to think of Rusty now, sitting here on a blue summer morning with Maggie so close. But she has asked the question.

Rusty certainly liked a performance. She was a singer, but frankly – well, she wasn't that talented. Good-looking girl, though, stunning. *A captivating presence*, he says, in an affected tone, as if he's quoting a review, All the men adored her.

Maggie writes down the exact words, trying to ignore the quick spike of envy.

Tell me something ordinary, she says, Something you'll always remember.

He tilts his head to one side and stares out of the window.

She was very tidy, he says, at last.

Tidy how?

He bats at the air in irritation.

Tidy. Liked everything in its place.

So, she was house-proud. It's hardly a crime.

No. She was a maniac, he says, She was obsessive. I could never find anything. When we had visitors, after they'd gone, she'd take their cups or glasses or whatever, and she'd soak them in bleach. Can you imagine? I dropped a spoon on the floor once, at dinner, and she made me fetch a clean one.

Well, says Maggie, That's not so odd.

It is. We could have eaten off that floor.

How times have changed, she says, quietly, Shall we try a nicer memory, Kenneth? Something you liked about her?

She was stunning, he repeats, slapping his palms down on the arms of the chair with an air of finality, And all the men adored her.

But she chose you, she says, head bent, Must have been love.

Love! barks Kenneth, as though the idea is absurd, People didn't marry for love in my day – in my set. But I did love her, and I suppose I was a safe enough prospect. I would be successful, you see, which was what women wanted, back then. And all a man wanted, apparently, was a beautiful wife. You made your bed. No living together then, you couldn't find out about each other first.

Maggie has an image of the bedroom upstairs, the dressing table covered in pots of face cream and dusting powder and elegant perfumes and silver-backed hairbrushes, and a pair of diamond earrings tossed casually into the middle of it all: placed very carefully in the middle, perhaps. And of her own room. Sink full of blood. Torn handkerchief spotted with stains.

But what would you have *wanted* to find out, Kenneth? she asks, struggling to keep her voice level, She was perfect, wasn't she? A woman other men coveted, and you won her. Wasn't that enough?

She liked to be made a fuss of, he says simply, Got terribly . . . low if she wasn't centre-stage. She craved attention, all the time, from anyone.

Ah, and you were jealous, says Maggie, sensing she's going too far but unable to stop herself, Is that why you left her?

I'm not having any of this in there, he says, pointing his finger at her, Don't think you can simply come in here and accuse me. Don't think for one minute I wouldn't send you packing.

He doesn't raise his voice, but his expression is livid. She puts her pen between the pages and closes the cover.

You'll have heard rumours, I'm sure, he says, About this family.

Maggie wants to say, I *am* the rumour, sitting right here in front of you; I'm the spectre at the feast. But she's afraid of him. Kenneth talks very quickly and firmly, as if he's rehearsed his response.

There was an incident, when Rusty was ill . . . it doesn't belong in there.

He gestures to the book in her lap,

That is not a period of my life I wish to remember.

The incident – she echoes.

A mother doesn't turn her back on her child, he says, But Rusty was unwell.

He moves over to the stereo, selects a record and puts it on. Maggie listens, waiting for more. In the long pause that follows, she hears her blood beating in her head, and then a song she knows so well: about a woman and a broken man, about a twist of fate. And she hears what she thinks Kenneth hears; the cruelty in the words, how everything that's in the past is lost, and how everything that happens now is built on that loss. She won't look up, dreading what she might see in his face, what Kenneth might discern in hers.

There was an opening for a consultancy in Bahrain, he continues, very quietly, almost apologetic, It was a busy time out there, in those days. And I thought, why not? Change of scene, might make all the difference. You think you've made plans, got your escape route, but then— he throws his hands up – All you're actually doing is running away. And you can't even do that without making a mess of it. Maggie, don't take that down. Please. Don't write that.

What do you want me to write, then?

He doesn't reply. He drops his head low and smoothes a desolate hand over his hair. She has a sudden, inexplicable urge to smooth it for him. Pulls on the sleeve of her shirt to stop herself. It's only the song that makes her feel like this, she tells herself, those silver guitar chords, that plaintive voice.

I want you to invent something, he says, at last, Something unexpected. Surprise me.

Like you surprised me? she says, eager now to reel back in the past five minutes and start all over again, With your lovely surprise?

He half shrugs in reply, and takes the needle off the record. Maggie slides the pen from the notebook, rubbing her thumb over the emerald cap as she does so.

Thank you, Kenneth, she says, It writes beautifully. But you shouldn't have.

Not a real gemstone, he says, Sorry about that.

It had better not be, I don't want anyone sweating their life away to provide me with a piece of rock.

So what would you rather they sweated over? he says bitterly, What should a man waste his life on?

She hesitates. To say the wrong thing now is to lose him. But the moment's already lost; he won't talk freely in this state. She feels the danger in him, the barely contained violence, and answers slowly, thinking it through as she speaks, articulating the idea for the first time.

What gets me up in the morning, what keeps me *sweating on* in life, is the possibility that it'll be better tomorrow.

And is it?

How can I know?

Kenneth gives her a warm smile.

Maggie, I'm so sorry, and you're so wise. Forgive me. Now, I've chosen this one specially for you, he says, lining up the needle on the track.

The sound is a big horse clopping slowly through the desert. Smell of leather, pink dusk falling behind the mountain. 'Lay Lady Lay'. He's playing her a love song.

How do you make the darkness shine? she asks, silently. And as if she's spoken, looks to him for the answer. In reply, he sits on the edge of the chair, places a hand lightly on her shoulder. She can smell his cologne. She can feel the slight tremor running through his skin, through the fabric of her shirt and through her own skin and through her bones and down beneath her bones. The place where she stabbed herself beats hot and sore. She would like to tell him everything. She would like to weep.

What does it do for you? he says, when the song dies.

It makes me very sad, she says, turning her face away, Because of course, she won't stay.

Kenneth's voice is ragged.

Why won't she stay, Maggie?

Because he doesn't know *her* story, she says, It's always *his* story. And what is he anyway? He's just some desperado. He's not a saint, and she's probably — she's probably just a whore! Kenneth, blurred, kneels in front of her.

Maggie, what on earth is it? What's happened? Was it me being a brute? Did I frighten you?

I'm no good at this, she says, You're right, the past is gone. We shouldn't go looking for it.

She holds her palms out, as if he might divine her grief this way, but he simply takes her hands in his own. They remain like this, like two supplicants, paying no attention to the endless hiss-click of the needle on the vinyl.

Will is coming today, Kenneth whispers at last, Invited himself for lunch.

Maggie dips her head down; she still can't look at him.

Best hide myself away then, she says.

Kenneth squeezes her hands tight; she feels his own parched warmth penetrate her skin.

No need for that, Maggie, I'd love for him to meet you. As long as you feel up to it. He can be difficult, I warn you. Overprotective. Has been, ever since—

Maggie raises her head and looks at him: she is willing him to say.

– ever since Rusty went, he says.

Where is Rusty, Kenneth? Locked in the attic?

Maggie knows from his face he won't answer.

Because the way you say it, you make her sound like a dog that's run off. And I think you might be able to trust me just a little bit. Don't you?

She removes herself from his grip, crossing the floor of the library with ringing steps.

★

William swings his Mazda round to the porch; Kenneth is waiting at the open door, wearing a pained expression.

Now I know the name perfectly, just can't remember the face, he says, holding his arms out in welcome.

Ha, Dad, you're such a wit. How are you? says William, climbing the steps and pushing his sunglasses up onto his head. Maggie watches as they embrace and disappear into the dark hole of the entrance. She waits for the door to close. Now they will be walking through the hall, now they will be standing in the kitchen. William will remark on the heat and he'll remove his jacket, looking for somewhere to hang it. Kenneth will fetch a bottle of wine from the fridge, and William will decline, and then Kenneth will offer him a glass of soda. He has already frosted the tumbler, has refilled the ice tray, has fetched a wrinkled lime from the fruit bowl and sheared off a thick uneven wedge. She knows all this; she has seen the evidence. When Kenneth went up to his room to change, she checked the kitchen, saw two bowls and two plates ready on a tray, saw the blue prawns defrosting in a sieve on the side of the sink, the shredded lettuce. He will leave nothing to chance: William is here to judge him.

A spider parachutes down directly in her eye-line; hangs there, twirling, so that Maggie has to move. Can't stand here, hiding in the bushes all day. The back of William gives nothing much away; his hair is greying, he wears a suit, he drives a flash car. He is tall, like his father, but was too far away for her to get a proper look at his face, and was wearing dark sunglasses. She would have liked to have seen his eyes. It can't be possible, but she's sure she could smell him: a scent of spearmint. Her palate is educated enough for that. Maggie slings her bag over her shoulder, turns her back on the house and walks into the trees.

fifteen

The pen helps her to write even faster than before. She feels her hand glide across the page, fleet black imaginings pouring from the nib.

★

Nell is asleep. She's left the radio on and the sound of voices fills her dreams. Leon's thick arm pins her to the mattress. They are both uncovered, naked, their skin cooling in the night air. The boy Will lifts the latch on the front door and eases it open. He knows how things are here, has waited a long while, and made preparations: he took the rope-bell when he was home at half-term, just in case he accidentally knocked it on the way back out, and last night he checked over the dinghy. He'd even planned to force a door or window, thought about how would be the best way to do it, but then had a stroke of luck when Leon and Nell had another fight last week and she tried to shut him outside. Leon bust the lock clean off. She'd asked Thomas if he'd fix it for them, and then changed her mind and said that Leon would do it. Will has seen what Leon has been doing this week: lying doped-up in the sun, or sitting under the shade of the willow tree, drinking from a pint glass.

Nell has taken to walking around half-dressed: a striped bikini top and long skirt, or nothing at all on top and tiny little shorts, always barefoot. She lets the little one run around naked. Will can't stand that; the little one's got no choice in the matter. He had to act quickly, before they finally got round to fixing the lock. Watched them to make sure. You can smell the weed from over the other side of the river. Will knows what it is; some of the older boys at school smoke the stuff, usually down the field behind the chapel, or leaning far out of the dorm window after lights out. If one gets caught smoking, they all get punished.

Will is careful going up the stairs: untried, he doesn't know where the creaks might be. Turns right. This is where she is. He has observed her from the tree on the other side of the bank. He was quite high up in the branches, Thomas's binoculars around his neck, and she was rubbing her hand across the window. He thought she was waving, but when he looked through the lenses he saw that she'd stuck a transfer of a rainbow on the glass. Here she is now, asleep; she's kicked the bedclothes right off the bed, but her skin is still sweaty and her hair is clinging to her forehead. Will has carried heavy things for Thomas; boxes of logs, a dead fox that Thomas said he planned to use as an example, a roadkill fawn. He goes to lift her but her eyes open like a doll's and she sits up and says, I'm thirsty. He says, OK, little one, come with me and we'll get you a glass of water. And she rubs her hands over her head and yawns and her open pink mouth reminds him of a kitten he once had. She twists her feet into her slippers, half stumbling against the bed, and as they turn to the stairs she takes *him* by the hand.

Very steep, she says, and he says, Shh, because they're passing Nell's bedroom, and Shh again because she's such a chatterbox and she just won't listen. When she starts to say, Where are we going? he moves her quickly through the door and down into the garden. More difficult now, more risky than he thought, trying to get her to go at his pace. At the river's edge, she starts to cry.

Nell won't let me, she says, as he's trying to lift her into the dinghy, I'll drown, No! and she's making no sense at all, and he has to shout at her, half throws her into the boat and she bangs her head—

Not her head. Maggie looks up into the emerald leaves on the tree above, crosses out the error and continues.

she bangs her ~~head~~ face on the rowlock, and it's such a shock, it makes her silent. Will pushes the dinghy into the middle of the river. The level's low enough for him to carry on pushing. The silt is gritty underfoot, the water sloshing around his knees; the child lies still as a sack in the belly of the boat. He feels the dinghy banking as he manouevres it into the reeds on the other side, thinking it will capsize and tip her out. His hands are shaking and his shorts are wet, and he lifts her out of the boat and leads her through the tangled weeds. It's all taken such a long time. He'd started in the black of night, no moon, perfect, and now he can feel the dawn lifting behind him as he propels her up the rise towards the house. Her face in the dimness looks very dirty. One of her eyes is shut, the skin around it swelling like a bubble. He tries to hold her hand nicely but she's shivering and her fingers keep slipping from his grip. He takes her by the wrist, striding fast into the courtyard, and in the far wall there is a low door and behind the door there is the trunk room. Will's prepared it, cleared the space, moved anything he thought might be dangerous up onto the high shelf – the fishing tackle and the tennis rackets – and has padlocked his school trunk. He thought about giving her a tennis ball to play with, and then imagined her throwing it at the door, the sound it would make. He's put his sleeping bag in here, and a chamber pot. He doesn't know what else a child of four might need.

I'm thirsty, she says again. Her eyes are like pips of light. He takes a packet of chewing gum from his pocket and unwraps a stick, holding it for her to take.

You mustn't swallow it, he says, feeling the terrible fear of finding her, in the morning, choked and cold, You must chew it and then spit it out. Look.

He shows her, folding the stick into his mouth and chewing it, making noises of pleasure, exaggerating the movement of his jaw.

And when the flavour's gone, you spit it out, see?

And he spits it in the chamber pot.

Here, he says, offering the packet, You have them.

But she wriggles back against the wall, puts her hands out in front of her, trying to push him away. It makes him feel hot, uncontrolled, when she does that. A guilty feeling, like when he's been caught picking his nose and wiping it on the cushion covers.

You mustn't talk, he says, Do you understand? No talking. She doesn't look as though she's listening so he puts his face very close to hers, like the older boys do to him at school when they want to frighten him, and he repeats the words very slowly.

You – must – not – talk. If the dog hears you talking – even a little bit – he'll jump in and rip your heart out. And Eat It. Do you understand?

A dog? whispers Maggie.

A very hungry dog, he says, satisfied he's terrified her now.

He leaves the packet of chewing gum on a boot rack where she can reach it and locks the door behind him. After the closeness of the room the dawn air is like diving into a swimming pool. Will feels the sweat running beneath his clothes. Tomorrow, he only has to wait until tomorrow, and then he can move her to the nursery.

sixteen

Maggie takes the bridle path into the village. The air has become sticky, the sun dim and lifeless, a flattened coin under a thin membrane of cloud. At the shop, she pauses to read the small ads in the window. Peering through them into the interior, she sees Thomas Bryce contemplating a row of tins on a shelf. Inside, the air is even thicker, and damp, carrying a vapour of rotting vegetables. Maggie stands close enough behind Thomas to know the smell is from him. She sees how the grime on his collar makes the fabric look wet. It has been a month since they last met.

Hello Thomas, she says, D'you remember me?

When he swivels his head to look at her, his eyes are filmy.

It's Maggie, she says.

Thomas selects a tin of tomatoes from the shelf and studies it.

I know, he says, I'm not blind.

I've been meaning to stop by again, she continues, ducking forward to try to catch his attention, I'd like to have another chat.

He replaces the tin and fetches down a garish-coloured plastic pot.

Noodles, he reads, considering, Bramble don't much like 'em.

Are you still up at Keeper's? she asks.

Where else would I be?

Only, I wondered if you'd had to move out. I heard the estate were thinking of selling it. I could put a word in for you.

He turns to face her again, weighing the pot in his hand.

They won't kick me out, he says.

Maggie clenches and unclenches her jaw.

And why's that, Thomas?

They won't kick me out, he repeats, That's mine for life. I told you before, I've got nothing more to say to you.

He puts the pot back and walks away, leaves her standing there at the shelves. As soon as he is gone from the doorway, the assistant fetches a can of air freshener from under the counter. She moves past the till and into the aisle.

He's a bit ripe, that one, she says, flapping a hand in front of her face, I dread it when he comes in. Only spends about a pound a week.

She holds the can aloft and squirts a spray of lavender rain into the space above their heads.

Don't suppose you sell antiseptic? asks Maggie.

Father and son sit facing each other. Earlier, Kenneth had erected a picnic table under the cedar tree and covered it with a white cloth. He'd brought out the cutlery and the napkins, trudged back in for the side plates: he wanted everything to go smoothly, was afraid of dropping or smashing things. Last time he had William over, for dinner, Kenneth had forgotten the forks, and then, after he'd gone back and fetched them, had to make a second trip to get the wine glasses. Grist to William's mill, the small details.

When they first went outside, William with his sunglasses covering his eyes again and carrying the drinks, and Kenneth with the salad, he noticed something was different; couldn't fathom what it was. Now he sees: there's a jar of wild flowers in the centre of the table. He doesn't remember putting them there; in fact, he's certain he didn't put them there.

Kenneth glances over at the flattened oblong of grass where the blanket had been, trying to recapture the memory of the night before. But instead he revisits that scene in the library. He was horrible. He sees again the terrible look on Maggie's face; pain, and fear, and bewilderment: he caused that. Bullying her, being an oaf. And then, stupidly trying to win her back with a song. Some hope. And what does she do? She leaves him flowers.

Throughout lunch, he glances surreptitiously at them. One has hairy stems and purple petals; another, long dark stems with flat white petals springing from a bulb of green. The other sprigs are rosemary. He would never think of putting a herb in a bouquet. Maggie, you're a wonder, he says, in his head.

William does most of the talking. He's telling his father about work, the latest gallery opening, but neither of them is fooled; he hasn't come to discuss work. As he speaks, William pulls absently at the purple flowerhead, dragging the others with it and almost upending the jar.

Careful! says Kenneth, You'll have it over.

What's this then, Dad? he says, drawing out the stalk.
Kenneth looks at it, pretends to be thinking.

It's called, um, I'm not sure of the common name.

But you'd know it in Latin?
William raises an eyebrow as he says it, shoots his father a quick grin.

Not your arrangement, then, he says.

What would you like to know? Kenneth asks. He waits, wiping his hands on his napkin.

Well, does she have any other talents, William says, Apart from floristry?
He resists the urge to put the stalk in his mouth.

She has, says Kenneth. He would like to list all that Maggie does, realizes that what she is to him is not definable.

I don't expect you to understand, or even like the idea, but it's a professional relationship.

I bet. So what is her profession, exactly?

William tosses the stalk on the table; the texture of it on his fingers is hairy and rough, and the peppery smell gives him an odd sensation at the back of his throat. He feels his father's eyes on him, flicks a greenfly off his shirt.

Dad, I hope you're not going to make a fool of yourself.

Why change the habit of a lifetime? says Kenneth.

Ali thinks she's a fraud.

Kenneth turns away from the table, unable to still the energy in his legs, kicking them out in front of him.

Bush telegraph works fast round here, he says, How dare you discuss my private business?

William leans back in his chair like a poker player, raising his sunglasses from his eyes and sliding them onto the top of his head.

Someone has to look out for you, he says, I'm just asking you to be cautious. You don't know what the world's like these days. There are lots of charlatans out there only too happy to con you. A lot of vile individuals, he continues, nodding, You hear about it all the time, old people robbed in their living rooms, shootings on the street, happy slapping . . .

Happy what? says Kenneth, incredulous.

William throws his arms wide.

You see, you've no idea what goes on. You just let this woman walk in, give her free rein. And you don't know the first thing about her.

Some things you take on trust, says Kenneth.

As soon as the words leave his lips, he knows it's the wrong thing to say. Kenneth watches as William turns his head away, his response delivered with feigned outrage.

No, Dad, you must *never* take anything on trust. Where's she from? What did she do before? How much are you paying her?

She's just working for me for a few months, Will. You don't have to feel threatened. I'm not some old codger, he says, and then, as if it might lighten the tone, I'm sixty-several, he adds, with a laugh.

What day is it today, Dad? asks William quietly.

Don't insult me, says Kenneth, tossing his napkin onto his empty plate.

OK. Something easier. What did you have for breakfast?

He leans forward again. Kenneth leans forward too, conspiratorial, a look of amusement on his face. He places his hands on the table, making the glasses rock gently.

An egg, lightly boiled, two pieces of toast. A cup of tea. I believe it was Twinings.

They haven't noticed the sky thickening overhead, but the two of them are sweating in the stifled air. They see the sheen on each other's face, the colour rising at the throat; both interpret these signs as victory. Kenneth feels the tremor in his hands and keeps them pressed on the cloth.

Let me meet her, then, says William, lightly, If she's *no threat*. Bring her up to town.

Actually, I think an evening here would be better, have some people over. Before the summer disappears entirely, Kenneth says, looking at the sky, You can meet her then.

He stacks the crockery onto the tray and carries it back into the kitchen. He's smiling to himself, humming a tune under his breath.

seventeen

She takes care removing her shirt: the fabric has stuck in places; she will have to soak it off. Standing in her bathroom, Maggie drenches a cotton wool ball in warm water and presses it against her sleeve, feels the water run down her arm and drip off her fingertips. A cluster of smeared brown stains indicates where the puncture wounds have rubbed. She notices a few more further down the sleeve; at some point during the day, it must have ridden up and opened the wounds again. When she judges it won't be too painful, she snakes her arm out and inspects the damage; gently touches the places where the ink has got under the skin. She will be left with a few black dots as a reminder, but for the most part the wounds will come clean. She dabs on the antiseptic cream she bought in the shop and covers the skin with a large square of plaster. Immediately, she feels better: healed, less frayed.

That's the very last, she warns herself in the mirror, ignoring the smirk of the woman staring back.

★

When William phones Alison, she sounds distracted.

Is it a bad time? he asks, hearing her struggling with the phone.

Terrible, I'm trying to learn how to play golf, although why is beyond me. Bloody wasp! she shouts – a rush of crackle on the line – Hang on.

There's a pause, a thunk, more rustling, and then her voice, low and ordinary again.

That's better, she says, Killed the bastard. Now, how was he? William tells her about lunch with Kenneth, and his father's plans to hold a party.

A soirée, she says, How elegant. Let's hope he remembers to actually invite people. That is, of course, unless he was making one of his jokes.

William feels the truth of the remark. Of course it was a joke. His father was just trying to fob him off.

What did she say her name was again? he asks.

Maggie, she says, That's all.

And she was a lot younger than him, you said? And pretty? Alison gives a little cough.

I didn't say pretty. I think I said 'bedraggled'. Much more your type than his.

Meaning? says William, sensing a trap.

Meaning a lot like those women who hang about the private views hoping for a free drink. You know, intense faces, intense mannerisms – intense bloody hair, she says, exasperated.

Ah, laughs William, Just my type. So, she *is* pretty then. That explains it. What we need to do is give the old man a project, something to divert him, to occupy his time.

The hotel idea? she asks, I thought he wasn't interested.

He wasn't, says William, But with you on board, he might be persuaded. You know, you can be *very* persuasive.

A long silence follows where all he can hear is what sounds like wind butting against the handset. Just when he thinks the connection is down, Alison speaks again.

I care about him, Will. I wouldn't want him to do anything he doesn't want to do. If he agrees, I'll help. But I'm not going to try to force his hand. Is that clear?

You're breaking up, he says, Thanks Ali, I'm counting you in.

★

In the prefect's office, Maggie rolls a sheet of paper into the typewriter. Looking at the notes from the morning, she hears again her own hysterical voice rising above the soft slow gravel of 'Lay Lady Lay'. The light from the window isn't helping her to see; nothing here will help her see. It's too dark.

You mustn't talk, he'd said, Do you understand? No talking. Put his face close to hers, repeated the words very slowly. His breath smelled of spearmint. No talking, he'd said, The dog will rip your heart out.

```
Big Girl Now
Not your surprise, Kenneth, but mine, to see
how desperate you were to bury the past. Like
father like son like son like father.
I didn't say a word in that place, Kenneth,
but I sang; I sang my heart out.
Just like that bird.
```

Maggie lays the typed sheet down on the desk, and strides through the hall, along the corridor, into the atrium. She has a clear image in her head, and she holds it there; it won't escape from her now. She knows where she's headed and what she will do. The French windows lead her out into the courtyard, and in the courtyard is the tree, and its eyes seem to slide sideways, beckoning her on. Beyond, there will be a wall with a low wooden door. And she will open it and go inside and see for herself what the fear looked like.

Here she is, standing in front of the tree, and beyond it, there

122

is the wall. There is the wall but there is no door. There is only a tree. There are only bricks. There is no door.

Kenneth leads her slowly across the back lawn. He has one hand round her waist and holds her wrist with the other, daintily, as if any pressure would cause her to snap in half. She leans against him and he catches the warm scent of her hair and an astringent, more medicinal smell he can't define. Really, he would like to carry her, pick her up bodily and crush her to him and wrap himself all around her, like a suit of armour, like a shroud. He wants to bury himself inside her. He wants to eat her. The knowledge makes him breathless. Kenneth understands for the first time how vast love is; how savage; how appalling. He sits her at the table under the cedar and goes to fetch her some water. A moment to think, he tells himself, to compose himself. But in the kitchen he doesn't think, he turns the cold tap on full and pushes his face under the flow, dashing up the liquid in his hands, coughing out the water like a drowning man. Still he feels a raw heat bubbling in his blood. If anyone has hurt her, if they've hurt her, he thinks, I will kill them.

Picking his way back across the lawn with the tray, the glasses chattering and the light sparking off the crystal facets of the jug, he sees her bent double, a clear stream of liquid spilling from her mouth. Even this, he would own. In the shadow of the tree, her skin is the colour of ash.

It'll be too much sun, Maggie, he says, You walked all the way into town. And back! No wonder you don't feel well.
She doesn't speak. She wipes her eyes with her fingertips. When he offers her the glass of water, she turns and splashes it in quick arcs over the grass, erasing the evidence of her sickness, then holds it up for a refill.

Perhaps you should lie down for a while, and I'll concoct something adventurous for supper. What do you say?
Maggie opens her mouth, sucks in a breath, closes it again.

Was it that scary tree, the one with the eyes? he asks, desperate now for a clue, Because I'll have it chopped down if necessary.

It'll have a restraining order, she says. Her lips are flecked with sticky blobs of white.

A preservation order, Maggie, he says, pointing a finger at her, Are you trying to catch me out?

He drags his chair nearer to hers, removes his handkerchief from his pocket and tilts the jug of water so a thin trickle runs on and off the cotton and drips through the gap between his knees. He dabs the handkerchief against her lips, and when she doesn't protest, he folds it over and wipes the flecks away from the corners of her mouth. The look of her: he could howl.

Thank you, she says, and taking this as an instruction to stop, he closes his fist around the handkerchief and then stares at it, mystified.

A handkerchief, a handkerchief, who said that? he asks.

Othello, she says.

They fall silent again. Kenneth stuffs it back into his pocket, gazing around for another distraction. He pours himself a glass of water and drinks it in one.

Now. Tell me about these, he says, pulling the flowers from the jar and laying them like specimens on the tablecloth.

This one's rosemary, she says, touching the needles, For remembrance.

When she doesn't continue, he picks up another and holds it out.

And what's this?

She smiles faintly,

Purple basil. To keep the flies away, she says, Also, for love. At this, he smiles back at her.

And for banishment, she says.

Banishment? Did you say banishment? I thought it was just for making pesto. And this white one? he asks, stroking the petals with his finger.

Bladder campion. It's a weed. Grows all over here.

I've seen it, says Kenneth, nodding, Horrible name for such a beautiful thing. They do say a weed is just a flower in the wrong place.

She doesn't answer that. They sit together under the tree. The sky has gone the colour of putty, there's no breeze to be felt, no air. He doesn't take his eyes from her, watches her sip at her water, watches the dance of light and shade on her face. He asks her once, twice, if something – someone – scared her. She must tell him, he says, he has a gun. When she meets his eye, he can tell it's to look for the joke.

I do, Maggie. And I would kill anyone who tried to hurt you.

There, he's admitted it, and the admission is a pure release. Her mouth moves but still she says nothing; something has shocked her, if he can only find out what.

I've tried to write up your song notes, she says, finally, It was hard for me.

Kenneth passes his hand over his face and feels how greasy his skin is. He's still quite tired. After William had left, he took a nap in his den, fed the fish, tried and failed to work on his catalogue of objects. He'd like a gin and tonic now, or better still a vodka martini. He can almost taste the tight, glacial pitch of it. He glances at his watch: half past four. Pours himself another glass of water and drinks it. But still he's thirsty.

I didn't really say anything, he says, Not very encouraging.

Maybe you should write them yourself, she says, Without me. Because – well, I'm not cut out for the job, am I?

Kenneth detects an edge in her voice.

Perhaps I don't want someone 'cut out for the job', he says, sounding petulant, Perhaps I want you.

You don't know anything about me.

With her head down again and her hair hanging over her face, Kenneth can't read her expression. He wants to lift the hair away, he wants to say, Don't do that, don't hide inside yourself like that, like a frightened animal. You're too good for that. Instead, he bends forward, trying to meet her gaze.

I know three things for sure, he says quietly, One, I do very much like having you here; two, you like music, thank God in Heaven; and three – and this is crucial – we both like Chablis! Maggie gives a slow blink.

Not the best qualifications for the job.

When I interviewed you, I said I wanted someone to sit in a corner and listen to me. What a frightful old bore I was. But look at me now, he says, bouncing his feet on the grass, You've taught me all sorts – how to get rid of unwanted gifts, how to cool the blood with cold water . . . and about herbs, and bats, and echo-thingy.

Echolocation, she says.

Echolocation. Exactly. I've read up about it. Bats use sound to see. They're like me and you, he says, We see things in sounds. How wonderful is that? Now I'll admit, I've no wish ever to replay that period in my life again, when Rusty wasn't well. But it's a small setback. Shall we just draw a line under it and move on? Nineteen seventy-six. That was *not* a very good year, he says.

It was a terrible year, says Maggie.

But surely you weren't born? he says, Or – or you were just a baby?

Not quite a baby. I was four.

She looks at him directly. Her eyes on him are full of light.

Seems a lifetime ago. Being four, that is, he adds quickly, I can't say I can recall anything before I started school.

Songs, says Maggie, I remember songs.

Do you? Maybe we could play them? When shall we do it? Do you have the records to hand?

She shakes her head.

Never mind, he says, We can find them again, Maggie. And then we can listen to *your* music. I'd love that.

He leans across the table to pour her more water, thinking

126

again of the bottle of Stoli in the freezer. But he won't leave her now.

They'll be easy to find, will they? There's a very good second-hand record shop in town. We could go hunting.

He offers her the full glass, holding it out in front of her.

If you had the Internet, you could probably download them, she says.

Kenneth pulls a baffled, ironic face.

God! You're beginning to sound like Will. Got the lecture again today, how cut off I am from the outside world, how – decrepit.

He hunches closer to her, lowering his voice.

Do *you* know what 'happy slapping' is? he whispers, Is it something to do with kinky sex?

Maggie tilts her head back, and Kenneth, like a child, copies her, sees the branches of the cedar hanging above them. He wonders if he's guessed correctly, until she says,

It's a form of bullying. Kids do it – one of them will hit someone, and the rest of them film it on their mobiles.

I'm definitely not getting one of those phones, he says, folding his arms.

It's not a requirement of the purchase, she says, smiling properly now, You wouldn't have to slap anyone.

Wouldn't dream of it, he says, and, cocking his head on one side, considers, Well, I'd quite like to give those buggers down at the golf club a swift kick up the arse. Balls flying every-where. Marching about in those ridiculous clothes. But that phone business, it's – it's beyond comprehension. Why would anyone do that?

It's a way of using technology, says Maggie, Ingenious, if it wasn't so cruel. When I was younger, it was graffiti on the toilet wall. So and so is a slag, phone this number for sex . . .

Has that happened to you?

No, says Maggie, patiently, I was just giving an example.

Good, he says, because I would have to shoot them too. I

hate bullies. Will was always getting picked on at school.
Maggie strokes her eyebrow with her finger.

He was bullied?

He was a lonely child, says Kenneth, Very secretive. And he had, he still has it, this . . . front. It made the others distrust him.

But *he* wasn't cruel? she asks.

No. Underneath all the bravado, he's hypersensitive.
She asks again.

He wouldn't hurt anyone, wouldn't get – violent?

No! He's soft as butter, that boy. He wants to meet you, by the way. He was very curious.

What did you tell him?
Kenneth lets out a theatrical sigh, hangs his head to one side.

I'd like to have told him that I think you're lovely and kind and beautiful and just what a chap needs in his dotage.

But?

But I couldn't remember the word at the time, he says, I couldn't remember 'dotage'. I went through them all, dosage, and postage, and sewage and—
Maggie lets out a yelp of laughter, presses her hand to her chest.

'These strong Egyptian fetters I must break or lose myself in postage'! she cries.

What's that, Maggie? That's Shakespeare, too, isn't it?

Yes, but *I* can't remember who says it, she lies, You know, Kenneth, I bet the archive was his idea, wasn't it? To keep you out of the real world, where people forget things all the time and have to face actual problems, like pain and loss and – and chaos. Some things are better left forgotten. And as for that rubbish in your den, you don't need a catalogue, you need a bonfire. You need to burn it.

Ah, but Will thinks I'm losing my grip on things, Kenneth says, He asked me what day it was.

And what day *is* it? she asks.

Haven't the foggiest, he says, grinning at her.

Me neither, she says, and he feels such a choke of gratitude that he has to look away. She looks away too. She can't bring herself to tell him what she's going to do. They sit together in the shade, staring out over the sloping lawn and into the trees. Kenneth sees a possible future beyond them. Maggie sees the glinting river.

eighteen

Oh Nelly you're a funny one got a face like a pickled onion, got a nose like a squashed tomato and—

Onward Christian shoulders, marching off to war. With the cross of Jesus, going on before!

She sang her way through the songs she knew, hymns she could remember from Sunday school, leaning against the sweating brick, legs pulled up under her pyjama top. She really wanted to pee, but there were things moving about on the floor: mice, or could be big mice. The boy had put his chewing gum in the bowl; that would make it a bin, not a potty. But she really wanted to go.

Maggie looks back to her last entry, flipping the pages of the notebook. It seems appropriate that she's working from back to front, as if the end will simply emerge as the beginning; the final page will become the first. She checks again, reading through what she'd written about how William took her away and put her in the trunk room. She's sure it was a trunk room; she's sure of the location. But it wasn't where she thought it was. Fine, she tells herself, That doesn't mean it didn't happen that way. A child of four, what could she know about geography? But something is still wrong with the entry. Reading her words again, it takes Maggie a moment to see what is different: she's removed herself from the memory; there's no *I*. She's managed, without thinking, to displace herself from the centre, and put William there instead. She has imagined what she thought would be impossible: what it would be like to be him. Maggie looks up to the stained-glass lady for guidance, sees the rain clouds beyond the window, their bellies laced with purple and black.

That's okay, she says, That's classic.

Maggie knows from the counselling she's had how she copes. She separates; she's very good at splitting and dividing: black and white, then and now, sound and silence. The first time she started to modify her body, it was random and awkward. She pulled her hair out, one strand at a time, then a few, then in the end, whole clumps. The feeling was delicious to start with, and painful; the waiting moment, the tugging, the release as it fell away through her fingers. She did it when she was bored, when her mind was racing, before she went to sleep. Like all habits, it was new and real and *something* in the beginning, and then after a while it just became the thing she did. She ate the evidence, crushing the fine filaments of hair under her teeth, rolling the strands around her tongue; a gritty swallow. When the bald patches became noticeable, she had to think of another way. She couldn't bear the thought of burning herself, although she knew girls who did it, with matches or lighters or more often the red tip of a cigarette. It was the smell she most disliked. They had a coven at school, the girls who branded and cut and etched. They called it 'contouring', as if it were a treatment you'd have done in a hair salon or beauty parlour. The girls who contoured knew each other without knowing how. Then one day Janine showed her how she did it; with a safety razor, on the inner arm, high up. When Maggie tried cutting, she marvelled at the small streaks of itchiness that bobbled red, the feel of secretly glowing in hidden places. None of them wanted to be found out: it made it bearable, to sit in maths or history, and let the heat of a fresh wound take you away.

It was reopening a wound that gave Maggie the greatest relief: like returning to the site of a hard-won battle. And she hated the bumpiness of a scab forming, she'd want the skin smooth and perfect again, so she'd slice or pick it off. Catching the edge of a long scab with her fingernail, she'd pull, carefully and slowly, astonished at the acute point of pain, at the way the old skin came away, leaving a shiny pink weal beneath. New skin. Incredible. Sometimes, it would well up again with freckles of blood, bright shiny beads of wet. And then she would lick the wound, or talk to it: How does that feel, does that feel all right?

She knew one morning, in needlework class, that it had to stop. She'd been watching the teacher demonstrate how to stitch a hem. All the girls had gathered round Mrs Evans as she bent over the machine, head down, following the rapid stab of needle into fabric, feeding it through with her slim fingers. Maggie saw how the material ran over the plate, how it glided, really; how the hem went in rough on one side and came out smooth and neat on the other. And then she was considering how that might feel. How it might feel to stitch through the skin, to stitch it together, smooth and neat. Fold it over, hide the rough edge from the eye. The surface would be perfect. That was when Maggie realized she was thinking of her skin as if it didn't actually belong to her.

There have been times since when she's actively planned to modify some part of her; gone to Boots or Superdrug and bought razors and antiseptic wipes and plasters, and then she would battle for hours to conquer the feeling. Like a recovering alcoholic, she would tell herself: just last this day, just this one day, and the urgency would gradually drain out of her. Or she'd argue herself out of it. This is so boring, she'd say. You are so predictable. Can't you think of anything more inventive than this? What are you like?

But occasionally she'd be caught, as she was when she discovered the fountain pen from Kenneth. She couldn't say then why his gift had made her so weak. Now she considers it: not because he likes her, but because she likes him back. She would like to be neat for him. Smooth. She would like to be as smooth and perfect as a neatly stitched hem. That's not supposed to happen. And the fact of it makes it hard to keep things separate in her mind: black and white, smooth and jagged, him and her, then and now.

When it gets to the edge of the bench it will be day. After a while, she stops staring at the thin line of light and falls asleep, her body curved like a comma on the wooden slats. The brick against her back is damp and then her back is damp, and when she wakes up she thinks she's had a dream about a boy.

Leon always says, What's up, babe? when she cries, and she can show him where she caught her finger in the cupboard door or slipped on the wet step outside when she was running in and banged her knee. He kisses the place and says, Looks terminal, Bird, which she knows is funny because Nell laughs and he laughs, and if it really is terminal, Nell will wipe it with a wet cloth and put a plaster on it. Sometimes, when she takes the plaster off, the skin underneath is a different colour, paler and lighter than the rest of her, and Nell will say, All better, and throw the plaster away. Then a sticky brown edge will show her where the plaster used to be, until eventually that too will be gone. She can't find the place, now, to show Leon where it hurts, because it's deep inside and it hurts all over.

It's very hard to see, even though the line is getting wider and brighter. She's thirsty and her eye is sore and there's a thing inside her belly that feels like when she's hungry but it's a feeling she doesn't really know because she's never had it before. She thinks it's a hungry feeling but it's not, it's fear.

nineteen

The market place is nearly empty. Three teenage boys lean against the lychgate at the clock tower, a man jogs by on the other side of the road, tugging a reluctant dog. Inside the perspex of the bus shelter, two elderly women, so alike in their appearance they could be twins, perch on the bench, swapping nods and pauses. Now and then one or the other will bend forward, investigating the distance for any sign of a bus. Maggie stands a little way away from them, her case jammed between her feet. She feels conspicuous, as if any minute now Kenneth will screech into the lay-by, fling open the car door, and ask her what she thinks she's up to. She relaxes a little when she remembers that he doesn't drive any more. She'd left him sitting in the garden, a volume of Shakespeare in front of him, having what he called a 'sundowner'. Except the sun wasn't shining; you couldn't tell where it was in the sky.

As the coach pulls up, it starts to rain, a rush of thick blobs smelling of road dirt and tar, but fresh, Maggie thinks, a good smell after the headache-inducing sultriness of the afternoon.

She'd hated having to deceive him. There was hardly any food in the house; an inch of milk, some dried goods, stuff in tins, but he'd used all the salad for his lunch with William, and most of the bread was gone.

Who needs milk when we've got wine, he'd said, And the

van comes round in the morning. We can manage, Maggie, we're practically old hands at awful dinners.

But she had insisted; she'd go into town before the supermarket closed and buy some vegetables, some fresh rolls, and anyway, she'd said, the walk would do her good. That was a mistake.

No more walking for you today, Maggie. Listen, I can't run you in – it's – I no longer have a licence. So perhaps, if you're very careful, you might take the car?

And then he'd offered to come too, to keep her company, and suddenly she was trapped.

I've got to go to the chemist, she'd lied, which made him throw his hands up in retreat.

The notebook is at the bottom of the case, and she will leave it there. When the driver asks if she wants her bag stowed, she says yes, to avoid the temptation of looking at what she's written, to stop herself from writing any more. There are hardly any other passengers on the coach. The two women sit together at the front, their walking sticks sliding companionably along the handrail in front of them, and the teenage boys head straight for the back. She smells cigarettes and chewing gum as they pass her.

★

The clock on the tower says eight, but she knows that's not the time: it read eight o'clock when she arrived, and was still eight o'clock when she got on the coach. It doesn't matter, she tells herself, there's no such thing as the right time, but then goes through it again: she left at six-thirty. It would have taken her twenty minutes to walk to the market place, and she waited for ten or so minutes for the coach to come. The urge to know makes her get up and lean over the headrests and ask the two women. They both consult their watches.

Quarter past, says one, Ten past, says the other, and she leaves them to argue it out and sits down again. She'll be back at Field Cottage within the hour, with nothing to show for it but a new wound, and a second, invisible one opening up, a small fissure of sadness and regret. Kenneth will have started on his 'concocting'. She imagines him standing in the pantry, holding a tin at arm's length, or trying to read the use-by date on a jar of soupe de poissons. Then he'll be sitting on the terrace, his best place, as he calls it, and he'll be looking at his watch, too, and wondering where she can have got to. It's not pain, she tells herself, it's pity, so put that feeling away. And it's not where I've got to, it's where I'm going, Maggie whispers to herself, wiping her breath from the window. You're not running away, she says, touching the smooth outline of the plaster through her sleeve, You're quitting while you're ahead.

He checks all the rooms on the ground floor and all the rooms upstairs. He goes and knocks on the door of her flat. The east wing – the suite of rooms beyond Maggie's landing – is unused, and the connecting door locked, but as Kenneth climbs back down the stairs, he tries it anyway, to make sure. He tells himself he's being silly, but then he saw something in her face this afternoon when he was talking about Will – an anxious look – that makes him return to his office and fumble about in the desk drawer and find the master key, and he climbs her stairs again and unlocks the door to her flat. He knocks twice, very loudly, before he steps into the room, only now considering the possibility that she might simply have fallen asleep. Bound to be tired out after the day she's had. He hasn't been in the place since she moved in, and although he can see at once that she's gone, he finds her everywhere. A square indentation on the quilt where she laid her case to pack it; a vase of flowers on the kitchen table; the scent of her on the bathroom air. He sees some bloodied cotton wool balls in the metal bin and he looks away. He has to be gone from here. Kenneth takes the stairs quickly, gripping the cold iron balustrade at the bottom; feels a sharp pain in his ribs from all the climbing up and down.

She's the last person on the coach. The boys jumped off at Boxford, and not long afterwards the elderly women got let off by the side of the road, at the intersection of two enormous fields. The driver dropped down out of his cab and walked round the side of the coach. Maggie waited, listening to the rolling engine, as he carried their shopping across the carriageway, then ran back to shepherd them over. Now, as the coach nears Welford, the rain ceases and a cloud break appears, low in the sky, just wide enough to glimpse a streak of sunset.

Kenneth tries to behave normally. He's hungry so makes himself a snack of peanut butter on toast, but as he's eating it he realizes why the jar has been in the pantry for so long: he isn't at all fond of peanut butter, the way it cleaves to the roof of his mouth. He wanders about the rooms with his glass of wine, wanders back to the kitchen to top it up. In the library, he puts on a collection of Chopin nocturnes, thinking it will soothe him, but all it makes him feel is depressed. He sits in the chair Maggie sat in and then moves from it as if bitten, paces the room, perches in the window seat, walks to the wall of records. She said she liked Dylan, and some other stuff. Martin someone? Folk, soul. He half-wishes she'd said she liked military bands, or Billie Holiday. Nina Simone. There's so much he didn't play her. All he's got in the folk section is a pristine Peter, Paul and Mary album. His soul collection is nothing to boast about either: a couple of Aretha Franklin, Al Green, a Motown Classics record that Will bought him one Christmas and which he's never knowingly played, and Otis Redding. He chooses this one, sliding it from the shelf, but his heart sags when he remembers the moment Maggie found it, her teasing: it would be torture to hear this now. He looks again at his watch. He'll wait until ten, and then he'll do something. He isn't quite sure what.

She unlocks the door to her cottage. The inside feels damp and airless, drained of light. She moves through the unlit rooms, opening all the curtains.

Kenneth sits at his desk with Maggie's letter of application in his hands. He struggles to read it, holding it further and further away from him, pulling it back in, slowly. The words are blear in front of his eyes. As far as he can see, there is no phone number, no contact details, and for her address, she's just put what looks like 'Fell Cottage'. Could be anywhere. Perhaps he should talk to Will.

Lying down fully clothed on her bed, Maggie waits for sleep. Her case is on the floor beside her, unopened. She tries not to think about Kenneth, but the shadows on the wall won't let her.

twenty

William trips up the steps to find the front door of Earl House ajar, the hall ashen in the half-light. It's only just past five, but the messages his father left on his machine gave him no choice. He shouts, Dad! Dad! hearing his own voice ring through the house. Kenneth appears from the kitchen, wearing his dressing gown and a look of surprise. The two men stare at each other; take in the stubble and the unslept eyes.

What's happened? they both say, in unison.

Your phone messages happened, Dad. You said it was urgent.

Did I? says Kenneth, When?

William grits his teeth,

About two hours ago?

Kenneth's tone is offhand, infuriating,

And you came straight down? How did you get in?

Through the door, says William, The front door. Which you conveniently left wide open.

Ah, *that* door, says Kenneth. Well, she's gone. All packed up. And I don't know where.

And you left the house unlocked just in case she came back? Why? Do you think she's a cat?

Worried she might have lost her key, says Kenneth, I suppose you'd like some coffee. I'm afraid there's not much milk.

She could have rung the bell, Dad, like a normal person.

William leans against the doorway and rubs a hand over his face.

I'd only just got in, he continues, And checked my messages, and there's you, gibbering on and on.

I was not gibbering, says Kenneth, putting the kettle on the hob, I simply wanted your advice. I did *not* want you racing over here at the crack of dawn.

Six messages, Dad, says William, All exactly the same.
Kenneth looks at him now.

Six? Oh. Well, I'd had a few drinks, probably.
Kenneth scratches at a blob of dried grease on the hob, inspects his finger, waits for the kettle to boil. He pours the water into two mugs, drops a teabag in one, and a spoon of coffee granules in the other. He does all this calmly and without spilling anything, without making a clatter.

Can't seem to find any way to contact her, he says. He can't remember whether his son takes milk or sugar. Decides not to ask.

But you've checked the silver? asks William.

I don't have a great deal of silver, son, not much call for it these days.

You know what I mean, says William, Has she taken anything?
Kenneth laughs to himself. He wants to say – Yes, indeed, she stole my heart – but he knows his son won't see the funny side.

I thought she might be in danger, he says, Wondered if I should call the police.
William nods his head, as if to agree.

Good idea, he says, Call the police and tell them that your secretary has quit. They'll send a squad car round straight away.

Shall we sit out to drink it? Kenneth says, passing him a mug, Only I do like the light at this hour of the morning.

The bath is ancient and too big, and the water runs so slowly that Maggie doesn't bother with the cold tap; by the time the bath is full, the hot water will have cooled enough to get in. While she's waiting, she cleans her teeth, and with the tooth-brush angled in her mouth she goes through a familiar ritual, opening the windows upstairs. She looks out over the fields at the back of the house: in the rain, the ancient stone of St Gregory's church shines like wet coal. At the front window, she takes in the mud-carved road, the solitary tree bent askew by a lifetime of wind, the river stretching out beyond it. Nothing is changed or altered in any way. She's been away no time. The road is quiet at this hour, although soon it will be rumbling with tractors and farm lorries. In the bedroom, Maggie shuf-fles through the piles of CDs on the dressing table, considering Nick Drake, Jeff Buckley, Joni Mitchell. She won't know what she wants until she sees it. Scanning the racks on the far wall of the room, tracing a clear line through the dust with her finger, Maggie finds what she's been searching for: *Otis Blue*. She puts the disc into the player, turns the volume up full, goes back into the bathroom and climbs into the bath.

Outside, the cows in the field turn their heads as one towards the window, listening to the crying of the song.

part three

the river

the river man

It used to be that Thomas Bryce knew the names of all the dwellings on the river; which ones were tenanted, which were grace and favour, which lay empty. There were four on the north side under his jurisdiction, an area of nearly fifteen miles from Welford to Snelsmore. Officially, his job was to check the waters, make sure the licences were in order: didn't matter who lived there or why, no one fished on his patch without a permit. Field Cottage stood alone at the very end; Keeper's, his own place, bang in the middle; then Meadow Cottage, then Weaver's, opposite Earl House. He knew the cottage when the Weaver family had it. They were pig farmers at one time, although they always claimed that their original trade was in their name. Then it fell derelict for a while until the Cranes got it into their heads to turn it into their holiday home, and that wasn't much of an improvement, from what he could tell. They spent one summer there and gave up. Mrs Crane not thrilled with the flies, apparently. So it stayed empty, and the youths from town would come across the water and camp there and have parties. Once, he turned up to check the licences on that stretch and saw all the windows had been put through. After that, the Cranes gave it to their son to look after. Thomas remembers the very first time he met him, when he was only a kid. Edward was very polite in those days, very interested in the river and the fish. The next time, years on, he was calling himself Ed and had a ponytail and was wearing a necklace. He remembers the girlfriends too: the one with the motorbike; the tall one with the miniskirt and all the make-up; that one with the baby. Sometimes he'd see her from over on the far bank and he'd hold his breath, not want her to notice him, because she was very nice to watch, when she didn't know you were looking. If she met you, she went stiff and terrified, like she was waiting to be arrested. She was a beauty, Nell, but not what you'd call modest. That wouldn't bother him now.

Edward was supposed to be taking care of the place, but he didn't know anything. Cutting down the trees! Thomas had a go at him for it, and Edward complained how they made the walls damp, the inside gloomy. Why live by the river if you don't like the wet, Thomas told him. He didn't listen, of course; none of them would listen. Thought they owned the place. And they did, the bricks and mortar of it; but Thomas told them more than once: doesn't matter what the deeds say, no one owns the river but nature herself. Then he didn't see Edward any more, but the other bloke with all the hair was always around the place, playing the bongos and singing. He saw her and him out in the back garden once, lying down like Adam and Eve. He thought to shout, You'll want trees now, you shameless hoboes, but he had the lad with him and didn't want to draw attention.

Four cottages down that stretch of river, very peaceful. Now, it's teeming; he can't put names to the faces he sees. There's the new development and the barn conversions, the leisure centre just past Boxford; there's the golf club. Meadow Cottage is up for sale again and Weaver's has been turned into a holiday let. The river's not his business any more, but it makes him want to spit when he sees it, all the rubbish, the way people think if they chuck the odd bottle in, the odd can, it won't matter; and they leave the trees to overhang, and the pennywort to smother, and think it won't affect anyone else.

Everything affects everyone else on a river life. There's only Field Cottage left tenanted. The river was always snagging up that way, on account of the bend in it, like a dog-leg, before it straightened again in a rush down to town. They gave it to Nell to bring her girl up, all grace and favour, like, and – more to the point – out of the way. But it wasn't much of a favour, was it, what with the damp, and the estate not wanting to spend money on it. She was doing *them* a favour, if anything. He knows who lives there now: he knows her name, and that she looks a lot like her mother used to, and that she won't be cutting down any trees round her way. She likes it gloomy.

twenty-one

Kenneth isn't surprised to find she's taken his song notes with her; they were her idea, and her invention, and he doesn't suppose they'd mean much to him without her interpretation. Alone in the dimness of the prefect's office, he rests his hands on the desk and stares unblinking at the typewriter, and the sheaf of paper, and the box file. He'd clicked open the lid as soon as he saw it, but found nothing inside. He was so hoping she'd have left the notebook. He remembers he'd written on the front, the crass joke he'd made about her being a hobbit. Unforgivable. Stupid, stupid man.

She's still here, and in every room of the house. Even the daylight has the look of her. A single sheet of paper wound round the platen is all she's left behind. He bends forward, grunting with the effort, and snatches it out with his fingers, holds it close to his face, then at arm's length. A short paragraph of words, very small, handwritten. Handwritten, but left on the typewriter for anyone to find. She's left him a message! And then he thinks on; perhaps he doesn't want to read it, perhaps it will upset him. He peers again at the sheet; it looks like a poem; not an address, at any rate, not a phone number: can't make out any numbers. He folds it carefully and slips it into his back trouser pocket. He must find his reading glasses. He'll have put them somewhere obvious.

For the first few days after she'd gone, he'd simply remained in the library, in the quiet, or stood under the shower and let the rushing water deafen him. Silence or roar; anything in between was unbearable. When the van came with his weekly delivery, Kenneth could barely bring himself to speak to the girl, Sarah, even though they had always been friendly; him helping her in with the boxes, and feeling for her, because it wasn't like driving a mobile library about, it was heavy work. And she had felt sorry for him, he could tell, up at the house on his own. Once, she'd asked him why his family didn't do his shopping for him, and he'd joked that he'd have no excuse to see her pretty face every week, then, would he? When she'd arrived this time, it was all he could do to answer the door. He'd told her he wouldn't be having any more deliveries, but then he'd had to fill out a form, because Sarah said she wasn't authorized to cancel on his behalf. The form had such tiny print on it, and Kenneth didn't know where his glasses were, and he had to breathe hard through his nose in order to stop the tears.

Standing there on the porch, full of self-pity, trying not to weep. Standing at the window of his office, looking out over the fields and the clouds rumbling low across them, with a great thick lump in his throat, impossible to swallow. Sitting on the rainswept terrace with his head in his hands. Can't remember what day it is, but remembers how it feels to cry.

The boxes remain on the kitchen counter where he'd left them. He sees the outer leaves of the cabbage have turned a yellowy brown, the lettuces have shrivelled, the carrots, in plastic, are silvered with condensation and dotted with mould. He visualizes the bottom of the box, the gathering of slimy liquid, the putrefaction, and has a fleet, clear image of the river man. He can't recall his name just now but it doesn't matter. He should do something with the boxes, and then he was going to do that other thing. Feed the fish, that was it.

★

William rings the bell – one steady drill – and waits. He follows through with a series of short jabs at the button. Finally, he places the wine he's brought down at his feet, and with both hands, bangs on the panel in the centre of the door. He resists the temptation to shout through the letter box, the urge to throw the bottle at the wood. Not so long ago he mentioned again the idea of him having a key, for emergencies, and felt the black taste of hatred at the back of his mouth when his father said it wouldn't be necessary.

At your time of life, William had argued, Anything could happen. And his father had laughed and replied, Oh, I do hope so.

He goes round the back of the house to the courtyard, kicking at the gravel like a truculent child. He'll smash the lock on the French windows if he has to. But there's no need, because the windows are open to the weather, and there's Kenneth, stretched out on one of the wicker sofas, swiping through a magazine. He raises his head when he sees William, standing in the rain with his collar turned up and his hair slick and dripping, and waves him inside.

You'll drown out there, he says, Come and give your father a kiss.

William crosses the tiles, bends over obediently. A hint of aftershave, lemony, on his son's fresh skin. Kenneth is about to ease himself out of his seat when William pulls up sharp.

Dad, don't tell me you've started smoking, he says, pointing to a cigar in the ashtray. Kenneth sinks back, smiles at him.

Thought I'd give it a try, he says, Can't do any harm at my age. It's quite enjoyable. I can understand what they see in it. William catches his breath. He wants to say, You'll only set the house on fire, no harm in that, but he has made a promise to himself that he'll go more carefully this time. And now a new promise to check all the smoke alarms. There are matters in need of attention, and if he loses his father now, it'll be a wasted trip. William knows how Kenneth operates: how forgetful he is, and how he plays on it. His refusal to see a specialist is his weapon, so there's no telling how absent-minded he's become, no way to be sure how much of his behaviour is the performance of an autocrat and how much is masking the truth. William puts the wine down on the coffee table.

You didn't answer the door, he says, unbuttoning his jacket.

Couldn't be bothered, says Kenneth, not looking up, And you said I should be careful who I let in these days.

William turns about, curls his fingers into a fist. He has a dizzying urge to take the wine bottle and hit his father on the head with it, smash his skull to pieces. He can almost hear the sound of cracking bone. The vision makes him sick to the stomach.

Is this an all day mood, or just for the next half-hour? he asks, trying to control his breathing. Kenneth keeps flicking the pages of the magazine, pretends to admire a set of bathroom scales.

Dad?

I miss her, he says, giving in, I know I shouldn't, I hardly knew her. She's young enough to be my daughter. But I do miss her. And it makes me really very angry.

William drags a chair across the tiles and sits on the edge of it. He licks his lips.

What do you wish to do? he asks, like a counsellor, What would be the ideal situation here?

I'd like her to come back, obviously, but I don't think she's going to. She was quite troubled, on that last day.

The day I came for lunch.

That's the one.

She probably realized that I was wise to her scheme, William says, And took off before I blew her cover.

Kenneth's eyes are steady on his son now.

Is that so, Miss Marple? Listen to yourself! She had no scheme. She had, um, she had—

Kenneth falters. What did she have? What the bugger do they call it?

– she had issues.

William smothers a laugh.

Get you, Dad. *Issues.* She was a flake, that was her main issue. Next time you want a secretary, I'll do the hiring.

There it is again, that tone, the same self-righteous timbre to his son's voice that Kenneth heard the last time they met. Triumphant, says Kenneth, nailing it at last: he thinks he's won a war.

What was that, Dad?

I said flood warning. Heard it on the morning news. Better batten down the hatches.

He rises unsteadily from his seat, grabbing the bottle of wine by the neck.

Fancy a picnic? he says, Before the deluge?

twenty-two

The clouds swell across the sky, blackening the hills below with their thick shadows. The lane outside the cottage is awash with tractor mud and run-off from the fields, alive and uncontained; but it is the river Maggie watches, how it gathers into a foaming swirl at the bend, fuller now than she's ever seen it. She thinks of Kenneth, alone in his house on the downs, looking at the very same river, and feels an ache, like a small hole, opening in her chest. It catches her out, this sudden stitch of pain, and she has to breathe carefully to ease it away. She should never have gone there in the first place. It's just made everything worse.

In the days after her mother's death, Maggie wasn't able to think about what she would do with the rest of her life. Without Nell in the background, it was as difficult to imagine the future as it was to forget the past. And it was this past, the pieces of it, that Maggie kept revisiting. She wanted to take it out, lay it side by side, organize it, as if it were a pack of playing cards. She wanted clarity, logic, sequence, and all with a new urgency, a sense of sudden desperation, felt more keenly because her memories were so fractured. She had no idea that trying to regain what was lost was in itself a symptom of loss.

Leon had come up for the funeral, so it was just the two of them, standing under the tall trees at the woodland site, wishing

Nell a safe journey onwards. Nell had taken care of everything beforehand; the burial and the coffin and the Portland stone memorial, the bulbs to be planted and the words to be spoken. All the practical work was done; it was the impractical stuff, the absence, the gone-ness of her, that no one could do anything about. Maggie realized that she didn't want to go back to Charmouth with Leon. An idea was taking shape in her head. Nell would never have allowed her to apply for the job at Earl House, but death had lifted the barrier: her mother couldn't stop her from doing anything, now. And it was Maggie, not Nell, who had to go on, who had to live with herself. She thought she'd make discoveries at Earl House, and she'd been right about that: just not the discoveries she'd expected.

And what a mess of it she'd made. If she's capable of nothing else, at least she has prepared for the weather, she tells herself. At least she has made the effort to do something before the roads got impassable.

On her fifth day back, with the cupboards nearly empty and the log pile low, she'd taken Nell's old bike out of the shed and cycled to the petrol station on Bear Lane, ducking the traffic and the blowing rain. The petrol station doubled as a minimarket, and had recently expanded into a souvenir shop and newsagent. Since the post office closed in the village, it had begun to sell greetings cards and stationery and stamps. Maggie stood, twirling the rack of cards, not so much drying off in the steamy atmosphere as simply getting warm again.

She'd bought a sepia-tone postcard of St Gregory's Church and a sack of logs. The man from the timber yard next door came dashing out of the dark lean-to when he saw her, and held the logs for her while she forced them into her panniers.

Criminal, he'd said, Burning logs in July.

I know, my mother would have a fit, she'd replied, trying to smile, But it gets so cold at night.

Only when she heard her own voice did she realize that she'd talked to no one for nearly a week.

That's a lot to shift on that bike. I could give you a lift home, if you want.

She thought he was flirting with her until he'd added,

Must be hard for you now, up at that place. Lonely.

And then she understood he was offering his condolences.

It's okay, really, she'd said, Thank you. It's okay.

Maggie returned to find a heap of sandbags had been dropped off outside the cottage. Every night on the local news the threat of flooding had been the first story, but Maggie hadn't been worried, didn't think it abnormal; it was just an abnormal time of year to have so much rain. With the arrival of the sandbags, she reconsidered: it did seem wrong, all this water. It did seem as if it would never stop. She'd dragged the sandbags to the front step one by one, and left them there. They might stop a river rise, but wouldn't prevent the rain from seeping in through the cracked slate roof, or finding its way down the chimney, where it battled the fire in spittering gusts. She heaved her panniers in one at a time, filling the coal bucket with logs and stacking the rest on top of the meter cupboard. The bed in the corner of the room was still made up. Maggie sat in the armchair next to the fire and stared at it. The room was darkening quietly, and the fire became brighter, and Maggie felt the heat of it burn her calves and sting her eyes.

I miss you, Nell, she said, to the bed.

Over the past few weeks, she had spoken quite often to the bed in the corner of the room; found it impossible, at first, not to. Even though her mother died in a hospital, the bed was where Nell had lain for most of the previous year. It was where they talked. At night, Maggie sat in the chair by the fire and Nell sat sideways on the bed, resting against the wall, and then, after the last round of chemotherapy, she'd half sit, with the pillow supporting her back. At the end, she lay with her head on the pillow, unable to lift it. She died on a late May morning so beautiful, so shining with promise, it was impossible to think that anyone could die on such a day. For a long time, Maggie couldn't believe her mother was gone. Often she'd hear her, singing, or talking back to the radio. Sometimes, sitting on her own by the fire and trying to read her book, she'd catch a hint of movement, and look up, and nearly see Nell, fidgeting in her sleep.

She knew this was grief. She understood it would take time. Hearing Nell's voice and seeing her turn up in unexpected places; Maggie had anticipated that. But grief didn't account for the smell. It arrived the day Nell died. Maggie came back from the hospital, unlocked the door of the cottage, and there it was, floating so thick in the air she could almost see it. Not the scent of her mother: she could have endured that. It was like leaking gas. They weren't on the mains at Field Cottage, so a gas leak was impossible, but still the smell was there, rising in a vapour at night to wake her, and Maggie would walk through the house, searching for the source, afraid to turn on the lights or strike a match. It was a dark punishment, she thought. She didn't know it then, but that was also grief; that was the smell of grief.

twenty-three

They sit under the tree, Kenneth with his umbrella in one hand and a crystal goblet in the other, watching the downpour. As they put their plates on the soaked tablecloth, William makes to clear away the remnants of the wild flowers, shrivelled now and broken into pieces by the weather. Kenneth stays his hand.

Leave them, he says, I like them.

The rain comes sideways in fast, unpredictable bursts, raking the lawn and bouncing off the flagstones. The cedar gives some cover, but when the water falls from the branches, it comes in a heavy rush, spiking the top of William's head and splashing down the back of his neck. This is ridiculous, he thinks, This is lunacy.

They said we were in for a hot summer, says Kenneth, throwing the crusts of his sandwich onto the grass, Another 'summer of seventy-six'.

Who said? asks William.

Those people on the news. The weatherman, Kenneth says, Here, have this.

He passes William the umbrella while he pours more wine. The glasses are glittering with droplets of rain. To Kenneth they look marvellous.

That was the hottest in history, he continues.

Until the next one came along, says William, covering his

glass with his hand so Kenneth can't fill it again, No more for me, I'm driving.

You remember the fields? he asks his son, How they would go up – whoof – without any warning. Spontaneous, that's it, that's the one.

It'll be climate change, says William, aching to move off the subject, They don't call it global warming any more, have you noticed? Go easy on that wine, Dad.

And the fish? The river dried up, and people had to go and collect the fish with their bare hands. Drowning in air.

You weren't around very much.

Thought you didn't remember, says Kenneth, piqued. William takes a short quick breath. Here we go, he says, in his head.

Dad, look, about this place.

What, this place here, under this tree? says Kenneth, jabbing a finger on the tablecloth.

Yep, very funny. We should at least talk about it.

I'm not going to live in a theme park, Kenneth says, You can do what you like with it when I'm dead, but while I'm here, it stays as it is.

Not a theme park, Dad, a boutique hotel. A select clientele. You don't use that half of the house anyway. You'd hardly know they were there.

Kenneth gives a silent laugh.

Troupes of yahoos dragging their cases up the drive, wandering about the flower beds with their video cameras and their maps and their *mobile phones*. I think I might notice them, don't you?

Ali wants to help, says his son, trying to coax him, She'd do all the interior stuff. And we've had this idea to turn the main hall into a gallery, you know, paintings, watercolours, the odd sculpture. You wouldn't have to do a thing – I'd act as agent, and Ali would manage it all. She quite misses you, you know.

Well, tell her from me that I don't need her help. Or yours.

And I don't miss her, either, says Kenneth, rising from the table, Now, if you'll excuse me, I'm going for a dip.

William thinks he must have misheard him.

A what? he says, A what did you say?

A dip, sighs Kenneth, as if he's talking to an imbecile. He moves off in the direction of the trees.

In the river? cries William, In this weather? Are you completely nuts?

The shout from his father is joyous.

Ha! 'Tis a naughty night to swim in, Will!

Kenneth removes first one shoe, then the other, tossing them over his shoulder. William watches as they bounce across the lawn. He thinks his father's bluffing, one of his tedious japes, but keeps his eyes on the retreating form. The belt comes off, leaping like a snake through the air, a pause until the trousers fall, and then Kenneth, stepping awkwardly out of them, hobbles in his shirt and socks down to the water's edge.

Sod him, says William, Silly bastard. I hope he drowns.

He wipes the rain from his forehead, closes his eyes and puts his face in his hands. Anyone who didn't know him would think he was praying.

twenty-four

Fifteen miles downriver, Maggie stands in the meadow, unsure of how to go on. She keeps meaning to get the bus into town, to stock up on groceries, look in the small ads for a job: something easy, temporary, to tide her over while she considers her next move. Then she forgets what it was she was going to do, and only remembers too late. Time flows away from her. Mostly, she's been buying what food she needs from the petrol station.

On her last visit, instead of the usual butterfly nets and straw hats hanging from the awning, she saw that the proprietor had lined up a row of wellington boots on the forecourt, from large to small, from black to green to rainbow-coloured. The only pair in her size were duck-egg blue. She tried them on, retreating a few steps to see how she looked in the reflection of the glass frontage: like a gigantic toddler, she thought. She was bending over, tucking her jeans in, so didn't notice the woman approach until she felt a breath on her neck.

Is that Nell's girl? asked the woman, catching Maggie's upper arm in a pinch. The tiny painted face poking out of the plastic rain hat broke into a neat smile.

Course it is. The image of her. You still here? We thought you'd have gone straight back.

No, said Maggie, There's still stuff to do.

There will be, agreed the woman, Sorry for your loss. You'll be on your way soon, though? That place'll be empty soon?

The man from the timber yard appeared at Maggie's side, swinging the door open for the woman. They exchanged friendly hellos before she dipped under his arm and ambled inside.

Old Mrs Moore. Her grandson Sam's getting married, he said, by way of explanation.

And they'll want my home, naturally, said Maggie.

The man shrugged.

I suppose she thinks you'll be giving it up. It's Maggie, isn't it? I'm Aaron, he said, holding out his hand, It's hard these days to get young people to stay, especially if they've got nowhere to live. They disappear. You know that.

Do I? she said, feeling a catch in her throat, What makes you say that?

You left. Went to live down south somewhere.

There must be other places. Ours isn't exactly plush.

There's the new barn conversions, but out of your league if you're a sheep farmer, or a carpenter – any of us, really, unless you're London based. And Weaver's is empty most of the year, he said, It's a holiday let. Your family used to live there, right?

I don't know you, she said, leaning against the wall and kicking off one of the boots, But you seem to know me: my name and my mother and where I live and where I used to live and where I went. Do let me know if I've left anything out.

Then he surprised her.

We *do* know each other, Maggie. Aaron Baggs. My family had Meadow Cottage, down the way a bit from Weaver's. But you probably won't remember us. I'm living at the Gatehouse now.

She did have a faint recollection of the family: three children, all younger than her. But there was something else about them that she couldn't quite recall; caught a glimpse of it on the edge of her memory before it slipped away entirely. Maggie looked at him properly, took in his eyes and the softness in them, thinking it would bring the moment back. His face was so lined and dark it looked dirty; the work had aged him. The work, or the weather, or the close embrace of village life.

You didn't leave, she said.

Oh, I went away, all right. And then I came home again, he said, Just like we all do.

Maggie paired the boots together and pretended to consider them. When she looked in at the window again, she saw two other women had joined Mrs Moore. They stood all in a row, watching her. Aaron was watching her too, smiling.

They won't cut much ice down on the gallops.

I've never been one for the pony club, she said, snatching them up. She could fling them at the glass; that would give them something to talk about.

Are you one for a barn dance, though, he asked, Only, there's one in Shefford on Friday. If you fancy it.

Maggie thought she heard pity in the offer.

Thanks, but as your friend in there says, I might be gone by Friday.

Aaron fished in the top pocket of his shirt and fetched out a phone.

Why don't you give me your number just in case?

I've left my phone at home, she said, and seeing his reaction, added, It's true! And I've no idea what the number is.

He put his hand up to stop her but she wanted him to understand: she was not a coward.

Really, if I didn't want to go, I'd say.

Then I'll pick you up at eight, he said.

She'd watched him walk away, his shoulders pulled back and the proud way he held his head, and decided at once she wouldn't go. She cycled home to the sound of Nell's voice in her ear, her mocking cadence. Some local lad. Going to a dance with a local lad. The thought almost made Maggie change her mind, as if she could still spite her mother, even now, through death's blunt severance. Nell's inability to keep her opinions to herself was one of the reasons Maggie left the village in the first place: that way her mother had, of making her feel very small whenever she tried to take a step on her own; ridiculed her if she wore perfume, or lipstick, or mentioned a boy; if she tried in any way to make herself fit in with the rest or be different from her mother.

Maggie's first visit to Charmouth had been a revelation. Leon had invited her down on the pretext of offering her a holiday job; he'd assumed, wrongly, that it would force Nell to follow. Nell didn't speak about it until the night before Maggie left, and then she said something that Maggie would never forget.

That shop was bought at a very high price. Remember that. Remember he's not your father. He's not a blood relation. Because he won't have forgotten.

It was meant to frighten her, of course: a malicious last-ditch attempt to stop her going. Leon was her father in every other sense, and had been ever since Ed left. Maggie had even taken his name. So she wasn't afraid of that, only of Nell: of missing her or of having to return defeated, having to admit that she couldn't manage without her. But Maggie had loved Charmouth from the beginning, or thought she did, which amounted to the same thing. So many of the people she met, through Leon, or at the craft shop or the pub, seemed to have simply landed there, as if dropped from the sky. She particularly liked the way they behaved; they were friendly and took an interest, but they didn't intrude, didn't care enough to pry. She was simply who she was, just like them. In Charmouth, she could be anyone.

She tried once, on one of her return trips to Field Cottage, to explain to Nell how she felt, hoping her mother would at least visit them, at least experience what it meant to be away from the village, to feel unbound, free. She was confused by Nell's response.

Have I taught you nothing? Places don't give you freedom.

It's what's inside makes you free. Don't kid yourself; you're not starting a new life, you're just moving house.

To be near the sea, to be away from Nell: in the end they amounted to the same thing. The next time Maggie went back to Charmouth, she stayed.

A spasm of shame jolts through her now. She'd abandoned her mother. She thought of Nell in those days as a belligerent sort of guard dog, a creature like Cerberus, all-seeing, ready to attack. It took death for Maggie to understood that Nell was protecting her; she was shielding her with her life. No one could blame a mother for that.

When she thinks of the years apart from Nell – nearly twenty of them – Maggie gets an odd sensation, as if she's emerging from a prolonged and unhappy dream to find she's still seventeen, still at Field Cottage, and Nell is downstairs making toast and tea. And she's had actual dreams of a time before Nell was gone, half-glimpsed moments of memory: her mother bending over in the garden, wrenching up a weed; breathless and tearful with laughter at some comedy show on the television; staring into the open kitchen drawer where she'd kept her medication, saying, No regrets, Coyote, in a fake American accent. Maggie wakes from this sensation to a heap of loss; the realization, fresh all over again, that Nell is gone forever.

Maggie stands in the clearing, lost and absent and ankle-deep in muddy water. Get a move on, Nell would say, You'll take root! She had planned to walk over to the Gatehouse and leave a message. She couldn't go to the dance with Aaron; the thought of it – having to meet people – made her teeth chatter with fright. They would remember her, of course, as Aaron did, as that old woman did. They would be polite to her face, but curious. She sees again those women behind the glass at the petrol station, their eyes on her. Thinking she can keep out of sight of the bungalows on the main road, she takes the meadow path. Except there is no path, just a spill of standing water and patches of treacherous bog. In her pocket she has the fountain pen Kenneth gave her and the postcard of the church. She tries out various phrases in her head; nothing seems right.

As she pushes her way through the dripping willowherb, nearing the flint wall at the western edge of the Gatehouse, she knows what she's going to do. She heads back onto the main road, ducks under cover of the bus shelter, and takes out the pen. She writes just three words – *Water over stones* – and addresses the card to Kenneth. Only when she has dropped it into the postbox on the way back home does she realize she's forgotten to put a stamp on it.

★

Aah! How very cold it is. Nice and cold. Cools the blood. Echolocation. Echo location. Echolocation!

Kenneth takes a deep breath and pushes down towards the riverbed, opening his eyes to a rush of silvery specks, and then a hand, an arm, greenish, dead, looming in front of his face. He rears up in fright, choking, scrabbling for the surface. You fool, he says to himself, It's your own bloody arm. And ducks down again. Below is oblivion, sightless, silent. There's Maggie, now, dipping one wrist, then the other, under the tap, and there again, lying on the lawn, her pale hand raised to the moon. And here, sitting on the edge of the chair in the library, tears falling in big splashes from her eyes. Afterwards, he noticed a trail of dark stains down the front of his trousers, thought they were grease spots, probably, and didn't much care. But later in the garden, baffled by William's attitude, he'd looked down again and the spots on his trousers had dried into faint blotches, glittering on the fabric like battered stars.

So strange and quiet. And so green. The current drags at his legs, pushes him sideways and back, he has to walk rather than swim through the water. And now he must breathe. He forces himself up again, feeling the mud slide away under his feet, sees from underneath how the rain pricks the surface of the water and the rain looks like a song. Not a song, a musical box, the one his grandfather had bequeathed him, when he was just a boy. He'd been so disappointed; it looked like any ordinary boring brown box, but then he'd lifted the lid and everything changed. Inside there was a glass plate through which you could see the cylinder. Shining brass. And when he turned the key, the metal teeth combed the pins on the cylinder so that he felt every single tooth of sound on his skin.

> *You should see me dance the polka,*
> *You should see me cover the ground,*
> *You should see my coat-tails flying*
> *As I jump my partner round!*

Standing under the umbrella on the far slope, William waits and watches as his father wades back through the mud, underpants grey and sagging, the hair on his chest glinting like wire wool.

They section people for less, William says, holding out a hand as Kenneth approaches the reeds at the water's edge. Kenneth ignores him, grips an overhanging branch and pulls himself up to the lip of the bank, teeters for a second, then slips and falls with a flat thwack back into the river. William tries to find an open spot to wade in after him, but still his father won't be helped, shooing him away with a dripping brown arm. As if he were a dog.

No point in ruining your shoes. I expect they cost a fortune, mutters Kenneth, finally easing himself up onto a patch of rough grass. William stares at his shoes, flecked with mud and strings of slime, and continues to stare at them until Kenneth is away, walking unsteadily back to the house; and then he trails him, seeing the long dark slash of red running from his father's elbow and wanting it not to be there.

You're bleeding, Dad, he says, his voice coming very small.

It actually feels quite warm in there, Kenneth replies, Relative air temperature, something like that. Womb-like. I suppose it's not the worst thing, drowning.

William won't be led into another meandering conversation. He's had enough. He makes to pass Kenneth the trousers he'd left slumped on the lawn, but his father bats him away.

I said it was warm. Didn't say it was *clean*. I'll need a shower. It's quite stirred up underneath, you know, soupy. What was the name of that chap who used to look after the river?

William stares at his father's back, freckled and soft as milk.

Dad, you're bleeding, he says again, putting a hand out to touch him.

Kenneth turns so fast, so full of wrath, it makes William flinch.

I said, what was his name? he says, teeth bared.

Cooper, says William.

Kenneth grunts, bending to the lawn to retrieve his belt. He wraps it round his hand.

The one before him.

I can't remember.

William shakes the rain from the umbrella and folds it closed.

It's hereditary, you know, says Kenneth, his eyes hard as marbles, Don't think you'll escape.

Escape from what, being a lunatic? A crazy old bastard? Well, I'm really looking forward to that, shouts William, launching himself up the steps and crashing the back door wide, I'm so looking forward to being you. Roll on dementia!

twenty-five

And there it is again, rising up to hit her as soon as she opens the door: the unmistakable stink of gas. Maggie slips off her boots and parks them on the newspaper under the stairs, throws her coat over the arm of the chair and pads through the house.

She's had weeks of the smell, trying to endure it, unable to endure it, checking the bins out the back and the sink in the kitchen, standing on the doorstep in the middle of the night, sniffing the air like a fox, wondering if it was a leak blowing in from the town, whether she should report it to someone: knowing all the time it was inside, in there with her, but not knowing what it was. It is worse now than before she left to go and work for Kenneth, as if the cottage is punishing her for her absence. It makes her furious, this invasion, and she longs again for the tawny scent of her room in Earl House, and for Kenneth, the trace of his cologne on the air.

She knows there's really no point in searching. She's been through the whole cottage, looked under the furniture and in the cupboards, opened and closed drawers, poked at the drains with a stick. But still. She kneels in front of the fire, breaks up the firelighter into smaller shards, relishing the squeak it makes, the sharp petrol tang, and puts a match to the kindling. Slowly, she adds sticks of tinder until the blaze is steady enough to support a log, which she balances on top. Rests on her haunches, sniffing solvent on her fingers but looking at the electricity cupboard as if it's a stranger sitting there, sitting there in the corner.

She opens the door, as she has done twice, three times before, but instead of staring at the digits slowly turning over, she glances down. Pushed against the wall, down low where the skirting used to be, is a dusty brown box. She knows it well. Made of wood, it has a carving of an elephant on the lid, the tusks inlaid with mother-of-pearl. Nell was given it by one of her travelling friends, before Maggie was born: her dream-catcher box. She used to keep feathers in it, and bits of string and beads, and that's what Maggie expects to find when she lifts the lid, some old beads and bits of string. After she's seen, she goes into the kitchen and washes her hands, tears some kitchen towel from the roll and takes it back in with her, because she doesn't want to get dirty prints on what she's found. Wipes the lid of the box, wipes her fingers, opens it again and takes out the photographs.

The first is of the three of them sitting in the garden: Ed in a deckchair with Nell on his lap, her face obscured by a lock of his hair blowing across it, and Cindy kneeling, as if about to get up, her blouse billowing open, her eyes surprised. Maggie stares at the photograph for a beat longer, sees how tanned Cindy's face is, how white and shining her breasts. Imagines what it would have been like to be Leon, seeing her that way, closing one eye, pressing the shutter at just that moment. The second is of a later time, of her young self in a broad-brimmed hat, clutching a doll; and the third is a portrait of Nell, looking hot and uncomfortable, dock leaves at shoulder height. Maggie knows this photograph. Nell had a series of them, all taken in the garden and the fields around the cottage, which she'd taped into an exercise book. She taught Maggie the names of the plants this way. Sometimes she'd cut a stem or flowerhead and press it between the covers. After a while they'd darken, go brittle, fall out onto the floor and be lost.

She studies Nell, takes in her beautiful auburn hair and her rueful face, and smiles with her, for her, asking her to please smile properly, willing the image to change so that Maggie can see that gap-toothed grin again. And in the background is the river, and beyond the river the trees, slightly out of focus, and a flare of orange low down on the forest floor.

Beneath the photographs Maggie finds a business card, clean and new, with Ed's logo and a telephone number. On the back, in her fat handwriting, Nell had scrawled another number and an Internet address. Maggie recognizes it: Ed's website. She didn't know that Nell knew. There are cuttings; one from a glossy magazine showing her mother's dreamcatchers hanging in a shop window, and a music review of Athame at Les Cousins. At the bottom of the box, wedged flat, is a bent piece of sugar paper. Maggie takes it out and looks at it: she drew this picture with the crayons Leon bought her. It was after she'd stopped talking. Most of the glitter has fallen off the edges, and the paper is faded, but the colours are still fresh. It was supposed to be a Christmas card for Ed, only it's here, in Nell's box. It shows a tiny red girl under a mountain. On the top of the mountain is some sort of animal.

It is the very last thing that makes her cry out. Tucked beneath the drawing is a folded square of newspaper, yellowed with age, and when she carefully unfolds it and looks, the sight of it stops her breath. Here she is, four years old, the whole of one side of her face a shade darker than the rest, as if it's been painted black; that slash of pain cutting across her forehead, darker still; and the left eye closed and swollen like a walnut. She's leaning forward across the picture, one arm stretching out of the frame. And the boy who is holding her is triumphant and smiling.

Birdie Crane Found Alive!
Below the headline, a single smudged line of text before the page is torn:

Schoolboy William Earl was said to be 'flabbergasted' when he discovered—
She never knew.

Nell says, Don't tell me, I don't want to hear, so Maggie doesn't tell her. It might be the words in a book she's reading, or a song she's heard on the radio, or something someone said on the television. It could be anything, and it will make the feeling in Maggie inflate like a balloon. But Nell will put her hands over her ears and block her out, or she'll say, You mustn't speak about it, do you understand? You'll get us into trouble. They'll take you away from me!

Maggie began to unlearn how to speak. It wasn't deliberate. She'd start to articulate something, but the words in her mouth felt like sharp gravel: her tongue couldn't move round them, and her voice would come out narrow and pointed over the stones, as if it had been slashed into ribbons. And then one day, Leon noticed how silent she'd become and said, What about singing for us, Bird, you used to do that a treat. And it was easier to sing, except Nell couldn't bear that, either. She'd shake her head and say, Stop, Stop, in a panicky way, as if Maggie was hitting her, and Leon would shout, What do you think you're doing? Poor kid'll have to open up some time. And you! Stick your head in the sand long enough and someone's sure to come by and kick your arse.

She was a child who couldn't speak, with a mother who couldn't listen. There was no way forward after that. Nell would talk, though, enough for both of them. They'd lie together in bed, Nell's arms wrapped tight round her daughter, and she'd whisper secrets, stories about her old life, before Maggie, before Ed and Leon, and the two of them would sleep, eventually, and dream of the past.

Maggie stares accusingly at the empty bed.

You never let me talk about it, she says, to the pillow, the

171

wall, Not even between *us*! Never. Like it never happened. You know, Nell, sometimes I think they should have taken me away from you. Sometimes I think I'd have been better off.

As if she's magicked her – of course, she has magicked her – Nell drifts into her vision.

Tell me now, then, Bird, she says, Go on. You can tell me now. No one can touch us now.

Sitting in the armchair, with the dreamcatcher box at her feet and the ghost of her mother lying peacefully on the bed, Maggie takes a breath to begin. But when she opens her mouth, silence follows. She swallows hard, feeling the knot of sounds stuck in her throat, gives a little shake of her head.

In there, you daft thing, says her mother, Go on, write it down!

Maggie picks up the notebook and reads the words on the front again, parting like a wave beneath the steady shield: *Veritate et Virtute*. Truth and courage, truth and courage, she says. She turns to the pages at the back.

★

Black again. Light goes thin like this. If I put my eye here, it goes black. The boy came with pop and a fruit. It had fur and a sandwich in silver paper. The paper was shiny. The boy sat on the bench. He smelled funny. He said, She's not ready for you yet. I tried to think but he was too close.

★

She can't do it. Maggie looks up from the page. Instead of the bed, instead of her image of Nell, she sees the plate glass window of the petrol station. Three women looking out at her, her looking in at them. The revelation makes her heart beat faster: they were seeing only her. But she was seeing them, and in front of them, like a frail replica of the real thing, she saw herself.

Okay, Nell, she says, I'm going to tell you. But I have to step back to see it.

★

The light goes very thin again, and then it's gone. If she put her eye to the crack in the door, all she'd see would be black. It must be years, she thinks, and to stop the fizzing in her chest, she plays I Spy.

The boy came earlier with a bottle of pink lemonade and a fruit. It had fur on it: a peach. And he had a sandwich wrapped in silver paper, but she wouldn't eat it. She told him she wanted her mummy, and he said, She's not ready for you yet. She's upset. And he's got to be on his plane. We don't want him coming back and spoiling everything, do we? And at first she thought he meant Leon, so then she worried about Nell, and what would she do all alone, and then she worried about the postman with the something eyes. Then she remembered a song they used to like singing. They were all going to look for America. When she'd asked what a merica was, Nell told her it was a massive country far away where all the westerns were filmed. You had to catch a plane to get there. She didn't know if Nell would go on the plane with Leon, or how she would find them in such a big place. It was a bad worry.

The boy must have seen it, the worry worming around inside her, because he sat close to her on the bench and said in a soft voice,

Do you like horses?

And when she didn't say anything, he asked,

Do you like boats? I like them.

And when she still said nothing, he said,

You must be very tired. Shall I sing you to sleep?

And in a quiet, high voice, he sang a song she'd never heard before. She listened very carefully. A song about a storm, about a boat on a stormy sea, about an anchor. She didn't know what an anchor was, but she didn't like the sound of it, the way the word broke in two inside his mouth. Or the way he laughed at his singing, made a joke about his pillows, how the pillows rolled. It made her think of Nell and Leon in the big bed.

She must have fallen asleep, though, because when she wakes, the boy is gone. But the worry is back again, crouched like a toad in a corner of the dark.

There's a lump on her eye with a cut down the middle of it, and she touches it, and the feel of the cut under her fingers is ragged like the hem of Nell's dress.

The line of light is wide again, and she wakes up and moves off the slats that have been hard on her back and looks through the gap into the open. She sees a lot of children crossing the courtyard, going under the shade of a tree and round to the front of the house. She's about to shout for her mother, but remembers that the dog will come and eat her if she talks, so she sings instead. But no one can hear her for the sound their feet make on the gravel.

She stays at the crack, smelling the air, which tastes like light. She wonders if she's been put in here because she has to be cured, like Nell's fur hat. She hears singing. It's very faint, but not on the radio; she can tell it's not on the radio because they keep stopping and starting, and when they stop there's a sound like a stick being tapped on wood. That's what makes them stop. And again, says a voice, and they start up once more:

> *Each little flower that opens*
> *Each little bird that sings*
> *He made their glowing colours*
> *He made their tiny wings.*

Maggie tries to focus on the words on the page, sees how some of them are blotched from where the ink has smudged. She wipes her nose with the back of her hand. What did you do, Nell? she says, You never told me that, either. What did you do when you found me gone?

★

Nell's not an early riser, so when she opens one eye to look at the clock and sees it's only just gone six, she rolls over into the middle of the bed and wraps her smooth leg around Leon's hairy one, and falls back to sleep. At nine, she sits up with a start and shakes Leon's shoulder.

Where's Bird? she says, because it's my habit to climb into bed with them as soon as I wake up, which is often quite early, and sing to them. Nell sees my empty bed and the open door and she knows in her bones that I'm in the river.

Get the river man, she says, Get the police. Why don't you do something?

Leon gestures wildly, as if, like a conjurer, he can make her panic disappear simply by waving his hands.

I'll get Bryce, he says, But no police, not yet. She might have just wandered off. Let's have a search round, okay? Okay?

They go to Meadow Cottage first, along the river and down through the back lanes, where Nell keeps looking over the hedgerows, expecting to find me in a ditch. Mrs Baggs, in her long apron, gathers her children into her body, as if they too are in danger of being lost.

My husband's not well, she says, her eyes flicking up to the closed bedroom curtains, But I'll tell him as soon as he gets up. Sorry I can't go myself, she says, lifting the smallest onto her hip.

At Keeper's Cottage, Thomas Bryce pulls on his boots, fetches his dog from the garden, and sets out to comb the river-bank.

But we should go in your car, cries Nell, Surely that's best?

Sonny'll find her if she's out there, he says, with what sounds like a boast in his voice.

At midday, Thomas climbs up through the nettles at the end of the garden, startling my mother. She's sitting on an upturned bucket, skin burning in the hot sun. She has searched the house and the shed and the nearby fields, and searched all over again. To try to stop the shudders coursing through her body, she has had a joint and a glass of rum. Leon has gone into town; his mate has a van, they'll check the roads. She told herself if he wasn't back in an hour, she'd go to the police, weed or no weed. But she hasn't moved; she's kept her eye on the river, as if it will rise up in a spume and spit me out onto the bank. Thomas treads silently up to her, followed by his dog, nose-down on the path.

Nothing this end, he says, And not much water neither. She won't have been carried away, if that's what you're thinking.

How can you be sure? she asks, not liking him.

Look for yourself – there's no flow. If she dropped in here, see, he says, pointing his stick backwards at the river, She'd have only been up to here, he says, sliding the stick across his shins to demonstrate the depth.

Nell tries to keep the disgust out of her voice.

Yeah, that's right, she says, If she were as tall as you.

Thomas catches hold of his dog as he pads up to greet her.

Some places it's bone dry. Like I said, she won't have been carried away. Not by the water, anyway. This here's a bourne river.

She hears 'born' river, thinks he's trying to tell her something.

You're saying a little child can't drown in that water? she

asks, squinting up at him, You're saying someone took her?

The river man shifts from one leg to the other. Under his cap, his head is prickling with sweat.

I'm only saying she won't have been carried away, he says.

Someone's got her, she says.

Or she's wandered off. Kids do that, don't they?

She can't open the front gate, says Nell, The latch is too stiff. She looks over his shoulder into the beckoning weeds.

Someone's got her, she says again, her voice like a siren on the air. Thomas reaches out a hand towards her shoulder, to comfort her; rests it instead on his stick.

Now hang on, he says, You have reported it, haven't you? You've been to the station?

He looks around the garden, at the burnt-out fire and last night's abandoned glasses, fixing his eyes on Leon's makeshift green-house. He takes in her silence.

Well, you must, then. Someone might've seen her. She might be there now.

Nell has an image of me sitting on the front desk of the police station, swinging my legs, the duty officer feeding me toffees from a crumpled paper bag. But she knows that's just an image in a film. She ~~knows~~ thinks she knows, because, despite what Thomas Bryce tells her, she can sense it: I've gone in the river.

Thank you, Mr Bryce, she says, rising from the bucket and leading him along the side of the cottage, My boyfriend's deal-ing with that.

Not her father? he says.

He can smell sweat on her, stale perfume and alcohol.

He's away, she says, showing him out of the front gate and thanking him again. She watches him walk down the lane. Now and then, he rustles the hedges with his stick, puts his hand up to his cap and stares out over the fields of wheat and barley, and the sun makes Nell see everything white and flinty, too sharp for her eyes to focus on. She watches until he is a small dark outline on the dusty road. A born river. She doesn't

177

know what it means, and thinks there's intent in what he said, as if he's giving her a clue to decipher. She touches the top of her head, feels her scalp burning. The dog trails behind the river man until he whistles, and then Sonny flies to his side.

★

Maggie puts her pen down and shuts her eyes. The fire, collapsed on itself, burns low; the room is airless. She knows that if she looks up she'll see Nell, her accusing stare, her mouth quivering with resentment.

You've no idea what I went through, she'll say, You're not even close. You can't imagine the agony, so don't you dare try. Maggie will not look up for that.

twenty-six

Kenneth admits defeat and decides to call William; it's late, but
he knows his son is often out until the early hours, doing God
knows what, and that he'll check his answerphone when he
gets back in. When the woman on the end of the line tells him
he can re-record his message at any time, Kenneth thinks hard
about what he will say.

Will, it's your father. I don't want to fill up your machine,
so ring me back when you get in. Bye. Speak to you soon.
Bye.

After he's put the phone down, he's unsure of how his voice
sounded. Did he sound drunk? Incoherent? The woman said
he could record his message again, so he redials.

Hello, he says, to William's voicemail, I'd like to re-record
that message if I may.

Nothing happens in the long silence that follows, so in the end
he simply repeats himself, puts the receiver back on the cradle,
and glares at it. Will's always telling him he should get a portable
phone: Kenneth squeezes his eyes tight to bring the right word
up – a cordless – and now, sitting at his desk, he wishes he'd
taken his advice. He'd like to go down and sit outside. But
then he'd have to shift pretty quickly, to his den or up to the
office, if Will rang back. He considers the prospect of getting
a new phone; he'd have one where there isn't a machine for

answering, but a service, and where the numbers are already stored in it and you only have to push one button. His address book is old, and tattered, and the words and numbers look very small these days. Will had suggested they go and choose one together. Kenneth's wondering whether the cordless one would be waterproof, when the phone rings. It's his son.

That was quick, says Kenneth, I've only just left a message.

Dad, you rang my mobile. What's wrong?

Did I? says Kenneth, peering again at the address book, Well, how clever of me. Nothing's wrong, no panic. I just wondered if you happened to know where I'd put my reading glasses. He hears himself saying it, the affected, offhand tone, and cringes with shame.

What? says William, and then, with a punctured sigh, When did you last have them?

Don't know, says Kenneth, About a week ago. Um, not sure.

Have you looked in all the usual places? There's another voice in the background, more distant, a woman calling Will, Will, saying something that Kenneth can't make out. He hears the muffle of a hand closing over the receiver.

Is this a bad time? says Kenneth, Because I can call back.

No, Dad, listen. Check all the usual places. Don't forget the cellar, and then if you still can't find them – hang on, what about your spare ones? Where do you keep them?

Good thinking, says Kenneth, desperate now to be off the line, Of course! I'll go and fetch them right away. He mislaid his spare pair ages ago. He hears a rash of laughter and the sound of a car engine, and William says,

Got to go, Dad. Speak to you soon. I'll call you in the morning. The silence is ringing. Kenneth does as he's told and searches again, in his office desk, and on the windowsill, and goes downstairs and checks the top of the fridge and all the kitchen shelves, leaving a residue of grime on his fingers, and then he goes to his den and rummages down the sides of the armchairs and pats all the surfaces he can think of. He's standing in the atrium wondering what to do next when he has a sudden realization. He can see them, clearly, in his mind's eye. Up the stairs, up what he always thinks of now as Maggie's stairs, and into the flat. There they are. The last time he was up here, he sat on the bed, and took off his glasses and rubbed his face, like a child waking up. And now he sits on the bed again, puts on his glasses, takes out the folded piece of paper from his trouser pocket and, with a tiny prickle of recognition he simply can't place, reads and rereads the words on the page.

We have an anchor that keeps the soul
Steadfast and sure while the pillows roll,
Fastened to the rock which cannot move,
Grounded firm and deep in the Saviour's love.

twenty-seven

The rain is unrelenting, and the air so drenched that the view from Maggie's cottage is opaque, elusive, like a half-remembered dream. In the distance, the river keeps a wide black shadow. Every day it thickens; becomes more sinuous, more alive. The sky has come down to meet the fields, throwing its metallic light over everything: the trees dissolve against it; even the cows are drained of colour. They gather in a steaming cluster in the barn, shaking their heads, lowing mournfully at the weather. There is the hiss of wet wheels on the main road, and beneath it, a hush of deep rain falling on the land.

The windows inside the cottage glow with condensation. Maggie banks up the fire with logs, covering them with a heap of coal slack: the dust sparkles pink and yellow with the effort of staying lit. She stands in the centre of the room and looks around, trying to see it as a visitor might. A lot of brown furniture, a bed in the corner, a thin veil of dust. The damp has invaded the sympathy cards on the mantelpiece, giving them an ancient, wrinkled look. She should have got rid of them weeks ago. She gathers them into a little pile, meaning to burn them, and then she makes another decision: she will burn the cards, and the notes she typed for Kenneth, and the notebook, and the newspaper cutting. It will all be burnt. Everything will be flame and ash. She will have nothing left to tempt her to look back.

She slides the folded sheaf of papers out of the notebook and opens them flat, not intending to read them but unable to stop herself.

```
Kenneth likes dancing to you. He says the
spaces in between are as important as the
sounds. Listen to the gaps, he says, They
are music too.
I'm doing that, Kenneth, I'm listening to
the gaps and I'm trying to fill the spaces.
Not dead yet.
```

She throws them onto the fire, watches as the pages fold in upon themselves, twisting black, blacker, and then a quick flare of lustrous blue. Immediately, she's filled with regret. The sound of the front gate saves her, and she rises from the floor to see Aaron dashing up the path with one hand shielding his head. Through the soaked glass, he appears as a series of waves and ripples, like a man under water. She opens the lid of the dream-catcher box and shoves the notebook inside it, quickly, but not quickly enough to avoid the face of the boy in the photograph smiling up at her. Behind the door, she hears Aaron clear his throat. He's grinning shyly when she opens it, one arm behind his back.

For you, he says, producing a large bunch of white chrysan-themums, Picked them fresh.

Maggie puts on her best smile as she takes them from him. The cellophane under her fingers is cold and sparkling with rain.

Fresh from the petrol station? she says, understanding that he was making a joke.

There's no getting past you. I see I shall have to do better next time.

She would like to tell him that there won't be a next time – that there won't even be a *this* time – but he's here now, standing so tall in her tiny living room that he looks like a giant at the funfair. She doesn't have the heart to do it.

I'm not quite ready, she says, taking the flowers into the kitchen, Have a sit down. I'll only be a minute.

She puts them in the sink and then stands there, twisting her fingers into a knot. The last time there were other people in this house, they were paramedics. Maggie had assumed they'd take Nell away quickly, that they'd be on their way in five minutes, but they'd spent a long while, the woman sitting on the edge of Nell's bed and whispering gently to her, the man standing with Maggie here in the kitchen, asking her to collect up her mother's medication, asking her about morphine and steroids and antidepressants and at what times her mother took them and whether Nell had free access to them. One question heaped itself upon the other, and Maggie couldn't concentrate. She tugged on the stiff drawer of the dresser, not knowing how to answer, yanking it out so it fell with a bouncing crash at her feet. The pills and packets and assorted debris of sickness spilled out onto the kitchen floor.

She understands now that they needed facts, but at the time she thought it a terrible intrusion. They bent down together to retrieve the mess. The man had a shaved head, and a hole in his left earlobe where an earring would have been, and his pale eyes looked tired in the morning light. Smell of antiseptic coming off him, antiseptic, and calm, and kindness. It was a torment to her, all of it; the questions and the delays and the sweet air of springtime as she opened the door for them to take her mother away. She wanted to scream at them, Get a move on! Can't you see she's dying? But they knew there was no point in rushing. They'd brought a folding wheelchair out of the ambulance, and lowered Nell gently into it, and the sound she made is in Maggie's ears right now. Like a child's cry, she thought then, and later, like an animal's.

I'm saying, what do you normally do for your winter logs? Aaron is standing in the doorway, leaning against the frame.

Only, you can't be getting them from the garage. You should order them direct from us.

Maggie frowns at him.

My mother gets them from somewhere. Um, a man from Boxford. Can't think of his name. He delivers. Logs and coal, oil for the burner. Anyway, it's only July. There's plenty of time. She hears herself, the unravelling, disjointed sounds she's making, and all the while, Aaron watches her face. He moves close to her and she's afraid he will touch her – put his arms round her – and he can't do that because it would be unbearable. She would cry if he did that. He rests one hand on the stove and tucks the other in the pocket of his jeans.

I'm really sorry about your mum, Maggie, he says.

Me too, she says, pressing her lips together. She would say, But it's all right, I'm managing, or, She's at peace, or any other stock response, but when she opens her mouth there is only silence: the words are stuck again and the stones are resting heavy on her tongue.

We'll get your winter fuel sorted, he says, But what about that barn dance? Sure you're up to it?

She could send him away now: he would easily forgive her. And then she would be alone with her ghost; with Nell, still angry, refusing to speak to her. Anything would be better than that. Playing for time, Maggie reaches up to the shelf to fetch down a vase, and as Aaron reaches up for her, she freezes.

Can you smell that? she asks.

He takes a deep breath in.

Smell what?

You can't smell it?

He smiles and shakes his head, as if she's teasing him, and he lifts the neck of his shirt and buries his face inside it.

I'll have you know I've had a shower, he says, Is it wood? We've been sawing birch all afternoon.

It's gas, says Maggie, suddenly furious, My own personal stink of gas.

She dumps the flowers, still in their wrapper, into the vase, and runs the tap on them.

Not on the mains, are you? he asks.

Nope.

It gets worse before it gets better, he says quietly, But it does get better. Honest.

What makes it better? Knowing, or not knowing?
He starts to say something else but she cuts him off.

I can't go to the dance, Aaron. I'm sorry, you're right, I'm not up to it. But would you mind dropping me off on the way? There's someone I have to see.

twenty-eight

The last time Maggie came to talk to Thomas Bryce, he didn't let her in; he simply poked his face in the narrow gap between the door and the frame and grunted his responses at her. Ran his hand along the metal chain, as if testing the strength of it, while she stood on the porch, clutching the bottle of beer she'd bought him. She told him that her mother had just died, and that she would like to ask a few questions. Got nothing back in the way of answers, only an instruction to leave the bottle on the step.

Tonight, he slips off the chain and opens the door, not even bothering to check who it might be. He knows straight away it's her, leads her in without a backward glance. As if he's been expecting her; as if, this time, he's readied himself.

Cup of tea? he says, and doesn't wait for an answer. She follows him through the hallway, eyes fixed on the floor, because it's dark in here, too dark to see properly, and the carpet underfoot is loose and torn. They pass through the living room, blue and flat in the television light, and down the step into the kitchen. The only illumination comes from a street lamp in the lane at the back of the cottage, casting a sulphurous glare into the room. It smells bad, as yellow and acrid as the sodium glow. Thomas fills a cup with water and tips it into the kettle, flicking the switch with a bent thumb, then remembers he has company and measures out another cup of water and tips that in too.

Mustn't waste it, he says, Never mind all that out there—he jerks his head to the window – We'll have drought again in a couple of month.

He opens the fridge, and in the clear white oblong beam it throws across the floor, Maggie sees that she's standing in a shallow wash of liquid. She looks at Thomas's feet, clad in a pair of grey plimsolls, the bottoms of his trousers turned up above the ankles.

Thomas, I think the water's in *here*, she says, Haven't you got your sandbags?

The windows of heaven were stopped, he says, Worst is over. He sniffs the carton of milk and hands it to her.

I don't reckon that'll be off.

Maggie takes it, looking around for somewhere to put it down, seeing the table heaped with boxes and containers and more cartons. She follows him back into the living room where he lowers the volume on the television and drops himself heavily into his chair in the corner. He motions her to sit on the sofa, which is cream leatherette, etched with scratches but otherwise bare. It squeaks whenever she shifts in her seat. Between them is an old-fashioned marble-effect coffee table with a battered metal trim, and a huge onyx ashtray in the centre, filled with spent matches. The tea tastes of iron, coating her tongue with the bitter dryness of sterilized milk.

I know what you've come about, he says, And there's a film on in ten minutes, so, you know, we'll make it quick.

We will, says Maggie.

She's prepared herself for this. She has gone over this conversation in her head so many times since Nell died, has imagined the whole scene; and now, since she found the dreamcatcher box, her questions will be direct. Maggie had braced herself for another battle, but he seems quite cooperative, almost friendly; she might not even need ten minutes.

Can you tell me anything about William Earl? she says, When he was a boy?

A sound of scratching as she speaks, and Maggie scans the room, looking for the source of the noise. Thomas shakes his head, twists around and takes his pipe and a crumpled paper bag from the shelf.

Don't reckon I remember much about him, he says.

He used to help you when you worked on the river.

Oh, him, yes, and quite a few other boys, too. They all blend together, after a while.

Maggie unzips the inner pocket of her fleece and takes out the newspaper cutting, smoothes it flat on the coffee table, and then, realizing he won't be able to see it from any distance, hands it over to him.

Will this help? she says, It's a picture of William. He's hold-ing me.

Oh aye, says Thomas, not taking his eyes off the television, Well, he found you, you know. You'd gone wandering. He found you.

I don't think he did, says Maggie.

Still he doesn't look at the photograph. He concentrates on filling his pipe, and Maggie watches, waiting, staring at his fingers as they paddle in the paper bag, drawing out what appears to be a knot of dirty brown hair.

If you look, Thomas – can you see? Can you see what's happened to my face? It's like – as if it's been painted.

Oh, he found you all right. You'd gone wandering.

She folds the cutting and puts it back in her pocket.

What's the use? she asks, trying to control her voice, Is there any point in me asking?

Ask away, he says, stuffing the clump of tobacco into the bowl of his pipe, pressing his finger once, twice, on top.

Thomas, please listen. I remember him, from back then. I know what he did. So there's really no reason to pretend, not for my sake. All I want from you is the truth.

Maggie stares at the ashtray. It's in the shape of an island. It's in the shape of a Mediterranean island. She can do this.

William Earl abducted me, she says, I was only four, but I remember it as if it were yesterday.

Thomas jerks the pipe at her, the ball of his thumb joint shiny and misshapen, threatening to split the skin.

A slippery thing, memory, he says.

Not this memory.

Thomas smiles to himself.

I used to have a friend when I was little, he says, and now, finally, he appears to be looking at her, His name was Vinny.

Maggie nods for him to go on.

He was a good friend, the best friend you could ever have. We used to go everywhere together.

Thomas fumbles around in his pockets, shifts in his seat, his fingers searching underneath him, under the cushion, in his pockets again.

Yes, says Maggie, urging him on, And this Vinny? What about him?

Finding the matches, Thomas strikes one and pushes the flame into the bowl of the pipe. Sucks and sucks and the flame leaps up in a rash of sparks, and the room fills with a cloud of smoke, so thick Maggie can barely see him behind it. The smell is immediate; dense and choking.

My mother killed him.

Maggie sits back, appalled.

Why are you telling me this? she cries, feeling the tendrils of the smoke curl around her.

Because it's the truth, says Thomas, And you want the truth, don't you? That's what you're here for, isn't it? His name was Vinny and he lived in a little box—

Thomas picks up the matchbox and rattles it at her,

– And he lived in my pocket. And one day my mother found the box and she stood in front of me and she said, 'What have I told you, boy, about bringing these things in the house?

What have I told you?' And she crushed the box in her hand, and I swear I could hear his bones go pop. Chock, like that— Thomas closes his fist around the box,

– And that was the end of Vinny.

He stares at her for a long moment, takes another suck on his pipe.

I was only little, he says, But it could've happened yesterday, as you say. I should have put him back, see? And he would've been all right, if I'd only put him back. Like you're all right. Some mothers can be very hard.

Maggie stands up, banging against the coffee table, feeling and not caring about the metal cutting sharp into her leg, and there's the smell of pipe smoke and that noise again, that scratching noise. It's close and hot, that smell, and that scrabbling, it's a dog, she says it, she hears herself saying it:

It's a dog. It's your dog. Thomas, it was your dog!

Ah, no, that'll be Bramble, he says, I've locked her in the pantry. You don't like 'em much, do you, dogs? Now that I *do* remember.

twenty-nine

In the corner of the cafe, Alison is pretending to read the newspaper. She hates waiting; she hates, even more, being kept waiting, especially in a place as dreary as this. She'd ordered coffee without a second thought, and now wishes she hadn't. It's bitter, and murky as a puddle. The news is dreary too; local stories of the past week's flood damage, with a centre-page spread showing photographs of the Cerne Abbas giant and a statement from the Pagan Federation.

Anything of interest? asks William, bending over to kiss her on the cheek.

Pagans, she says, tapping the picture, Apparently it's all their fault.

William drags out a chair and cranes his neck to read the story.

Ah, the rain, yes, it'll be them all right. They got all upset about Homer. Threatened to cast a spell to wash him away.

You've lost me, says Alison, raising her head and trying to catch the waitress's eye, Don't have the coffee. It's like gravy browning.

Someone did a chalk drawing of Homer Simpson next to the Cerne Abbas giant, says William, I saw it on the news. It was quite funny, he was holding a doughnut. The Druids were in uproar.

Now that would have been worth seeing, she says, A Druid in uproar. How're things?

William nods, blinking rapidly, licks his lips. Alison waits. She'd never heard him sound as tense as he did last night when he rang her, and now she can feel his leg bouncing under the table, keeping time to some hectic inner rhythm.

Awful, says William, He's pretty bad. I don't know what to do.

Have you spoken to anyone else? she says, at last catching the attention of a waitress. As the woman approaches, William drops his voice.

He's refusing to see the doctor. Ali, he's refusing to see anyone. He's got . . . this . . . thing.

She hands the waitress her coffee cup and orders a pot of tea for two.

Can't wreck tea, can they? This *love* thing, is that what you mean? she says, You did mention it. But I thought the girl had vanished?

Not in here, says William, tapping his chest, You know what he's like when he gets fixated on something. Well, he's worse than ever. Paranoid. And bonkers to boot. I think he may do himself some damage. Last week when I was there, he went swimming.

Alison shrugs, until he tells her it was in the river, and then she grins.

Oh, he's just trying to wind you up. Succeeding too, I'd say. Again, the table vibrates steadily to an unseen count.

If your father wants to drown himself, let him.

William fixes his eyes on her, waits for her to relent.

You didn't see him, Ali.

Exactly. And haven't since that girl showed up. D'you know, Will, I don't think I care any more what happens to him. I've known your father for nearly ten years, and we've been close in that time.

193

William looks at Alison's face, sees the blush growing beneath the make-up as she lowers her voice.

But never quite close enough. He's always had the brakes on with me, always kept me here—
She puts an arm out in front of her,
  – And then along comes little Pippi Longstocking, with those cow eyes, and suddenly, I'm ancient history.
Must hurt, he says.
She tilts her head sideways; her own resentment has caught her out.

I suppose I've always known, she sighs, Men are such idiots when it comes to love. They haven't got a clue. I'd leave him to it if I were you. He gets what he deserves, the vain old twit.

You really think he's in love? says William.

I'm only going on your reports. You clearly think so. Has he thought any more about your suggestion?

The hotel? Not a chance. He'd burn the place down first. It's hardly fit to live in as it is; if it wasn't for Freya, he'd be knee-deep in filth.

And what does all this have to do with me? I told you last night, I've given up trying.
William leans forward, puts on his most appealing face.

I need you to go and see him.

Not a hope, my dear, says Alison, flicking an imaginary crumb from the table.

Ali, I really think he needs our help. I wouldn't ask, especially – given the way he's been treating you. But it's not him. It's like, like he's possessed. He's started smoking cigars, he drinks all day, and all night from what I can tell. He's reading bloody Shakespeare!
Alison lets out a hoot of laughter.

That serious, eh? Any play in particular?
William fishes in his pocket for his phone and presses three digits. He passes it to her.

Listen, he says.

He studies her face while she puts the phone to her ear, feels a quiver of satisfaction as her smile falls away.

Sounds like he's crying, she says.

Go on, he says, motioning for her to keep listening.

After a minute she holds it away from her ear. They stare at each other as the shouting continues, the wild booming of Kenneth's voice trapped inside the handset.

Those are just the ones I've kept, he says, taking the phone out of Alison's hand, And when I ring him back, he's absolutely normal. Doesn't remember calling half the time.

They are silent for a while, and the cafe is silent too, apart from the distant clatter of dishes in the kitchen, the clink of china on metal.

Last time I went over—

He pauses as the waitress brings the tray and lays out the cups and the milk jug and the teapot,

– he pretended he wasn't in.

Alison flips the lid on the pot and fishes about inside with a teaspoon.

Well, maybe he wasn't, she says, One measly tea bag. Typical.

I could hear him, though. Singing. Some old hymn by the sound of it.

You could always force him to see a doctor, she says, For his own safety.

William shoots her a look.

I don't want to turn him totally against me. I'm all he's got.

Alison knows better than to correct him. She rests her chin on her hand, considering.

I suppose it wouldn't hurt to pop by, she says, Although I swear, if he behaves badly, it'll be the last time.

I knew I could rely on you, he says, It'd be such a weight off my mind. You're an angel, Ali. Thank you.

She takes a paper napkin from the dispenser and wipes it round the inside of her cup, angling it to the light and grimacing at what she sees.

There's a very nice bar just down the road, Will. Good range of single malts. Next time you want to entertain *this* angel, I suggest we meet there.

thirty

It sounds like the music Leon used to play on his tabla. The noise was soft and muted for a little while, but now it's hard and rapid, and it's in the house. Maggie sits up in bed and listens. This is it, at last. She should have paid more attention: sandbags at the door, the cows shifted to the barn at the top of the field. There were men in sou'westers pumping frothy brown water down the middle of the road, but they'd given up days ago. These were the signs and she'd chosen to ignore them. The noise is fierce, insistent, like someone knocking, wanting to be let in. But then, she'd heard opposing views too; the villagers talked of nothing else.

Welford's never flooded in my lifetime, said a woman queuing at the counter in the petrol station, And it won't now. Maggie glanced at the woman, thought she looked ancient enough to be believed. And then the voice of another, behind her, which she realized belonged to Mrs Moore.

Yes, Susan, we'll be all right. Boil your water, mind.

The rain chases down the roof, finding the old cracked slates and working on them, hammering away until they collapse, sink sideways, splinter into shards. The rain, throwing itself from the sky into her house. But there *is* someone knocking. Maggie pulls on her clothes and pads barefoot to the top of the stairs, taking comfort in the feel of the boards under her feet, dry still, and the rug dry, and sees below her a shiver of light through the glass of the front door, the ripple of a figure. There's something not right about it – the figure and the wavering beam – something dreadful. Something . . . she's reaching for the memory and she's very nearly there . . . of pipe-smoke and dogs, and the way the light moves, like a sharp edge slicing an egg.

Maggie, it's me, shouts Aaron, through the glass.

She reaches for the light switch and flicks it, and the lights go on and off with a fierce clap. The wall under her fingers is soaked, the rain running down in a clear sheet.

The river Bourne's breached, he's saying, You've got to come. Maggie stays very still.

Aaron raps on the glass with his torch, pushing at the flap of the oblong letter box so that Maggie has to flatten herself against the wall to stop herself from seeing his mouth there, open and wet like a gash in a hole. The rain soaks through her shirt and she can feel it now, pooling at her feet. Again that light, dancing on the darkness.

She waits until she hears his truck pull away. Now she can breathe. Pressed against the wall at the top of the stairs, the smell is old wallpaper, electricity. She closes her eyes and sees the torch again cutting its way inside her, and the smell that follows is spearmint, wet earth, dog.

The River Man

What he'd wanted to say was, Not everything is as plain as it seems, not a hundred per cent straight. What you think you know, you don't. But then she took fright. Just like her mother, that one, fear creeping all over her. Except she's more serious than her mother, that's clear enough; more intent in herself. Nell, she was easy, let things stand. Didn't like to stir things up.

The way Thomas remembers it, Nell was that happy to be getting her girl back, there was no questions asked, no fuss. Not at the start, any road. It didn't matter who'd found her – who'd lost her in the first place, that's what people were saying. Who'd let her wander off in the middle of the night? Thank God no harm had come, they said that too. Nell, she was hopeless. Couldn't say how it was that her child could just get up and go off like that, how come there was no lock on the door, why no police got called. Because she's been stoned out of her brains, that's why, not paying attention, that's why. Drunk with that waster with the beard and bongos. That'll be why.

Thomas considers his supper. Completely lost his appetite now. He opens the remaining half of his sandwich and removes a slice of gherkin, tossing it into the fire where it hisses and sparks. Bramble watches the whole flight of it, trying to intercept it, immediately switching her hungry eyes back to Thomas's fingers. He feeds her a long piece of crust, but even as she wolfs it down, her attention is on his plate, assessing how much of the food is left, how much is hers, wanting it all.

You are a beast, he says, smiling.

He'll admit, his eyesight isn't so sharp these days. But Maggie's a good-looking girl, just like her mum was. Why Nell'd let herself get dragged down by that Leon is anybody's guess. He'd started it. The whole, My daughter's said this, and My daughter's said that, coming round, asking for an explanation, making threats.

I'll give you an explanation, says Thomas, alive again to the argument, and the way he says it makes Bramble slink away to the sofa.

Try explaining how you think you're her father, for starters. Thought it was Edward Crane, 'cause if he ain't the father, what's the woman doing there? Or don't she even know who it was? Try keeping a civil tongue in your head when you speak to me. There's a word for what you're doing. Extortion. Don't threaten me with the law. There's only one law that counts, and that's God's own. Take it up with the Earls if you're so eager. See where that'll get you.

Then a visit from Mrs Earl, totally different manner about her. Perfumed up, smiling. Wanted to know what Thomas knew. Not speculation, not what village talk says. Complimenting him on his vigilance. Complimenting him on how nice he'd made the cottage, how they would simply *hate* to lose him, despite the business with the dog. Said he wasn't to worry about anything, there'd be no police involved; they'd got his statement and she'd be very grateful if he should stand by it. The whole family would show how indebted they were to him for his . . . loyalty. Said she'd speak to Leon too, put him straight. And everything went tidy after that, after a fashion.

Thomas presses his fingers into his sternum, waiting for the burn to pass. There's gherkins for you. When that doesn't work, he makes his way down into the kitchen, searching amongst the boxes and cartons on the table for the tin of liver salts, feeling the cold water wash against his ankles. She was no fool. Only Sonny, it was a terrible shame about Sonny. He should take Bramble upstairs; she never was one for getting her feet wet. Not like Sonny. He was a proper water hound. Tell him to go, and he'd be in. He was a hard worker; they both were. Not like some. Some are born lucky, never have to do a day's turn.

Not like us, eh, Sonny, he says to Bramble, Some people get to live for free, make others do their dirty work. Some people get to open a nice little shop somewhere on the coast and live off the profits. Some people don't know they're born.

part four

hole in the rain

thirty-one

The silence wakes her, and a draught blowing on her face; the air, cool and dewy, carries a faint tang of the sea. Maggie flies up from under the mound of blankets to see her bedroom soaked in light, a curt breeze blowing in. Last night, enduring hours of unceasing rain, she'd made a decision: went downstairs and collected everything she thought she might need; a couple of bottles of drinking water, some food and candles from the pantry, a carton of milk from the fridge. She wrapped up her books and her most vital CDs in blankets, and put a change of clothes and the dreamcatcher box in her holdall. Methodically, with only the guttering light of the candle to see by, she checked and double-checked that she'd rescued the most important things. The furniture couldn't be saved, and Nell's collection of vinyl would have to stay lined up along the walls downstairs. Maggie reckoned the sleeves would be ruined but the records themselves would survive. She didn't consider that the river would leave its taint on everything.

She lay on the bed with her possessions close by, waiting for morning, or the flood, whichever came first. In the early hours, the rain began a new pattern, of fits and starts, sudden gusts, momentary gaps of silence. Maggie noted and then grew accustomed to the sirens, a helicopter thwapping in the distance, the way the wind sang through the roof tiles. Just before daybreak came a lull so quiet, she imagined she could hear the river lapping at the front door. The worst *is* over, she thought, Thomas was right. She began to feel herself drift off to sleep, only to be jarred awake by a noise outside: not wind, not a helicopter, but a noise she could feel: a deep, guttural roar. The branch punched through the window, in and out again, like a giant's maw. Maggie could only stare at the gaping hole it had left; in the dawnlight, the rain was lit up and trembling like piano strings.

From the window she can see that the tree is still standing, the branch torn from the trunk like a severed limb. The wound is butter-yellow and so fresh she can almost smell the sap. The branch itself is gone, submerged, or carried away, and the field opposite the cottage has been transformed into a broad swim of water. Maggie watches the run-off pass below her, rapid and brown, hurrying away with its loot of tangled twigs, an up-turned dinghy, a child's buggy. She follows its progress down into the valley and then switches back to look in the opposite direction, back up to the bend in the hill, where she sees that the road has become visible again, emerging from the water like a drawbridge.

thirty-two

```
At  the  start  thes  ound  is  as  sweet  as  a
summer morning
The sound  is like
If  you  imagine    all  the  sum  er  mornings
wrapped up inone
```

Christ-All-Bloody-Mighty!
Kenneth puts the tip of his finger in his mouth and sucks
on it. Holding it under the lamplight, he sees a purple line
darkening along his fingernail, a thin streak of a bruise from
the tip to the bed. He waits for the throb of pain to pass. He
has been trying to describe Ravel's string quartet. Beside the
typewriter is a bottle of Glenfarclas and a cup containing rehy-
drated mushrooms. Occasionally, he'll fish one out and feed
it into his mouth, chewing slowly on the salty, rubbery sliver.
It's only early evening but he's on his second whisky and his
eighteenth sheet of paper. The rejects are crushed and scattered
around his feet: some of them have tumbled away across the
floor to nestle beneath the furniture. He takes another mouth-
ful of his drink, then another. His trousers are rolled up to his
knees, and on his feet he sports a pair of William's old trainers.
There's a draught blowing in around his ankles. Kenneth's
gaze searches along the library windows: all closed, the

raindrops on them twinkling like diamonds. He takes another sip of his whisky.

When he woke this morning, he made a promise to himself: he would start again with his project, without anyone's help, first thing. He delayed the start by rewarding his idea with a cooked breakfast. He planned to have eggs and bacon and mushrooms and beans and just the one slice of fried bread. In the cupboard, he found a tin of pilchards he couldn't remember ordering, an untouched packet of crispbread, and a can of borlotti beans. Some dried mushrooms, like toenail clippings, sat in a dusty cellophane wrapper. There was one egg left in the tray, and he couldn't read the tiny red print to see how old it was, but he'd learnt a trick years ago about how to tell if an egg was fresh. You put it in a pan of water, and if it sank to the bottom, it was fresh. Or if it floated to the top. He couldn't remember which way round it was supposed to be, so when he tried it, and the egg floated, he decided that it was a fifty-fifty chance, and what's more, he was going to eat the damn thing anyway. Looking in the fridge, he was delighted to find a half bottle of champagne that had rolled to the back. There was some sort of healthy spread William had insisted that he buy, a jar of pickled onions and an opened pack of streaky bacon. This was going to be a good day. Kenneth ate an onion or two while cooking, steeped the mushrooms in a cup of boiling water and forgot about them. His breakfast – of bacon and egg and borlotti beans covered in tomato ketchup, with a slice of the healthy crispbread on the side – tasted completely superb. The Buck's Fizz (without the orange juice) made the meal twice as enjoyable as the real thing.

After breakfast, he carried the typewriter from the prefect's office to the library and set it on a low table in front of his chair. He would do the washing-up first, then get cracking. Back in the kitchen, he turned the radio on to hear the news, ran hot water into the bowl and leaned over it, peering into the steam.

The view from the terrace was like shot silk: beautiful, hazy; the air soaked and the birds like black buds in the trees. The lawns were under water, so it was all river, practically, up to the steps. Kenneth decided that it would be nice to have a glass of wine, maybe a few slices of crispbread with some of the pilchards on top (it was nearly elevenses, after all) and he could sit with his raincoat on, in his best place, and admire the weather. He took down the key from the top of the door frame and made his way into the cellar. Immediately, he could taste the change of air, slightly sulphurous, a damp match. The grille of light at the back of the shelves showed him: the cellar was flooded. Retreating, Kenneth thought about what to do. He could call William. The last thing he wanted was to talk to William. He knew the idea of phoning a plumber was ludicrous; he'd heard the bulletins. Kenneth took off his shoes and socks and rolled up his trousers. There was nothing else for it, he would have to rescue his stock: the water would go down eventually, but he couldn't take the risk of leaving the wine in there, the damp getting to it. The concrete floor felt gritty under his bare feet, gritty on the first journey in and out – Kenneth leaving a wash of water in his wake – then atrociously sharp and painful on the second trip. He'd almost dropped the bottles. Limping out to the bench, he sat down and tried to raise his foot to see what he'd done. The effort of lifting his leg so high filled his head with blood and made him dizzy. He wiped the sole of his foot with his hand and felt again the stab of broken glass in his skin. He stood on the step and paddled his foot in the river water, gingerly at first, then with more vigour. Underneath, the grass was giving and sweet to the touch, and he raked it with his toes until the pain went away. He'd need to put some boots on. Bound to be wellies in the trunk room.

Only when Kenneth had hobbled round the side of the house and in through the courtyard gate did he remember: the trunk room no longer existed. The door that opened into it had been bricked up years ago, and the space inside knocked through to create a bigger wine cellar. He traced the wall with his hand; such a close match to the original brick, he could barely make out where the outline was.

It took five journeys to bring up his most vulnerable wines. He put the bottles anywhere on the worktops, admired the dust on them, his fingerprints in the dust, and didn't worry about laying them down; stood them up all around, a very dusty, priceless cityscape in his own kitchen. Kenneth promised himself he'd start work on his song notes straight after he'd had something to eat. He felt ravenous: thought it had to be lunchtime. It took an effort to open the tin of pilchards, having to fiddle with the ring pull and getting oil all over the worktop and on his fingers, but finally, he managed to concoct his lunch. With the pilchards smeared on three brittle pieces of crispbread, a glass of wine poured, and his book on the tray, he was ready. He took his meal outside, all the better to watch the weather, shivering a little but relishing the wild thrashing of the trees, the scouring rain. In a while he would light the chiminea, if he could find something to burn. That was one of Will's better ideas, unlike the fish tank, the electric toothbrush that raked his gums, the motorized pepper mill. Always buying him some present or other, as if to make up for, apologize for – he can't imagine what. You need to burn that stuff, she'd said. Too wet for a bonfire, and the chiminea too small to contain all the things he would like to burn. And the neons; he must remember to feed them. She'd said to eat them, hadn't she, fried like whitebait. Would be more palatable than the sardines. Sardines? Pilchards. Had fresh sardines once in Sicily; not the same taste at all, even if they are supposed to be family. And so his mind wandered away, little wisps of thoughts and memories and vague ideas and inspired ideas, and all the while Kenneth looked at the trees. The trees, and the river overflowing, and the smell of fish on his fingertips; something was floating to the surface. From deep in the house came the sound of the telephone ringing. Smell of fish on his fingers, metallic, faintly nauseating; the trees bending in the breeze; the sound of a telephone. Kenneth closed his eyes to see it more clearly.

It was the water bailiff calling, his words coming sharp and fast through the handset. Kenneth had been avoiding him since that business with Will and the child – must have been three months ago now – but occasionally, when the land agent wasn't available, he'd have to give him instructions or ask him to look in on one of the properties. And then he'd feel it, a new and uncomfortable familiarity, an unspoken guile. Nor did he care for the way the man looked at him these days, as if they'd made some fiendish pact with each other. In truth, he preferred his employees to be a little more servile.

Despite the early hour and his half-awake state, Kenneth knew that something was very wrong. He'd asked him to slow down, repeat himself, but couldn't get any more information beyond: You must come at once. Kenneth took directions and told him to wait until he'd arrived. He'd set off in his Range Rover, driving quickly through the lanes, empty at that time of the morning, then slowing at the bend in the valley. The view dropped away before him; a sweep of brown and ochre, the earth blasted into hollows here and there by the recent storms. The fields, with no time to recover from the drought, looked devastated. It had been wet again overnight, but now the skies were clear, hazy; there was a soft September trace in the air. Kenneth wound the window down to let in the morning, and at once saw a young boy waving madly from just below the verge on the opposite side of the road. So, the bailiff had got himself another helper; it was to be expected. The thought of Will, away at his new boarding school and hating it, gave him a momentary flash of rage.

What is it? he barked at the boy, younger than William, smaller at any rate. The boy simply pointed to the river with a switch of wood, where Kenneth could just make out two heads proud of the bushes.

What? he repeated, and the boy replied,

They said I've got to stay put.

Kenneth slid down the side of the bank, using the bushes as a brake. Thomas Bryce and another man he couldn't name were standing at the bend of the river, beside a clump of willows.

Thomas Bryce, said Kenneth, alive to the moment, That's the devil. That was his name.

It came back quickly then. Thomas Bryce and Freddy Peel were standing near the water, and a third man, unshaven, runty-looking, was on the deck of a small dredger – Flynn; he was known only as Flynn. The three of them were all speaking at the same time, but it was Bryce who broke through.

Ah, Ken— Mr Earl, I thought, not again, not another child. His voice was thick with drama. As Kenneth approached, Bryce put his hand out and gripped his arm.

I thought: Not another one.

Flynn braced himself on the deck of the boat and pushed his pole into the willows, trying to clear an overhanging branch so that Kenneth could see.

It were tangled up here, he was saying between thrusts, After the storm, right, and these needed cutting back, right? That's when I found him. Or some of him, any road.

The men laughed at that. Bryce took his cap off his head and flattened it against his chest. He put his hand out to Kenneth again, this time to stop him from getting any closer; and then Kenneth saw. That was the source of the smell, fish but not fish, flesh but not meat; putrefaction. A man's clothed arm, the full length of it from shoulder to fingertips, lay like a landed carp in the undergrowth. Kenneth crept closer, not entirely believing what he knew must be true, believing instead that these idiots were playing some kind of trick on him. He bent over it to make sure, because the arm didn't look remotely real. It was clothed in a checked fabric that was dotted with a patina of green slime. The fabric had been torn away at the shoulder; at the cuff end, the hand was open, the fingers fat as sausages. He took a breath and wished he hadn't.

Rest of him's in there, said Flynn, gesturing to the branches with his pole. The end of it gleamed black and sticky.

I tried to hoik him out, see, but look what happened.
The three men turned as one to where the limb had been tossed.

I'm going to fetch the police, said Kenneth, And call an ambulance.

Might be a bit late for an ambulance, said Peel. And the men laughed again. Flynn, aware of his audience, leaned forward from the waist and launched the tip of the pole back into the branches. His gaunt face split in a grin.

Here, give me a hand and I'll fetch him down, he said, to more guffaws.
Kenneth spun on Bryce and whispered loudly, emphatically:

You will need an ambulance for the body. And the police will need to be present. Show some respect.
The men sobered immediately. Flynn put down his pole and climbed onto the bank, and Bryce went looking for his lad. At least, thought Kenneth, he had the decency to keep the boy away. But the smell was the thing; how could they bear it?

Peel made to shake Kenneth's hand then thought the better of it, settled for wiping his palm down his trousers.

He will have fall in, he said, An' got caught up in them, see? He were famous for his drinken.

You know him? said Kenneth, not sure if anyone could identify a body in such a condition.

Baggs, he said, Just look at the size on him. Been gorn more'n a week.

★

The pilchards untouched, the wine, untouched; the book, unopened. Kenneth sitting very still, remembering how it felt to be a young man then, lording it, thinking he should be in control of his life, and really, how terrified he was. He imagines dealing with it differently. He wouldn't have gone there; would have told Bryce to call the police if there was a problem. But after the trouble with Will, and with Rusty, with the talk going round – he couldn't take the risk. Everything he'd thought was safe, solid, had turned to liquid. Rusty was leaving him. She was leaving him, and leaving William, too, and this was it, this was the problem he could hardly bear to admit to himself: Kenneth didn't want the child. He didn't love him. Standing on the riverbank with those three buffoons, he was thinking, This is what my life has become, a series of unending horrors. I'll be stuck here all my life with these imbeciles and their narrow, artful ways and their knowing looks. No Bahrain, no fresh start. Can't ever have a fresh start with a child like Will.

He'd tried to take control as best he could, step by step, giving the appearance of stability, of order. But he was sickened at Flynn's idea that they pull the man piecemeal out of the branches. Kenneth had fetched a blanket from the car and wrapped the arm in it, rolling it up, retching at the awful smell and wanting to put his hand over his face and trying not to breathe, only trying to take control. As best he could. No one would ever be able to say that he didn't face up to his responsibilities.

The smell is here again now, festering on the air, and with it follows his putrid life and how miserable it has been. How selfish he has been. How cruel.

thirty-three

The rain that falls on Kenneth and Maggie is the same rain that falls on William, but in London it takes on a city-fuelled quality, as if it comes not from the sky but from the towering structures that enclose his terrace block. It is more noise and light than smell and feel. The sound of tyres on tarmac, slick, abrasive, is as regular as the glimpses he gets of shining wet metal speeding on the road beyond the lush cover of the trees. To look up is to see an oblong of flat grey cut like a window-pane between the darker concrete forms of the surrounding buildings. The rain can only be seen at an angle, gathering light from the city as it drops to earth.

He abandons the desk where his computer shares space with his coffee cup and his diary and his empty glass. He is tidier than this normally – pristine, in fact – but today has been an off-day. He can't seem to think straight; as if he has become infected with his father's malaise.

The first answerphone message came mid-morning: his father couldn't find the number for the plumber, did Will happen to know it?

Recently, William has come to dread the sound of the tele-phone, and, since his father had discovered he could call his mobile too, is equally cautious about answering that. The calls were not merely rambling and disjointed, although that was unsettling enough; they were sometimes strangely impersonal, as if his father had forgotten who it was he'd phoned and was on his best behaviour. More frequently, they were appeals to William to confirm some snatch of a recollection, to restore certainty to an idea. Could you make a steak sandwich with mince or did you need a fillet? Was there any harm in burning barbecue briquettes in the chiminea? Did he have a clue where his boots might be?

William imagined he could see the holes being burrowed inside his father's head; pictured it as a labyrinth where beetles gnawed away at the soft tissue. Not for the first time, he felt the irony; while his father panned for long-forgotten moments, what escaped him was the day to day, everyday, unthinking normality of existing. Going on with life, without setting the house on fire or doing himself some serious injury. But to give voice to those concerns was to invite ridicule, or rage, or indifference.

It made William more determined to spend his day off as planned; searching online for support, finding out what was on offer. He'd discovered a place called a Memory Clinic in Slough, but it was the one in Southampton which held his attention; they had a Specialist Memory Nurse who would do home visits. Nowhere could he find mention of the need for a referral, knowing that his father would refuse to see his GP. He wrote down names and numbers in his diary, invigorated, but cautious enough to realize he would need to speak with him first. If he could implant the idea of a pretty young nurse coming to visit, it might make Kenneth more amenable.

The second call, in the middle of the afternoon, was a confused, messy recounting of an event William could barely recall; something about a body washed up in a tree. And by the way, had he mentioned he'd found his reading glasses? And by the way, did he remember a song about an anchor? Did that ring a bell? And did he mention the business of the body in the tree?

If William could only put his own memories to use instead of avoiding them, he might understand that connections were forming in his father's mind, might detect the synapses firing, creating sparks, reigniting a long-doused flame. But he thinks of his father now as a spent force. It wouldn't be his first mistake.

The final call comes as he's preparing dinner. He has planned to cook seared tuna with a mizuna and sorrel salad, mainly because Nat is coming over and the only other time he'd made her a meal, she teased him about the rice he'd used for the risotto. The wrong kind, apparently, as if there could be a wrong kind of risotto rice. He'd even shown her the box.

Blame my father, he'd said, trying not to feel hurt, I've inherited his culinary skills.

And she'd said,

You blame your father for everything; the wine you put away, your frankly obsessive cleanliness – the way you drive.

And what's wrong with my driving? he'd asked, knowing what the answer would be. He'd brought her round though, made her laugh. And she ate the risotto without complaint.

William considers answering the call, but knows from the others, and from the time of day, that it's better to wait. The booming of his father's voice makes the speaker vibrate.

Will, it's your father again. That water bailiff, he was called Thomas—

There's a pause during which William can hear what sounds like pages being shuffled.

– Thomas Bryce! That was it. Forgot to say the first time. Don't suppose you know if he's still about? I wouldn't mind having a word with him.

And just like that William is implicated. Two words, a name he pretended not to remember, only for the old bastard to find it in some murky corner of his brain.

★

He was first taken on by Thomas when he had just turned ten. It was a proper job, his father had warned, which would take up all the holidays and involve early starts and some responsibility. William didn't mind; the house had become so miserable since his mother got sick, since Grace had to leave, and the latest nanny, a local woman with fat goose-pimply arms, reminded him of the matron at school. She insisted he call her Miss Sharon, although no one else did, and said things he didn't understand about birds pecking out little boys' eyes if they spied on people. He wanted to tell her: I'm not a spy, and I'm not a baby. So there. But she had a look that frightened him. He didn't even need a nanny any more, but his father had insisted – William had heard him, talking to his mother about it. He wasn't spying; he was going to her room to see if she was feeling better, and heard, from behind the heavy wood, the clipped, angry tone of his father's voice. He'd waited before knocking, and that was a mistake – the voice getting louder, then the sound of the door handle, then his father, in a rage suddenly, sending him to his room. Someone to be a mother to him, since you're not capable – that's what he'd said. But his mother was sick, she couldn't help that.

Thomas wasn't like the other adults. He didn't speak to him like they did, like he was a small child, or worse, an idiot. Thomas's words were plain and direct and had nothing hidden in them. He'd worked with Thomas that first summer, then every holiday afterwards. At school, when things were bad, he clung to the memory of it: gliding down the river in Thomas's boat; hooking worms onto the line the way Thomas showed him; lying under the trees with a ham sandwich and Sonny at his shoulder, waiting patiently for the last crust. He loved the dog more than anything. During the first year, he'd petitioned his parents for a spaniel of his own; obliquely with his mother, who was so pale and tired and stayed in her room all day, suggesting in his sly, boyish way that a dog would be company for her too. Just a small one, a cocker, perhaps. He was more honest with his father, who would see through any pretence at altruism. And who would look after the animal while you're at school? his father demanded, Take it for walks, feed it, all that? William didn't have answers to the questions. Later, he thought Sharon could have done it, but by then the idea had been dismissed. Still, there was always Sonny.

The job was easy at first; all he had to do was sit with Thomas in the boat and call out when he saw anything unusual – like the time he'd spotted an upturned bicycle in the reeds, and that morning when he saw his first heron flying like a pterodactyl down the middle of the river. Sometimes he'd follow a step behind as Thomas surveyed the trees or checked the licences of mute fishermen, with nothing else to do; but by the second year, he was entrusted to take water samples. Thomas complained about the new regime, about the factory discharge, about the levels, about how much more work there was. William happily volunteered himself for any task. He was never late, never spoke out of turn, laughed in the right places, knew when to be still, silent, stealthy. He was strong, he could lift things, heavy objects: a fox, a fawn, a sack of logs.

He remembers Peel and Flynn, Thomas's drinking buddies. The River Rat gang, Thomas had called them, and Flynn especially looked rodent-like, with his long nose and his pointed, eager face. During their last summer, William had been allowed to sit out in the pub garden and 'keep the bench warm' for them while they went in the New Inn for a drink. They would appear a while later with a treat for him: a packet of smoky bacon crisps, and a half of bitter shandy in a knobbly glass.

William loved the taste of it, and the way the men would smile as he drank, nodding encouragement. He'd have to make it last, that was the trouble. One drink and you're on your way, my lad, Thomas would say, but if he took small sips, he could stay with them and listen to their talk. Often it was uninteresting stuff about the river, or the latest plans for the golf course, but now and then their voices would sink into whispers as they discussed the latest events at Weaver's Cottage. That was their chief delight: what the foolish boy had done now, how that girl went about half-starkers. Next time they passed the spot, William made sure to have a good look. That was when he first noticed Birdie.

★

Kenneth puts another record on – Keith Jarrett, the Köln Concert, because he's always considered it to be the most languid, summer-rain music. Not, he tells himself, that he's thinking of Maggie, of what would be the perfect piece to listen to at this moment, but because he *wants* to hear it. He sits again in front of the typewriter, takes a sip at the dregs of his whisky and positions his fingers above the keyboard, like a pianist about to perform. At this moment he believes – because he's read it somewhere, because he wants to believe – that the words will flow through his veins in a river of harmonious notes, spill from his fingertips in a cascade of meaning. But his mind is blank. There is just the sound of the concert in his head. He should be grateful for this after the day he's had; it would be reviving simply to follow the notes, as he would have done the first time he'd ever heard it; that intricate, vital quality, like a promise, like heartache, like nothing words can ever begin to describe. And he knows this piece will change even as he listens to it; recognizes the sleight of repetition, the subtle way it opens, spreads, like ripples on a pond. That's partly why he chose it. He has stopped fighting; has given himself over to whatever may come to mind.

Were he to have the conversation William so desperately wanted, he would tell him that he's not forgetting at all; on the contrary, he's just making room, letting the past take precedence for a while. He's discovered that his memories aren't fixed, that he can't control what comes in. It's like the weather; he can watch it, he can feel it, but he can't alter it. But nor can he fix on how he would like his memories to look, how he might describe them in words: thinks if only he could it would be easy. He imagines seeing inside his own head, into the inner workings of his mind. There was a programme about it once, how you can have a scan which shows the brain lit up like a fairground ride. Kenneth thinks his brain would be dark, with winding corridors, trapdoors, like the ghost train, or a dungeon. He follows this thread, now, satisfied he's found a way to visualize the invisible, and puts up no resistance to the thoughts meandering in and out. Here's his mind then, a dark cell – no, many, many cells – the shape of a panopticon; each cell positioned so that the prisoner is available for scrutiny. A thousand former Kenneths jostling for space. He would be the gaoler, too, an idea he relishes for the power it bestows. He's there as overseer, to keep his memories from escaping, wreaking havoc, murdering each other. He thinks he's the only person in the world to have this thought. He considers making a note of it but can't be bothered to move.

For now, he listens to the hollow, emptied-out sound of the opening bars, more an ending than a start, and lets it sweep over him. He feels the music as he never has before, with perfection, and anguish. It's only sensation; no rainy-day memory to examine or relive, although he knows he first heard the piece the year after its release, and played it regularly for months, to calm him sometimes, sometimes to take him away. Still nothing occurs to him. As he holds his hands up, waiting for the words to drop out of them, he understands that he has no words. A welcome wave of fatigue laps over his body. Closing his eyes, Kenneth rests his head back, drops his hands into his lap, and listens to the change in tone; cautious now, full of doubt: the spaces in between seem to ask him questions.

Are you sure you're doing the right thing? What about the boy? How will he cope, at this difficult time? Kenneth's answer is to remain silent. He doesn't know how Will might feel about him going away, only that he must. Rusty has revealed herself and he, in turn, has been honest with her. At first, wanting to patch things up – because they always patched things up, didn't they? – he thought there might be a way forward. But she was so contemptuous, so reproachful when he mentioned Grace.

Grace? The nanny? How unoriginal. It'll be the stable boy next.

There was no stable boy, of course, no horses. She was being ridiculous. But then he realized that it was he who was ridiculous. And stupid, and vain, so utterly selfish. His answer was to run away. Except at the time it didn't feel like running away; he was simply trying to make a life out of a mess.

The knocking on the record becomes his footsteps echoing through the hall, and Will, a slight, shadowy figure behind him, anxious, it seemed, for his father to be gone. And then he was in the cab, being taken off up the drive, his son waving briefly from the step, then dashing off quickly, like a cartoon boy. The knocking is louder, more emphatic; and here's the lull now, a not-quite-silence, just as suddenly eclipsed by the euphoria, the swift ecstatic cry of release. He was on his way to Bahrain; he was going to be free! There would be no more Rusty, the charade that was his marriage, the stifling presence of the boy. Such blissful release, whooping for joy inside, and his body jittering with the pure joy noise coming from the record, pure joy, only that, all that, joy so immense and sublime it is also a sorrow: and slowly he travels over the curve of sorrow; so many tears, so much rain, the widest ripple on the pond, a gradual expansion into nothingness.

He emerges to the sound of applause, and to repetition, repetition, such insistent repetition; the insistent repetition of the rhythm, and the rhythm becomes music, and the music sings the motion of a train on a track. From the window of the carriage he sees Maggie, very small, very far away, standing on the river towpath, a bright red stain on the collar of her blouse. From a crushed insect, a spider mite or beetle. And then she's gone and there is just sweeping scenery, yellow and brown and arid and baked, and the insistent repetition of the rhythm returns and inside it there's singing, there's shouting; it's William, in his Boys' Brigade uniform, cradling something in his arms. He's landed a carp. The river man's at his side, squinting at him with those eyes of his just two slits under his cap. They're on a dredger. Not a carp, a man's arm, a tear in the shoulder, ready to spill. Blood pooling in a long line from the sleeve. No. He's holding a child. Pink mouth open and wet. The rhythm pauses and resumes and the image of the child is carried away by the insistence of the rhythm. And the clouds race over the sky above the big house on the hill inside which in the library in the chair sits Kenneth. Kenneth sits in the chair in the library inside the big house on the hill and the clouds race over the sky.

He is fully awake now. He remains entirely motionless, eyes wide, his mind fixed on the images in his head. The concert is in its third phase, the rhythm still insistent, but the melody plaintive, full of longing. A different picture emerges with the sound: here is the countryside, in darkness, lights from the towns flying past, a covert bonfire glowing in a field, a funfair in a valley where the big wheel is lit like a jewelled crown. Here is the train again, but he's returning this time, suitcase forgotten, probably still on the tarmac at Heathrow, and he's stepping back down onto the platform at Newbury station and the stale air hits him in a blast of fumes and failure. He was so close.

★

His mouth is very dry. He leans forward and finds his glass.

The heat: the impossible, unremitting dryness of the heat that summer he'd decided to leave. Fish drowning in dry riverbeds, the fields going up instantly, as if sparked from under the earth. Words couldn't describe it, though the very same words were used over and over, as if repeating them brought them closer to the truth: baking, scorching, flaming. It was dryness and tiredness, and the air was second-hand and there was the smell, constant and toxic, of burnt paper in the atmosphere. There were no clouds. There was no breeze: standing on the porch on the morning he left, looking over the lawns into another clear sunrise, saying goodbye to the house, and struggling to get a breath. People said, At least you'll be prepared for Bahrain, and laughed, as if the heat was a joke, or he was, or the idea of going. He knew there would be something to stop him; understood there would be no escape, that no one escapes, not really, try as hard as they might to climb out. In the end they just fall back down into the hole.

Keith Jarrett plays on. Kenneth hears the piano as the bells of the church in which he and Rusty were married, and hears how much he loved her. How pale she looked as the bells rang out, as the photographer posed them here and there in the shadow of the lychgate. Just as a new bride ought to look. He couldn't believe his luck.

The house felt empty on his return. It was filled with darkness. He paused in the hall like a stranger and the clock ticked and the sound his footsteps made on the staircase beat time with his heart.

Rusty was in her room. He didn't forget to knock, he just chose not to, opening the door and finding her at the dressing table. She was drawing the spike of an earring from her earlobe.

He's in his room, she said, turning to look at him and then swivelling back to her own reflection, I do not want to see him.

Kenneth noticed she was heavily made-up, and dressed as if she'd just returned from an evening out.

What have you done?

Did he say that? Didn't he mean, What has *he* done?

And she swung round again, her beautiful face a long thin strip of hatred, and said,

Me? I lost a baby. Hang me for it.

★

William has cancelled Nat; he thinks about calling his father, holding the handset to his chest as he paces the living room. The view from his window is slashed with diagonal blurts of rain. Through it he sees the surrounding towers have lost their shape; they are flattened by the darkness, the individual apartments illuminated here and there into a mosaic of colours, like a Klee painting. He imagines the people inside them going about their lives, cooking, watching television, arguing, making love, and he is sick with loneliness and longing. He thinks of Sonny, how thick his fur was, how trusting his eyes, his soft mouth; wonders how anyone could have believed him.

thirty-four

Alison doesn't bother to ring the bell; she peers in through the front window, looking for signs of life. Not a shadow, not a flicker of movement within. Holding her umbrella sideways, she presses a pearly ear to the cold glass and listens.

This is how Kenneth sees her, backlit in the faint glow from the carriage lamps, like a neighbour eavesdropping through a wall.

Clear off! I said no Gypsies!

Sensing his shadow in the hallway, the ghost of Kenneth passing the clock, Alison thinks he's making one of his jokes. But the wait – presumably he's gone to find the key? – gets longer, and the rain bouncing up from the gravel is speckling her ankles.

William should get you certified, she yells, rapping her knuckles on the window. When he doesn't reappear, she decides to try round the back of the house, to get in through the courtyard or the terrace. Except the gate in the adjoining wall is locked, and on the terrace side, a veiled moon shows her the steps are under water. Alison paces the driveway, unsure of what to do next. She'd promised William, but if he won't let her in, what can she do? There's the sound of a sash sliding open with a fierce clap, and then there's Kenneth, poking his head out of an upstairs window.

How now, you secret, black, and midnight hag, he shouts. His face is impossible to read, but he's not so far away that she can't smell the whisky coming off him.

Actually, dear, I'm the eight o'clock hag. I was thinking you might need rescuing. I did phone, several times.

A knell that summons me to Heaven or Hell.

You can pretend all you like, Kenneth, you don't fool me. But William is worried, she says, to the blunt shape above her, What with the valley cut off and you up here alone. That's William your son, by the way, not Shakespeare. He asked me to call. Well, I've called.

When Kenneth doesn't answer, she makes one last attempt.

Oh, and I've had a change of heart about witnessing your will. Call it an 'advance decision' on my part, but I don't think you're entirely *compos mentis*.

He is down the stairs and has the door thrown wide before she has even got back in the car.

Open Sesame, she says, shaking the droplets from her umbrella, Now, shall we talk?

★

You see that?

The men stop loading and watch as the figure draws into view, only to disappear again as the road dips. They pause, and in the rain's respite, Sam Moore seizes the opportunity to flex and bend his aching fingers. Clamped rigid between his knees is a disgruntled ewe. Eyeing her at close range is a soaked Border collie, licking his lips with intent.

Have a look, Sam says. Aaron leaps up onto the flatbed into the stew of waterlogged sheep, craning his neck to catch any sign of movement through the trees.

Can't see. Must've gone back. Hang on, there he is. He's coming our way.

The figure appears to wade slowly upwards out of the wash, turns back on itself and swims away into the black.

He in trouble?

Dunno. Maybe, Aaron says, jumping down again. At a nod from Sam, he grabs the spongy rear end of the ewe and to a count of one they hoist her into the back with the rest of the flock. Aaron swings the gate of the pick-up closed and leans on the battered rim.

We'll give him a minute, he says, See if he appears.

Let's go get him out, decides Sam, Stupid tosser.

★

Alison says nothing about the state of the kitchen. She fills the kettle with water and lifts two cups from the draining board, but she can't resist inspecting them, tilting them under the spotlights while Kenneth searches among the wine bottles.

Had a disaster in the cellar, he's saying, But I've saved most of them, look. Trouble is, when you clap eyes on them – temptation!

And you can resist everything except temptation, I know, she says, But we're having tea.

No milk.

We're having it with lemon.

Kenneth shrugs.

No lemons.

It's the first chance she's had to study him properly. She expected to find him unshaven, unkempt, was ready to be confronted by a shambling wreck. She's surprised – and slightly perturbed – to find he looks as he always does; tanned, upright, a hint of mischief about him, a little boy hiding a secret. Better than he always does, in fact; less vague, more focused. Despite the rolled-up trousers and the ridiculous running shoes, or perhaps because of them, he has a youthful look about him.

But when they carry their cups into the library, Alison notes the mess. He may look perfectly fine, but the old Kenneth would never let the records lie around all over the place, out of their sleeves, out of sequence. The floor is decorated with a criss-cross of muddy tracks; a sheer film of dust covers the surfaces.

Where's Freya when you need her, she says, by way of comment.

Visiting her daughter in Cheshire, says Kenneth, Not that I need her, really. I manage well enough.

Well enough, indeed, she echoes, gazing at the typewriter and the rank mug of mushroom water and the whisky bottle and the papers everywhere. She snatches one up from the chair as she bends to sit in it. Kenneth doesn't try to take it from her; he makes a little nod of encouragement.

`Thoma Vryce`, she reads, `Was the water bailiff at the t ime it happened`.

At the time what happened?

Kenneth settles back in his seat, attempts a quick sip of the tea, flinching as he scalds his lips.

Will found a child in the barrow field. You remember? Years ago.

Alison nods, jiggles her foot at the floor and the balled-up papers dotted all over it.

And it's taken you a ream of paper to write that?

The point is . . . the point isn't what's written down, Ali. It's what's not written down, that's the point. There was something not right about it. He'd found a child, and the child – you remember, there was a dog, belonged to the bailiff – the dog had savaged the child?

I don't remember the details. It was before I moved here. And, she says sharply, No one ever spoke of it.

I know. He'd found a child and the water bailiff – Bryce – had got there just afterwards, and he took the dog away and he shot it.

Good thing too, says Alison, You can never trust them once they've turned.

Kenneth rubs a hand over his face. He doesn't know how to get the words out in order, in a sequence she will understand.

The thing is, there was a great hoo-ha in the village, the police and reporters and so on. The child had been missing, you see.

So?

So, Will hadn't just rescued a child from the dog – he'd *found* her. He was a little hero.

Nothing changes there, she says, trying to lift the atmosphere, He's such a sweetie.

But it didn't seem heroic. It didn't even seem real. I mean, when I came back, Rusty was incensed. She wouldn't speak of it, not to anyone. And you know how she loved the limelight. Alison's about to say that actually she doesn't know, but Kenneth continues his line of thought.

She wouldn't even look at William. Wouldn't be in the same room. We had to send him away again, you know, find another school for the poor chap. And he was strange too. He loved that dog, absolutely adored it, but he never said a word afterwards.

Well, that would explain it, she says, stifling a yawn, Grief has that effect. And maybe Rusty was really angry with *you*, Kenneth, for ditching them both like that and running off with the maid.

He checks her face to see if she's joking. Satisfied that she doesn't know about Grace, he shakes his head as if he's already considered and dismissed the idea.

No, Rusty was glad to be rid of me. And rid of Will too, as it turned out. How can a mother abandon her child?

The same way a father can, says Alison.

And Bryce. Always in the thick of it. Always something vaguely . . .

230

Kenneth searches his mind for the right word,

. . . Repellent about him. He was behaving oddly. I thought it was because he was worried he'd be prosecuted over the dog. The child's father was Godfrey Crane's son – the judge, you know – but we didn't know that then, not for a while. There was another man about, making a nuisance. Can't think of his name. Thing was, I was only gone a day or so, but when I came back, it was like that place.

Alison looks askance.

What place?

In that film, where everyone is the same but different. Like they've been—

Invasion of the Bodysnatchers, she says.

That's it. Even Rusty was different. As if she'd suddenly come to life, as if—

A snort of laughter from Alison stops him.

I think the opposite's supposed to happen, my dear, she says, By the way, how is Rusty these days?

She's agreed to give me a divorce.

The news has the effect of darkening the room. Alison can't keep the surprise from her voice.

After all these years! Has she given up the faith?

I went to see her a couple of weeks ago, says Kenneth, Told her I'd made a will, told her what kind, what was in it. Said I was in love and would she set me free.

This news is much more interesting to Alison than the heap of memories Kenneth has been forcing her to sift through, but she composes her face. She's forgotten about Maggie and what William told her the last time they met. Instead she's enjoying the tiny quickening of her pulse, the faint hope forming in her mind.

All that's out of the window now, of course, he says, actually getting up and moving to the glass, as if the word has suddenly reminded him of the object itself, Silly old fool that I am.

231

From behind him comes Alison's voice, low, defeated.

A silly old fool and a most insensitive one, Kenneth.

★

She'd been making good progress. The water in the lane outside the cottage was barely up to her calves, not much deeper than inside it. She sensed the daylight falling behind her, but couldn't wait any longer; no one was coming. For all anyone knew, the place was deserted. Maggie wouldn't spend another night there. It wasn't the smell, nor the sensation that the walls had turned to blotting paper and were sucking up the river stink: it was the rats. She hadn't anticipated rats. At first she thought it was someone at the front door – someone in trouble, perhaps, or that Aaron had come back and was trying to force his way in – but when she stood at the top of the landing and looked down, there was no one there. Then she caught a flash of movement in her peripheral vision, something alive, swimming through the hallway. For the next hour, as she sat in the middle of the bed and considered what to do, she could hear them squeaking and scrabbling in the rooms below. Time to leave.

Maggie thought she could manage if she kept on the verge side, where the water was bound to be shallower. But the verge had disintegrated here and there, once collapsing underneath her, tipping her into a half-submerged fence. She'd tied her holdall around her neck to keep it safe, and it was heavy, much heavier once it had got wet, and kept slipping round her body. She cradled it like a baby in front of her. After half a mile, she lifted out the dreamcatcher box and threw the holdall away. Didn't watch it jink and bobble over the surface; kept her eyes fixed ahead of her. Something glinted through the trees. Following the curve and dip of the road, she saw it again; white, hard-edged: a truck or van. The ford would be treacherous; already the noise in her ears was much louder, like the deafening rush of a weir, but the truck was a good sign. She broached it slowly, gripping a spindly hedgetop on one side of the field until that too was sunk, and then she waded through, holding the box above her head for as long as she could bear it. Knee-high now, nearly at the middle. It had grown so dark ahead of her she could no longer tell where the flood ended and the road began. Beneath the water, her boots had filled, liquid became solid; she could feel lumps of debris banging against her legs. She paused, trying to free herself of the sucking mud, but a quick twist of the current knocked her askew, almost snatching the box from her hands. So, let it go, then: let the notebook swim free, wash the past away. But she thought of the photograph of Nell, how it was all she had; and the part of her that wanted it to end dissolved in the froth breaking over her head. Under the surface, the water was brown as an old penny. Maggie slid sideways, backwards, choking, slipping, trying to regain her footing, trying to hold on to the box, choking and slipping and clawing water, clawing mud; fighting the pull of the current at first and then allowing it to carry her along.

thirty-five

After Alison leaves, Kenneth positions the stylus at the start of the record and plays the concert over again. He hears the music like rain, and there is still the actual rain, falling in shifts and shivers on the long windows, but Kenneth's listening is much more intent than sound on a surface: he's trying to hear his son.

The boy was lying on his bed, pretending to read a copy of *Mad* magazine. Kenneth stared at the boy's feet; how ugly they looked, how filthy the soles were, and it filled him with fury, the sight of the boy in shorts and a T-shirt, lying there on the clean white linen with such dirty feet. Kenneth had come all the way back, and his son wouldn't even look at him. He doesn't remember what they said to each other.

A message had been sent to his club, telling him to return home immediately, but he didn't get it because he wasn't there. He had booked into a hotel. Had Grace with him, wanted one last night with her before he left. He was tempted to persuade her to follow him out there. Lots of ex-pats needing nannies in Bahrain, lovely weather, a fresh start for both of them. She had hair that looked like silk but felt like wire. Extraordinary texture. And her mouth was too big for her face, but he liked that, it suited her. It was sexy. He'd reserved a table for dinner but in the end it was room service they had, very late into the night, and they both got quite drunk. It didn't matter; they could sleep in, maybe even spend the day in the park, like a pair of lovers, lying in the grass, getting sunburnt. His flight wasn't until the following evening.

They didn't go to the park and she didn't see him off at the airport, because it was so far and the trip was a bit of a drag in the heat and she was meeting someone at World's End and really had to shift. It was a blessing really; he remembers feeling as if he were duty-bound to make the suggestion, but the thought of the two of them at the airport together brought home the reality of the idea: he didn't want her in Bahrain at all. She promised him she'd think about it; said it over her shoulder, walking casually away from him, the tanned outline of her body clearly visible through the thin cheesecloth of her dress. She turned back once, and seeing him standing there in his suit with his case at his feet – watching her go – she put her hand up and smiled, and so he knew that was the end, of course. What would she have seen? A married man in an unfashionable suit; an older man, seventeen years older. Old enough, just about, to be her father.

He was paged in departures. The public address announced an urgent message for Mr Kenneth Earl, and although he heard it, once standing in the toilet cubicle, and once again while he was washing his hands in the basin, he didn't connect the name with himself. And the third time: he was looking for a novel to take him through the flight, hearing the creaking carousel of books, and, above it, the exact same message delivered in the same staticky monotone.

He would like to remember what he'd said to William. He has to put himself back in the hole.

Kenneth sat on the edge of the bed, laid his hand on his son's bare feet and said,

Will, I take it there's been some adventure. You're quite the hero, so Sharon says. What happened, son?

But the boy wouldn't talk.

In another cell of his memory, the cell where such moments are hidden from the light, Kenneth sees himself and his son in the room, and the preferred, imagined memory evaporates like dew. He sees again the dirty bare soles of William's feet – how it makes him rage to come back to that – and he's towering over the boy, his hands curled into fists; he's towering and shouting.

Stand up, boy! Have you forgotten your manners?
And William slides off the edge of the bed and gets to his feet.

Kenneth lets out a small, baffled cry: now, he wants to hear his son. Didn't want to then. He thinks of his own father, who held to the dictum that children should be seen and not heard, and marvels at how, like some process of genetic osmosis, he had absorbed the rule. But his father had never hit him; can't blame that on heredity. Rusty was quite different with the boy. They were always – Kenneth strains the word out – canoodling, him and her. Her little man. Wanted to take him places with them; the opera, the theatre. Why didn't he want that too? He was only ever home for the holidays as it was. Why did he want the boy to have his own sitting room, for Christ's sake? So that William could leave them in peace. To do what? He can't remember because he doesn't know. What was *wrong* with him? He gets up slowly, stiff and chilled from sitting so still for so long. He has an urge to light the fire, remembering at the last second, a lit match between his fingers, that William had stuffed the chimney with bin bags last winter to stop the heat escaping. Who'd light a fire in July, anyway? But everything's so damp. He wants to light a fire and he can't fathom why. Immobility, he says, taking himself off to the kitchen and refilling his glass. Immolation. He can't sit on the terrace for the stink. What is it with this weather, that it smells so bad?

★

Sam Moore pushes his crook further into the swirling mass. Behind him, Aaron is breathing heavily from the run down the hill. He tries to keep the torch steady so the light won't bounce around, but even so, only the surface is lit, broken like glass into hundreds of tiny shards.

See him?

Sam doesn't reply. He wades further into the wash, feeling about in the cold and dark. He lifts a dripping holdall from the middle of a nest of twigs and tosses it onto the bank, flinging up beside it a bent bicycle wheel, a length of plumbing hose, a single wellington boot. When he reaches the other side he puts his hands on his knees and bends double, scanning the ford for any sign of life.

Not a hope, he says, We can go to the centre, ask if anyone's missing.

And then to the pub, just to make sure?

Too right. Even if it's only bottled. I'm gagging.

Aaron turns away and immediately back again, grabs the boot and shines his torch over it.

Hang on a minute, he says, We need to look further downstream.

★

William drives like his father: fast, confident, music too loud in the cabin. Nat had made him a compilation CD and he plays it now, feeling the rush of adrenalin he always gets when he thinks of her. A CD is a step forward; it means she cares enough about him to share her tastes. She has thought through the music carefully. He recognizes a Seth Lakeman song, and

237

Coldplay, but doesn't know the next three bands and has to keep glancing at the track listing after that. He stops paying attention midway through; the CD case, nestled with his mobile phone on the passenger seat, is hard to read in the dark. And anyway, he's never been one for that kind of obsession. Perhaps when all this business with his father is over, when he's cured or better or something less histrionic, he'll bring her down to Berkshire.

Meet the family, he says out loud, grinning, Mad and very, very bad.

It's not often the roads are so empty, and he tries to enjoy the feeling of space it gives him, like being in a car advertisement, almost. Except his car isn't shinily manoeuvring along a winding road to the sea. His car is covered in grime and muck from the lanes, negotiating the blocked-off and sealed-off and impassable byroads that will, he hopes, eventually lead him to Boxford. He's going to visit Thomas, renew their acquaintance. Put an end to the mischief.

★

Kenneth knows now that his mind is not the dodgems or the ghost train; certainly no fun house. It is the hall of mirrors. There is before and after, and squeezed in between them is the actual moment itself, distorted by time, by what he knows now, what he didn't know then. And what he chose to ignore. Rusty was pregnant. He couldn't prove it wasn't his, of course, because she was clever. So, here's the next reflection: how did he know it wasn't his?

She'd called him up to the nursery to deliver her news, opening the door and smiling at him in an odd, peculiar way, like a child trying to please. She said something about the room coming into its own again, but he wasn't really paying attention because they'd been here before; once, twice, and she had

238

been so bitterly disappointed. And for a while after each failure she'd go quiet, and he'd think she was happy, or at least coming to terms with it, and then she'd begin again, the same arguments, the same fanatical cast in her eyes. One child would never be enough for her. She simply longed for a baby. And William needed a playmate, someone to draw him out. She never asked Kenneth what *he* might need. Then she'd had a stillbirth, and they both agreed there would be no more attempts.

Had they both agreed? He holds up another memory for scrutiny, squirming at the deformed shape of it: he had said, There'll be no more; it's ruining your health. That's my final word.

Afterwards, he'd taken every precaution – or thought he had – so the news was a shock. That was how he knew it wasn't his, then? The idiocy, the stupidity of him. And of course, the baby wasn't to be. Third recollection: Rusty in the middle of the bed, pillows stacked high around her, and the sheet pulled up to her chin. Like a disembodied head, floating in an Arctic sea. She had a look on her face, and once Kenneth had seen it the first time, he would never fail to notice it again: a kind of smirking contempt. He was trying to apologize, to share her sorrow, even though he didn't quite feel it in the same way.

Come on, Kenneth, he says to himself, What was it you really felt?

And Keith Jarrett plays out a rhythm of not-quite-repetition, and the answer comes in the spaces between the sounds: relief. Huge, sparkling relief. He'd already made plans for his love affair with Grace.

Grace. He'd kept it secret for a good six months: four of planning, when only he knew what he was about to do; two of snaring, although he preferred, in those cunning, deceitful days, to think of it as romancing. Now he knows the name of it, and is full of shame. Grace wasn't one of the more beautiful ones. But she was happy and free, and freedom is a kind of beauty in itself. When he'd had enough of a particular dalliance – when it became a problem – he'd enlist Rusty, confess all (not quite all) and she would deal with it. If the girl worked for the estate, she'd be promoted. If she was a friend of a friend, she'd be welcomed by Rusty with a full and overpowering benevolence. Rusty was so clever.

Kenneth wanders into the hall and opens the front door. His leg is aching from the big toe to the calf. The sole of his foot is throbbing. He continues out towards the rhododendrons, the bushes fused into a block of saturated shadow, and stares at them. The earth underfoot yields to his weight; his feet sink into the cold and wet. It feels good. There's a noise in the distance, some sort of siren, like atonal singing. A million years ago, it seems, a woman sang to him.

★

The journey from Boxford to Earl House is hazardous, and William has to take it more carefully. The motorway has been closed off, with diversion signs taking him in the wrong direction. He feels, although he can't know, not in this glossy darkness, as if he's circling the estate without getting any closer; as though he's stuck on an unending loop. Twice he's had to take a detour, found a river where a road should be, has had to double back on himself, and the scenery looks exactly the same; closed-in hedges and the tarmac like Vaseline; no houses lit, no people, nothing. At Westbrooke he climbs the hill, and as he rounds the bend, sees an unearthly sight; a caravan of horses crossing the horizon. One follows behind the other, nose to tail in a line, like a paper cut-out. Then no one and nothing again for another mile or two, except the sodden trees, and the road ahead, empty and straight. The CD has played through and returns to the start, the frenzied violin on the opening track making him press his foot harder on the accel-

240

erator. Really, he wants to rip up the tarmac, soar through space: he wants to fly, like the car in *Chitty Chitty Bang Bang*. Like the ones in *Blade Runner*. At this rate, it'll take ages to get to his father's house. That meddling old bugger, with his interfering ways. He thinks again about Thomas's watery eye through the crack in the door. Yes, someone had called. Someone was asking, is what he'd said, but Thomas swore he'd said nothing. Really, he'd said nothing. Swore it on his dog's life. And then – extraordinary – that pitiful cry. I'm an old man. As if age ever made a difference. William licks his lips, tasting salt and iron; the flavour, faintly shocking, of his own blood.

He dips his hand into his inside pocket and takes a stick of gum, unwrapping it and folding it into his mouth before he tries his phone again, reaching across the console and fumbling about on the seat to find it. Still no signal. When he glances back up at the road he slows down, to be sure of what he's seeing. It looks like a fallen branch but as he nears it he thinks it's a figure, a scarecrow, maybe, wrenched from a field by the weather and thrown onto the fence. As William flicks his main beam on, the scarecrow lifts its head and looks at him. The eyes are fawn-like, lit up, blazing green.

★

She sees the car beam as a torchlight. It reaches up high as it crests the hill and then she doesn't see it, only the shape of the dog, low, fast, racing down towards her with the moon behind it, and she moves into the shadow of the trees.

thirty-six

William arrives to find Kenneth sitting in the hall at the bottom of the staircase, a damp wind blowing through the house. He can tell at once that his father's had trouble; an abandoned pair of mud-crusted trainers on the doorstep, bloody footprints in a wandering pattern across the flagstones. Kenneth is bent double, trying to unravel a length of bandage. Without speaking, William kneels in front of him and takes hold of his foot, lifting it, looking at the bent toes and greenish toenails, the mud and gravel embedded in the skin. Gently, he sweeps his fingers over the sole until the ragged gash is revealed.

It hurts a bit, his father says.

I bet it does. It's pretty deep.

Kenneth lifts then drops again the strip of grey crepe bandage in his lap.

Couldn't find any more plasters. How did you manage to get here?

With great difficulty, says William, The roads are – well, they're not roads any more. I asked Ali to call. We were worried about you.

She called, says Kenneth. He pushes William's hand away, but his son persists, and they battle for a few seconds over the foot, Kenneth pulling his knee to his chest, his son tugging on the ankle, until Kenneth gives up the fight and leans back against the banister. William scrutinizes the wound, angling his father's foot to the light.

It'll need cleaning, he says. Stay here and I'll fetch some antiseptic. You'll have some, won't you? Bathroom?

Freya keeps it in the kitchen – under the sink.

Stay here. Don't move. Hold that foot up.

Kenneth stares at William's retreating figure, at his confident, brisk walk and at the sheer grown-up *manliness* of him, and is amazed. When did that happen? When did the awkward, sly boy become this person?

I'm sorry, he yells, I shouldn't have left you all alone. It was wrong.

William heads off along the corridor. He doesn't know what gremlin idea has crept into his father's mind this time, and now, when he would really like a drink and a moment to himself, he doesn't want to hear it. There's Dettol under the sink, a plastic bottle lying on its side among an assortment of old jam jars and rags and a box of tired-looking fish food. Everything feels sticky and unclean. He pours a capful of the antiseptic into a bowl and adds warm water, trying to still the trembling in his hands, trying to concentrate only on the milky liquid and the ticking sound of the house. It's the most bizarre night. The horses on the hill, and the roads awash, and that thing leaning on the fence; his father, like a lunatic, and that real lunatic Thomas. Behind him, Kenneth half-hops across the floor and lowers himself onto a stool next to the sink.

Is your phone working? asks William, My mobile's dead.

The phones are down, says Kenneth.

But you said Ali called?

She called in person, says Kenneth, And I sent her away again. Don't want her to be stuck here if it gets worse.

Don't want to be stuck with her, more like, says William, and Kenneth gives him a broad grin. He puts out his hand and catches his son by the arm. He would like to say it again, how sorry he is, but William interrupts.

It's worse in the valley. Up here's not so bad. And it said on the traffic news they're reopening the motorway. Crisis over.

Not in my cellar, says Kenneth, That's how I got my war wound.

William ducks back down and replaces the bottle. He has an urge to pull the jars out and wash them, run a cloth over the shelves and throw the fish food in the bin. There's a smell in the air, cutting through the antiseptic, of rotting vegetation, rank water. He's only half listening to his father, some nonsense about how his mind is a prison and he is the prisoner. When he emerges again, Kenneth is looking at him: he has asked him a question.

What's that, say again?

I said, when I left for Bahrain, were you sad?

William decides he will have that drink, goes to the stash of bottles on the counter and picks one at random.

How about some wine? I won't be going anywhere tonight. I suppose I can stay?

Of course you can, son, says Kenneth, But what did you feel, at the time?

It's so long ago, I can hardly remember.

Well, try, insists his father.

William would like to tell him how he was much more concerned about his mother. Not concerned: devastated. How he'd heard them, the doctor, and the nurse they'd hired, and the river man – the river man, again – talking about her nerves. How she was on the edge, how she so badly wanted another child. And he says,

It changed everything. Of course it did. But at least it meant I was more like the rest of them.

The rest of who?

The boys at school. Everyone divided their time, Dad, between one parent or the other. Or I should say, between one nanny or the other.

Ah, says Kenneth, swirling his foot in the bowl of water, So it wasn't a ruse?

What wasn't?

That business with the child. You hadn't concocted some story with the water bailiff to make me come back?

It's a bit of a stretch, William says, Even for me.

You really found her?

William studies the label on the bottle. He knows he should be able to read it, but he can't make the letters form words. He did find her, every day: found her running naked along the riverbank, a clown's smile of dirt around her mouth; holding the hand of the man in the market place while he sold his drugs to the older boys; with her mother, the woman topless and shining like an oyster; sitting alone in the long grass, talking to herself, flexing her fingers to the sky. He would like to say, Yes, I found her. She needed us. Instead, he says,

I found her all right – showing the bottle to his father – How about a glass of this?

They remain in the kitchen, Kenneth with his foot in the bowl of water, William leaning against the fridge, both back in the same time and both remembering that same time differently.

Did you get my message, asks Kenneth, About the plumber? Can't find his number anywhere.

William nods. He won't let on about the other calls. To distract him, he begins to tell his father about the journey down, and then another thought occurs.

What were you doing out there anyway? he says, nodding to the hallway.

Kenneth puts his head back and shows his teeth in a grimace.

Don't go saying I'm potty, he warns.

I won't, says his son.

I thought I heard singing.

You're potty, says William.

I'll drink to that, says Kenneth, and they both raise their glasses in salute.

Maggie sits between the two men. She has to keep wiping her nose; it's dripping wet, and her eyes are sore and gritty. The dreamcatcher box is on her lap; the wood feels slimy, cold, and water seeps from the underside, soaking her knees. Sam clicks open the glove compartment and fishes about amongst the assorted debris before he finds what he's looking for; an old patterned tea towel, folded into a triangle.

For emergencies, he says, smiling as he hands it to her, Plus, it's the only thing that's dry.

She takes it from him. It smells faintly of petrol but she wipes her nose and her eyes anyway. The view through the window of the truck is smeared by the wipers and the weather; she can't tell whether she's able to focus or not. There's not much space in the cabin, and despite herself, her leg is pressed close against Aaron's thigh; she can feel the heat of his body against the wet of her jeans, and another kind of heat, an anger, thrilling through him. It's in the way he drives, the way he doesn't speak. Even though they'd caught up with her on the edge of a field, Sam is proud: his first proper rescue, he calls it. He talks animatedly, so fast and excited that Maggie tunes out now and then; it's all about the weather, the havoc; how they discovered a fox in a bathroom, and a pair of kittens on a high shelf in the kitchen of another house, as if they'd been put there for safety. So still, he thought they were china ornaments. How the water cut off this farm or roared into that house, sneaked up through the skirting boards, fell through the roof. The roads like rivers. That madman in the Mazda. All she wants to do now is sleep. The warmth of the cabin makes her drowsy; the proximity of the two bodies pressed on either side of her makes her skin prickle: perhaps she is creating her own humid air.

We tried to tell him, anyway, he finishes. Silence resumes

for a moment, and then Aaron leans forward to turn up the radio.

Sorry, she says, What did you try?

We told him, there's only one road up from Snelsmore and he ain't on it.

Where was he going? she asks.

The Earl place.

thirty-seven

She leaves Aaron sleeping, moving swiftly past his living room, where he has spent the last two nights, and lets herself out of the house. She gets to the main road at the end of the Gatehouse before turning back. It isn't fair. Not right to disappear like that.

After they'd picked her up, Sam wanted to take her to the centre with the rest of the evacuees and get her checked over by the nurse, but Aaron overruled him. He was going to keep an eye on her, he said, she'd caused enough trouble. And he did just that; didn't ask her any questions, but watched her carefully, attentively, in a manner that suggested she wasn't to be trusted. The following morning, when Maggie asked if it might be possible for them to go back to Field Cottage to pick up some more clothes, he snapped at her,

We're not here at your beck and call. The village is flooded, you'll have noticed. People have lost everything. People have drowned. *You* could have drowned.

It was only then she remembered his father, and how he'd died. Even though she should have been thinking of Aaron and of all he did to help her, Maggie's mind chased in a straight line back to Kenneth, standing in his den, peering into the fish tank. The water gives up her dead, he'd said, when he'd told her about finding Baggs. He was right. People are lost and people are found. Aaron's father hadn't been saved, but he *had* been found. Everyone must be found, even her. But she hadn't been found by William, she'd been lost by him. He'd made her vanish. What remained, said Kenneth, they'd found what remained of Baggs. She turned it over and over in her mind; the losing of her, and then the discovering of her, as if she were a object, a buried thing unearthed. And what remained of her. She'd been living her whole life with the remains. Until today. Not dead yet.

She rehearses her speech, so when Aaron answers the door, barely awake, and squints at her in the shimmering morning light, the words tumble out of her mouth.

I wanted to say how very sorry I am about your father. And how sorry I am about me and the way I've behaved. I'm really grateful to you, for everything.

Aaron passes his hands over his face, blinking at the dark shape of her, noting also the dark shape of the dreamcatcher box under her arm.

Maggie, my father died years ago. What's all this about?

He opens the door wider to let her pass through, but she shakes her head at him, turns to walk away up the path.

I just wanted you to know that.

His voice comes hoarse, baffled.

Where are you going?

I have to find someone, she says.

Are you coming back? he cries, Only, it would be nice to know, you know.

Maggie turns again, her faint smile creasing into a frown.

Yes, I'm coming back.

Taking a direct route from the Gatehouse, she manages well on the road for a while, then, as the land dips and curves – showing her the standing lake of river spill – she heads for higher ground, only dropping beneath the shade of the rhododendrons for the last half-mile. As she walks, she practises what she will say, the movements her mouth should make, the noises in her throat, casting them out onto the air. They sound guttural, broken, like the cries of a raven. The main roads aren't flooded any more, and William may have gone by now; if so, she'll tell Kenneth. And if she can't manage that, at least she can show him the newspaper cutting and the notes she has made. But she *can* tell him now, surely? Yet the thought of it makes her throat close up, as if a hand is squeezing her neck, compressing her vocal chords; she has to force the not-quite-words through the narrow opening. She pauses, breathes slow and deep and begins again; steps back from herself to say it.

That – child – is—

she begins, her face a mask as she stretches out the words. Her tongue feels thick as a slug. Relax, she says, but the word makes her mouth widen into a tight line. Calm. An open-mouthed word. Easy – a subtle word, a word she can say – Easy.

That child is still missing, she says, I've come to take her home.

When she reaches Earl House, she goes diagonally behind it, across the field and along the river, past the cedar, its needles sequinned with sunlight, up to the terrace. The water has retreated, leaving the top lawn covered in a plane of shining mud. She slips once, putting her hand out to save herself, then a second time, fumbling the box as she skids. She's come this far. There's a ladder leaning against the wall and a spade caked in sludge; someone has been clearing the flood residue from the deck. She finds the kitchen empty, the floor freshly mopped and smelling of pine; she leaves footprints as she walks across it. A neat row of wine bottles are lined up along the counter, a bowl of water in the sink releases a thin veil of steam. At the entrance to the library, she pauses. There's a figure in the corner of the room, sitting in Kenneth's wing-backed chair.

And who might you be, says William, with no question in his voice. She steps backwards, putting space between him and her.

Maggie, she says.

The famous Maggie, he smiles, At last.

I've come—

The words retreat. She feels them slip away inside her, feels them spiralling down.

You've come to see my father, he says, Well, he's still asleep. Maybe I can help you.

He never sleeps – late.

So he says. But I wouldn't take his word for it. I'm William, his son. Forgive my manners, it's not every day we get a visitor just walk in off the street.

Maggie tries to look at him, but there's stuff falling into her eyes, specks of dirt; gritty, sharp. The effort of controlling her limbs makes her dizzy.

Would you like to leave a message, Maggie?

When she doesn't reply, he rises from his seat.

Something to give him, she says at last.

Afraid she might drop it, she rests the box on top of the glass cabinet. Beneath the lid, the sheet music seems to quiver; notes appear and disappear, jumping along the stave like performing fleas.

William nods at the box, his hands open to take it.

I can give it to him when he wakes up.

I want to make sure he gets it.

He lets out a brief, exasperated sigh.

Then I'll make sure he gets it.

She's about to lift the box away when the sheet music comes into focus. She takes a sharp breath in, and quotes, very clearly and precisely, as if from memory:

We have an anchor that keeps the soul

Steadfast and sure while the . . . billows roll.

William shoots her a quick grin, close now, almost at her shoulder.

It's a hymn, he says, Used to sing it at Boys' Brigade.

Maggie snatches up the box as he motions for her to follow him. He strides ahead, brusque and confident, telling her that she's welcome to make an appointment to see Kenneth, and perhaps she'd be kind enough to telephone first before she next decides to visit. He dismisses her as he might a servant. As he leads her along the corridor, she focuses on the back of his head, the small bald circle in the thatch of hair. Nell was right about power; it releases itself like a vapour, coming off him now in a kind of languorous heat. He couldn't care less what she thinks of him: she's nothing in his eyes. It makes her furious, the sensation sparking through her, quick and bright. Not just the arrogance of his clipped heels on the flagstones: something's wrong with what he's just said. He breaks his stride, looks back to check she's following.

You told me it was pillows, William. You used to sing 'pillows'. You thought it was funny. Remember? she says, turning away as he opens the front door.

She takes the stairs, up and up, the light from the windows chopping her into pieces, feeling William gaining on her, a pace behind, calling out. She flings open Kenneth's bathroom door and slams it shut behind her. William on the other side, the flat of his hand slapping the wood. There's a rising nausea, full and bitter in her throat, and the room moving around her. A sudden red pain on the side of her head. She turns to find the cause of it. It comes from high up: he was so much taller than her then.

The adjoining door, the one she knows will give her Kenneth, retreats as she moves towards it. Maggie sinks onto the edge of the bath. Someone's hand on her face, and then the river man, holding her, wrapping her up—

the river man

In a piece of cloth, see. Just here, round your head. Just to stop that running now. You've got very nice hair, young lady. Who'd you steal it off? That's it, you're all right, I've got you. Don't take no notice of him now, he'll make a fuss but he won't hurt you. He's a good old boy, Sonny. Wouldn't hurt a fly.

Thomas's eyes are wide and his breathing shallow. The knuckles of his right hand are satisfyingly swollen, the pink blotches deepened now to black and purple. He dangles his hand over the edge of the chair for Bramble to lick it. She must be hungry; he should get up. He will get up, in a while. In a little while. Should have done that at the time. Smacked him one, the lying little runt. A dog can bite, but a dog can't put a child in a hole. The distant past is yesterday, and then it's today, right now, and as he relives the moment, Bramble waits at his side. He'll get up, in a minute.

thirty-eight

Kenneth's touch is gentle. She would like to tell him why she came back, but her mouth is filled with dirt. He moves her over to sit on the chaise longue, the briefest caress of his fingers on her hair.

I've sent William for a glass of water.

He looks bleary and ruffled, a man emerging from sleep, and he smells that way, warm and faintly acidic. He's smiling at her; even now he can't contain his delight. Fighting the urge to be sick, Maggie lowers her gaze to his feet: one bare, the other with a bandage hanging from it. She puts a hand up to her head to check. Strewn across the tiles are the contents of the dreamcatcher box. The newspaper cutting, a sodden remnant, disintegrates as she lifts it, but the picture of Nell is safe, the notebook is safe. She gives it to Kenneth.

I want you to read this, she says, her voice echoing in the space, and Kenneth simply nods.

When William arrives with the water, Kenneth tries to snatch it from him, jealous, guarded. His look is accusing.

You can leave us now, Will. We'll be fine.

Why don't you get dressed, Dad, and I'll look after Maggie for a minute? he says, and only then does she see that Kenneth is wearing pyjamas. He retreats to the far door, but leaves it open. From inside the room, he talks to Maggie, telling her how astounded he is to see her again, overjoyed, how he'll take care of her. He pokes his head through the doorway now and then, eager to share the moment. She has to sit back to drink the water, afraid she will topple if she doesn't concentrate, and her eyes take in the plain white wall and the outline of the frieze beneath it.

Birdie Crane, says William.

This used to be the nursery, didn't it? she says, giving back the empty glass. They both look at each other, William and Maggie, and what passes through them is something that Kenneth can never share: the same memory.

Rusty is standing at the window. As they enter, she turns around, and sees the dirty child that William has beside him; a child like a vole, like some kind of subterranean creature, with her smeared face and her pinprick eyes. A horror. Rusty takes in how abhorrent the child is, and says to William,

Wherever did you get that from?

From across the river. I got her for you.

And why would you do that? she says, pulling her chin back, as if avoiding a bad smell.

They said you wanted a child. *You* said. I heard you! And they don't look after her.

You are going to return the child immediately and I am going to contact your father, she says, her voice rigid and controlled, You are in serious trouble.

But I got her for you, he says, a tremor of panic coursing through his body.

No. You found it. Do you understand?

Rusty turns back to the window – she won't face them again – and says,

Go now.

Maggie and William look at each other and their look remembers how dark it was outside, another warm, dark night, and how they went down to the kitchen and William – quickly, because he was afraid of his mother's strangeness and needed to get Birdie away – washed her hands and face with a dish-cloth and she stuck her tongue out as he washed her to taste the moisture. He stopped at the garage door and told her to stand there and he went inside and fetched the big torch, not because he was frightened of the dark but because she was, and he didn't want her frightened. They held hands crossing the field and their hands were hot. William didn't know what to do. He couldn't put her back in the boat and push it across to the other side; people would be searching for her, they'd be waiting and they'd catch him doing it. He'd thought she belonged here. He'd convinced himself. He'd thought his mother would get better, that he could make her better.

He would have to be quick, now, but she was so slow, she couldn't move fast like him and it was annoying, how slow she was, and the torch was heavy and he switched it off, thinking at the last minute that someone might see the light. And in the darkness, a new thought: he could leave her; he could just put her in the culvert and tell her not to move and then – and then what? What if she wouldn't stay? What if she tried to follow him? He didn't know. It was hard, trying to think what was best. What if she told on him? Best if she couldn't tell.

He was trying to think, and it was so hard, standing there, clicking the torch on and off in the culvert and worrying about everything, whether she would be afraid out here on her own, what his father would do to him, and whether she would tell on him, holding her hand very tight, squeezing it. And over the hill, with his twisting low run, came Sonny, scenting him, excited, racing towards them.

I saw him too, her eyes say, And I screamed, didn't I, because he was going to eat my heart out. And that's when you hit me.

Birdie Crane, William says again, and Maggie nods at him.

thirty-nine

Dear Nell,
You'll know about the flooding, I'm sure, and I'm sorry about
the state of your bed and your records – and everything, really.
It's a terrible mess. At least that awful gas smell has gone, although
I can't say I prefer the new one; eau de sewage, Aaron calls it.
You'll understand why I have to leave, and why I'm writing to
you now. Can't stay and talk, not yet, anyway, not here. I won't
be far away, though; I've finally decided to quit my job with that
slave-driver Leon (that's a joke, Mum). I'm only going up the
hill a bit. (We never travelled far, did we?) And don't worry about
this place going to rot – Sam Moore's having it. He breeds sheep
for the estate. Next time you look out of the window, there'll be
a flock of them in that field. And his wife's expecting a baby, so
there'll be a family here again too. It's only right.
I miss you, Nell.

Maggie pauses. She has more to say, but Aaron sounds his horn
again, impatient to be gone. As if Nell is reading her thoughts,
Maggie adds a postscript:

He's local, but don't worry, he's a good friend. I know, you don't
approve.
I love you,
Birdie

She folds the letter once and kisses it before she stows it in the box. She doesn't know yet what she will do with the box, or with the notebook, and listens hard for Nell to advise her. She can't carry it around forever, can't keep clinging on to it like a piece of driftwood. She has to let it go. There's only silence at first, and then, very faintly beneath it, a soft burring sound: the gradual shift and settle of the house, the water's retreat, and her own withdrawal, an eliding of all that's gone before in preparation for what's to come. She picks up the box and goes to join Aaron in the truck.

forty

William finds his father in his office, asleep in the chair, a pair of headphones clamped over his ears. He studies him for a minute before tossing the postcard onto the blotter, waiting for him to sense the change of air. Kenneth opens his eyes.

That, says William, pointing at the card, Cost me ninety-seven pence.

His father removes the headphones and leans over to scrutinize the picture.

What? What's this?

It's daylight robbery, says William, and seeing his father's bewildered expression, explains, There was no stamp on it. You have to pay extra. It's addressed to you.

Kenneth's hands swim about on the desk, shifting papers and CDs until he finds his glasses.

Water over stones, recites William, Pretty cryptic, if you ask me.

The handwriting is familiar to Kenneth, but he just can't place it. He pushes his finger behind the lens of his glasses and rubs his eye, trying to press it into focus. He's seen the writing recently somewhere, searches his mind until he finds the loose thread.

What time is it, he asks, not waiting for an answer, Why didn't you wake me, boy? I'll be late for Maggie.

★

She's hearing things: the noise of her shoes being sucked into the sodden earth, the regular sweep-squeak of her jacket as she moves, a crow laughing in the treetops. There's a melody playing in her head: 'All Things Bright and Beautiful'. A right bend leads her to the clearing. From here, set back behind the rhododendron bushes, she sees the upper half of Earl House, its tall windows full of purple clouds. The wheat on either side of her is battered low, as if parting the way, but further on it's alive, swaying and bowing in the stiff breeze. When she gets to the bowl barrow, she climbs up and sits on the mound to wait.

It had been her idea to have the burial. They were in Kenneth's den when she made the suggestion, inspecting the fish, scooping the dead ones from the surface with a spatula. He was upset by the sight of their dimmed bodies, and by William's accusation.

I had *not* forgotten to feed them, he was saying, But the power had gone off and I don't know how to reset this thing. What shall we do with them?

And then she asked him, straight out, if she could bury the box at the bowl barrow. She gave him no reason, although she imagined he would think it cathartic, or therapeutic. She really didn't mind what he thought.

It's an ancient monument, he said, Protected. I don't think it's allowed.

But only we will know, Kenneth, and it's not as if it would be the first time. People were buried there, once. I'd like to bury the box, and the notebook, when you've finished with it.

Burying the past? he suggested.

Burying what remains, she said, because she knew, once he

260

had read what she'd written in the notebook, that the past would be anything but buried.

Here he is now, making his way down the sloping lawns, half running, a garden spade under his arm. They meet at the barrow, where Kenneth, pink-faced, leans his weight on the handle and tries to get his breath back.

I'm not late? he asks.

I'm grateful you're letting me do this. I thought we could put it here, she says, tapping her foot on the turf.

They both look at the box for a moment, the wood split and swollen, the lid cloven.

Oh! I got your postcard, he says, Which reminds me, don't worry about the song notes.

He takes the notebook from his pocket and hands it to her. She studies the crest, the front page striated with watermarks. Her name, written in capitals, is smudged out of all recognition.

The 'song notes'?

Yes, in there. They don't matter. Like you said, I shouldn't be wasting my life worrying about the past. Time to get out in the real world again.

He looks intently at her.

We have more important things to think about now. We must plan our trip! You will come, won't you, Maggie? Say you'll come?

She stares back at him, taking in the measure of what he's just said.

You haven't read it.

Can't. I'm sure they're delightful. I know you worked hard. But the ink, it was washed away, some of it, and it's all stuck together. Anyway, as I say—

Maggie considers for a moment, flicking quickly through the notebook. The pages are stiff and rippled, and on the ones which aren't glued together, the writing – her neat, particular handwriting – is ghostly, vanished. There'll be no burying today. But surely, she can tell him now: if she can find the words. If she can say them. And he will believe her now. Surely.

Then I must tell you, she says, taking him by the hand and leading him back up the hill, There's something you ought to know.

On the top floor of the house, standing at the window, William is watching.

acknowledgements

Many thanks to Paul Baggaley and all the team at Picador, particularly to my editor, Sam Humphreys, for her patience and belief.

I'm indebted to Derek Johns at AP Watt for his unstinting support, and to Linda Shaughnessy for her keen editorial eye. I'd like to thank Tadzio Koelb and Penelope Williams for their help with the early sections, Peter Edwards for his knowledge of wine, and crucially, Arthur Foster, who supplied me with nearly all of Kenneth's jokes.

My love and thanks, as always, to my family, but especially to Stephen Foster, without whom nothing gets done.

John Martyn fans will notice the allusions throughout. This book is dedicated to his memory.